Part One

DARK SIDE

An Unexplained Case File

BRANDI GIBSON

Copyright © 2025 by Brandi Gibson

ISBN: 978-1-966343-55-4 hard cover
ISBN: 978-1-966343-56-1 soft cover

Edited by: Melisa Graham

Published by Warren Publishing
Charlotte, NC
www.warrenpublishing.net
Printed in the United States

"Don't dream it, be it."

—*The Rocky Horror Picture Show*

Acknowledgments

Hey guys! I just wanted to say a few words to the people who helped me. First, a big thank-you goes out to Sofie Martinez and David Sims for letting me bombard them with questions about how the legal system works in certain situations.

Second, to those who kept my drive alive, I also want to thank you. You guys were my cheering section before anything got started.

Last but not least, I want to thank Warren Publishing for taking care of me and my book. You people are amazing, and I hope you stick around for the next book! See you then!

Chapter One

I have discovered firsthand, while living in Waco in my twenty-five years of life, that there are just some things you don't do, like burn symbols into the high school football field, ask a policeman if he wants a doughnut, or borrow a crane to put the principal's truck onto the school roof. Not saying I did any of those things …. Well, maybe just a few. They were *hilarious,* but inadvisable.

I do love a good prank though. Mine were relatively benign and more along the lines of throwing lit smoke bombs down the hall while my peers were changing classes or letting a few white mice loose in the girls' locker room. A few bystanders knew which shenanigans were mine and kept quiet for reasons known only to them. Maybe they shared my sense of humor. Who knows?

Still, I avoided people from high school whenever I could. Not that I didn't have wonderful memories about getting shoved into lockers, among other things. I just had no desire to reminisce with a bunch of people who thought they were better than me, then learned the hard way not to underestimate me. To be clear, most people are thrilled to see old classmates; they spend ten years eagerly awaiting the reunion where they catch up and compare job status and what car they're driving. Not me.

I shifted a stack of cold-case files in my arms so I could reach my office door handle.

"Hey, Miar!" a colleague shouted in passing.

I jumped, sending the files to the floor, my coffee onto my shirt, and me into a round of cussing.

"Damn it," I grumbled, tossing the useless coffee cup in the trash and crouching down to gather the files. I had most of them sorted out when a pair of shiny shoes stopped in front of me. I'm not talking about a half-assed shine job either. Oh no, I could see my face in these beauties. Only one person in the department had shoes that shiny ....

"Hey, Chief." I reached out to tap his shoe. "Think you can move your foot, Boss Man?"

He grunted in response, and I heard the creak of stiff leather as his foot moved enough for me to retrieve the file. I stood, pushing my hair out of my face, and added the folder to my stack.

Chief Newburn took in my disheveled state and shook his head. He was impressive at six feet tall, clean-shaven, and built like a fridge. He was like a bull in a suit and had the attitude to match. He held up a folder. "I have something for you."

I stood up straighter. *Something new? Yes, please.*

"Aw, you shouldn't have," I said, grinning as I tried to wipe coffee off my shirt—to no avail. With a sigh, I flicked the napkin into the trash. Good thing I had extra shirts in the office. "My birthday isn't until the end of the year."

Newburn chuckled and motioned for me to open the office door.

I carefully arranged the files in my arms so I could unlock it. Once I heard the click, I nudged it open with my foot and made my way inside. "Careful," I said over my shoulder. "Make sure you don't trip. And before I turn on the light ... sorry about the mess." I heard a soft thump and a grunt in response. I sighed again and flipped on my lamp when I finally reached my desk.

My office was a good size, but the reason I got put in an office in the first place was simple: No one likes looking at extensive blood and gore, no matter how seasoned an officer you are. The cases that found their way to me were either cold cases that held long-dead leads, solved cases that needed to be given a home, or cases that needed to be added to the new database the station had slowly started creating a few months ago. Translation? My office was a glorified storage room. It housed two steel file cabinets that had seen better days, my desk—with room for another if the chief decided to force someone to share the space with me—a rather comfortable couch that I had slept on more than once, a giant dry-erase board, a rickety old ceiling fan, and a heater that barely worked. The carpet was worn and littered with coffee stains in varying sizes. The bigger ones pooled around my desk like an archipelago from times I'd fallen asleep while working and knocked cups to the floor.

"Allen, how do you find anything in all of this?"

"Carefully," I answered, putting the files down on an empty space on my desk. "Have a seat, and don't stack anything on top of each other. It took me over a week to get all of this sorted."

The chief snorted before moving a stack of papers to the ground and sitting on one of the chairs facing the desk. He glanced around, a look of disgust flittering over his face. I almost laughed. Almost. But I didn't because I'm a professional …. At least that's what I'm told.

I eased down into my own chair and studied the man across from me, steepling my fingers to make myself look as shrewd as possible. As I'm only five foot five, I've found other ways to make people take me seriously or even to intimidate them. The tone of voice I use when asking questions makes people think twice about trying to lie to me. How I stand can show that I mean business or, conversely, have people thinking that I'm a joke if I want them to underestimate me. On the other hand, I also get the occasional crack about me being a distant cousin to a dwarf and then get sent out of the room.

"So," I said, settling back, "what brings you to my paper jungle?"

Newburn tapped the folder against his leg, ignoring my antics, and held the collection of papers out to me. "Dallas PD sent me something that is right up your alley."

I leaned forward, trying not to look like an eager puppy as I took the folder. While it was true that I was known for getting cases solved no matter how long it took, it was rare for the chief to hand me an active case still in its infancy. If a detective or officer was completely stumped on a case, they would make the unwanted trek to my office and knock on the door. Most would get too spooked and just try to shove the file under the door before bolting back to their desks in the main bullpen. The only person who didn't seem to care about catching whatever supposed disease I had was the chief.

"Must be really bad," I murmured, testing the weight of the folder. "I mean, most of the time we have to jump through hoops to get in on an active investigation."

"No one knows what's going on. The best people have seen this and are completely confused," he said. "They were going to file it away as a cold case …. Until they saw the news a few minutes ago."

Newburn's words finally filtered through, and I tore my gaze from the contents in the folder. "Wait, what was on the news?"

The faintest hint of a smile came over the chief's face.

I frowned, then carefully began sorting the file's contents into small piles on whatever space was available on the desk. Most of the paperwork was normal, nothing standing out to speak of. But then again, if anything was extraordinarily odd at the crime scene, the officers wouldn't have put it in the report—too much of a chance of being sent to the loony bin.

I flipped through the pictures, pausing when I came to a wide shot of the crime scene. It looked like a hospital emergency room with just enough overhead lighting for me to make out the bed and the monitors. My stomach began to turn. Now I knew why the chief had come looking for me: The room was a bloodbath, as if someone had taken a gallon of red goo and thrown it haphazardly over half of the room. The cabinets were partially covered, as was the chair beside them. The other half of the room was dark red with lumps sticking to the walls and bed. The normally stark-white sheets were bunched into a heap at the foot of the bed, as if the patient had kicked them off in a sudden fit. I got a bad feeling about those lumps.

"Um … Chief," I started, still looking at the pictures, "where's the victim?"

A shadow fell over the desk as Newburn's arm moved into my line of vision.

"Here," he said, picking up the next photo in the pile.

My stomach heaved, and I closed my eyes for a moment. The photo was nothing but red. From the quick glance I had, it looked like something close to a skeleton had somehow been imprinted on the ceiling—oddly resembling a Rorschach inkblot, except this one had bits of clothing and other things mixed in.

Newburn stood and walked to the door. "The nurses said the victim came in complaining of body aches and chest pains. They got her into a room and, thirty minutes later, heard a scream and a loud bang."

A loud bang? *Wonderful,* I thought as I took a few deep breaths. I have a healthy respect for anyone who can hold their own around an insane amount of blood: nurses, morticians, first responders of any kind. After all, a strong stomach is your best friend in any of those professions. Mine, on the other hand, revolted when milk smelled sour. Yes, ironic given my chosen profession, but having a big brain doesn't automatically come with a strong stomach, unfortunately. "Now I don't think I want to know what was on the news ...."

"A similar crime scene here, at Saint Mary's Hospital," Newburn said. "You're wanted .... Now."

I groaned. "Seriously? After you showed me that?"

"You aren't taking tea with the queen of England," he answered, his voice firm. "Zack is already there, and they are waiting on you. Get your ass down there."

I nodded, my eyes drifting to the photos in my hand. One crime scene at a hospital was odd, but two? And both showing up in my office at the same time? Not a chance it was a coincidence.

I started looking for a fresh shirt. "Guess I'm going to a crime scene."

***

I straightened my suit jacket and made sure my shoulder-length hair was still mostly in its tie as I walked through the doors of the hospital's ER.

The seating area was empty of patients but full of staff and police officers. Part of the waiting room was cordoned off by yellow crime scene tape, and a screen of thick white plastic had been erected to shield the crime scene from the public and any prying reporters. What bothered me was the smell, like swimming through a sea of rotten pennies.

My hand went over my mouth, and I reminded myself that I was a seasoned detective, a pro. Professionals don't lose their cookies at crime scenes. Still, I really didn't want to see what was on the other side of that plastic wall, professional or not.

"Sir?"

I blinked a little and noticed a few people looking at me, and a nurse was standing in front of me. I must have stopped walking at some point. She asked me if I was all right, trying to focus my attention. I held up a finger.

"I'm good," I said, after a moment.

The nurse didn't look convinced and stayed where she was, a hand barely touching my back.

"Can you tell me what happened?" I asked, waving in the general direction of the plastic.

"She came in complaining of chest pains," the nurse answered after a minute, looking a bit uneasy. "I went to get her some aspirin …. It was only a few moments, I swear. I came running when the screaming started, then—"

"Bang?" I asked, the statement slipping out before I could stop it.

It was the nurse's turn to look ill. Guess I was right, and if what happened made a nurse queasy, my stomach and I weren't going to like this in the slightest …. I wouldn't solve the case just standing around though, so I thanked the nurse and forced myself forward.

"What was all that about?" an officer asked, holding up the crime scene tape.

"What was what about?" I asked, ducking under his arm.

"You looked ready to hurl there for a second," the officer said, smirking.

I hooked a thumb over my shoulder at the plastic. "I smelled that …. Anyone would react that way."

"Pretty sure it's just you, Detective," the officer answered, turning back around.

Most of these guys are very Captain America in modern-day dress, unlike me …. I'm more of a Tony Stark meets Batman kind of guy. Stark for the brains and Bat for the unyielding stubbornness of serving justice no matter what, minus the vigilante part.

Other people would say that I have a bit of a temper, and I do, but only when I'm backed into a corner. They would also say that my interest in poisons, urban legends, and knowing what common household things could kill you keeps me from having any kind of normal relationship with people; also correct.

I reached the plastic wall and took a breath before stepping through and letting the sheet fall back into place. I turned to survey the area and stumbled back into a waiting pair of hands as I felt my world tilt sideways.

Red. The entire area was covered. Late-afternoon sun filtered through a reddish-brown film covering a large window, casting a sick shadow over the stiff plastic sheets. Bits of cloth lay nearby, ragged and torn. Clumps of muscle and tissue sat in dark brick–colored piles that, I assumed, had been started by the crime scene techs attempting to gather the remains. The gruesome piles reminded me of the dinner scene in *The Rocky Horror Picture Show*, when everyone found out what happened to Eddie, or the detailed scenes from Stephen King's *The Tommyknockers*. Ugh. My stomach flopped again.

"Is he—"

"Nope," someone answered as I felt the hands leave my arms and move to my shoulders. "He can't handle a lot of blood."

The hands guided me to a clean spot on the wall and put my back against it before making me bend at the waist.

"Deep breaths," the person coaxed. "In and out."

I did as I was told and tried to ignore the clump of something near my shoe. It looked like a finger.

"Feeling any better?"

"Not really," I said weakly as I slowly straightened up, "but I'll live. Thanks, Zack."

Zack's face broke into a grin, and he gave me a pat on the back.

I've known the guy since college and have been working with him for around three years now. He's the most annoyingly cheerful person I ever met in his profession. I once asked him why he didn't work with the living. He explained that if he wanted to be cheerful 24/7, he would have applied to be a teacher.

I dusted myself off and took another look around.

"You have an age for my victim?" I asked, slipping on the plastic booties Zack handed me. For the record, getting those things on over your shoes while trying to remain standing requires a crazy amount of balance.

"She's about twenty-six," Zack said, starting farther into the mess.

I nodded and pointed out a nearby shoe that needed bagging. "Her name?"

"You know I won't be able to confirm a name or anything else until I can get her back—or most of her back—to the lab," Zack said as he waved to get someone's attention. "I have protocol to follow, just like you do."

I didn't respond as I picked my way carefully through the mess of what used to be a human, trying to see what I could make of it before everything got sanitized onto a piece of paper for me to study later.

The room looked exactly like the pictures Newburn showed me earlier of the Dallas case—blood everywhere, along with lumps or strings of what used to be the squishy insides. I took a pack of cigarettes from my pocket and pulled one out. I knew I couldn't smoke inside, and I wouldn't. I'm not that much of an ass. I crouched down to get a better view of the splatter pattern and rolled the cigarette between my fingers, occasionally bringing it up to my nose to break up the copper-tinged assault on my senses.

The victim had been sitting in one of the seats lining the big window in the waiting room. As a result, the design on the window behind them was interesting. The rest of the seats along the window and pretty much everything in that little plastic area was either completely covered or partially sprinkled with blood, the degree of coverage lessening as the radius from the blast zone, so to speak, increased. It reminded me of a child's artwork—you know, the kind where the kid starts coloring within the lines but then lets chaos take over and scribbles wildly all over the paper?

Crime scene techs were moving around, carefully bagging and tagging anything amid the sludge that might be helpful. In a far corner of the room that remained clean and clear, a small check-in station had been set up for the evidence bags and whatever else was found. Several cold-storage units no doubt held the more identifiably human remains. Plain plastic boxes held any bones, clothing, or miscellanea that were found.

A few techs looked my way and scowled before going back to their excavations. Besides my obviously weak stomach, I wasn't often allowed near crime scenes for a reason: I had no respect for protocol when it got in the way of getting the job done or getting answers in a decent amount of time. Of course, it didn't help that if I wasn't careful, I tended to ruin crime scenes. Oops.

"Any theories?"

I glanced over my shoulder and found Zack holding a few plastic evidence bags, with a few more sticking out of his back pocket. "Unless you have one? No. But I do have questions," I answered, getting carefully to my feet so I didn't slip in the booties and end up on my face. "The biggest one is what could have done this?"

"Alien?"

I side-eyed him. "As in the little facehugger guy who bursts out of the man's chest in *Alien?* That's your best guess?"

Zack shrugged. "You never know."

I frowned as I gazed at the mess. "Well, for one, the pattern is too big. And we wouldn't be using a vacuum to get our victim out of the carpet if this was caused by an alien; there'd still be whole pieces of her body. This is more like someone shoved a bunch of firecrackers down this poor lady's throat and lit the fuse. Is that even possible?"

"It shouldn't be," Zack answered with a shudder. "Now I'm going to have that image in my mind. Thanks a lot, Allen."

"I aim to please," I responded, my eyes still scanning the room. "Did anyone find a purse of any kind?"

One of the officers looked over at me and shook his head. "No, sir. Right now, we're still trying to figure out what's clothing and what's not."

"It should be somewhere near there." I motioned toward the chair in the center of the splatter pattern. "Should make Zack's job a bit easier once we get the ID."

The officer nodded. "Yes, sir."

I rolled the cigarette between my fingers again. "I'll need photos of the crime scene. Ceiling, floor, wide shots, and close-ups."

He gave me a short nod and turned away. "Whatever you say, Detective."

"Do your thing, guys. I'm heading out."

Zack snickered as he watched me struggle to get the plastic booties off once we stepped out of the plastic zone. He held out a bag, and I gladly chunked them in once I managed to get them off my feet.

"Sooooo?" Zack asked as he followed me out of the nearly deserted lobby.

I glanced over as I fished my lighter from my coat pocket. "You're really keen on what I think, aren't you?"

"It's a small ray of excitement in my otherwise boring life."

"Don't I feel sorry for you," I said, putting the cigarette between my lips to light it. I took a drag and blew the smoke into the air. "Honestly, I have no clue."

Zack shot me a dubious look.

"Really," I responded, taking in another lungful of smoke. "This crime scene is something new for me. I don't think Waco's ever had an exploding body before. Although this does remind me of some of the gorier Grimms' tales my mother used to tell me."

I heard Zack's feet shift a bit. He knew how sensitive a subject my mother was. Zack was one of the few who respected that boundary and was actually the one who pulled me off an FBI agent last summer when a rather nasty comment was made. I made the front-page news, fist and all. It's not like I fly off the handle every time someone decides to insult me; we'd been on a rather difficult case that hit a bit too close to home. The guy had taken a cheap shot, and I lost my temper. As a result, I ended up getting suspended for a week without pay and sent to anger management classes. That was all kinds of fun.

"Allen ..."

I stopped walking, not realizing how far ahead I'd walked until I was looking behind me for Zack. He was watching me carefully, his hands shoved into his pockets.

"Hmm?" I replied, flicking ash onto the pavement.

"Maybe you should look through them," he said, clearing his throat a little. "Your brothers' rooms, I mean. It's been years since they left."

The rooms. I felt a small knot of disgust form in my throat and turned to keep walking. "I'd rather wait …. Now's not the time."

Zack sighed and yelled something about calling me later. I didn't answer. I had one too many thoughts to sort through and too much information to digest—but I was just handed something very interesting, and it was guaranteed to occupy me for more than a day. That was the problem with having a high IQ, you get bored so easily.

I was almost to my car, a black Nissan Sentra that had seen better days, when my phone started ringing. I took another long drag, stubbed out my cigarette, then fished out my phone.

"Well?" the chief asked.

"No one can put the victim back together again," I said dryly, propping my phone on my shoulder so I could retrieve another cigarette.

"Think you can handle both cases at once?"

I leaned against the car and weighed my options. Two victims dying in the exact same way had my attention, but the one in Dallas was out of my jurisdiction …. Sort of. What's a hundred miles when lives were on the line?

"Hmm," I said, releasing the smoke I was holding. "Dallas PD is cooperating, right? No miles of red tape?"

"Less than normal," Newburn answered. "They want to catch whoever is doing this …. Just like you."

He knew he had me. I grinned and breathed in a lungful of tar-flavored air. "Well then, Boss, let the games begin."

Chapter Two

My house ... where do I even begin? Most of the things in the house came with it: couch, love seat, dining room table and chairs ... I didn't have any problem with this since it meant I didn't have to go out and buy anything. Yet it made me a bit sad because it had all belonged to my mother—as did the house.

Built in the late eighties, the house itself had seen a lot in its lifetime—more than many humans, I'm sure. It had seen my father's murder, my brothers' betrayal, my mother's downward spiral into grief, and eventually her death as well. Yet the house still stood, as if it had an iron will. I'd like to be like that one day. But I'm only human.

I jogged up the three steps to the porch, then stopped short. The front door was ajar. *What the hell?* I carefully drew my gun, flipped the safety off, and used the muzzle to nudge the door open, silently thanking Zack for yelling at me to oil the hinges.

I crept into the house—avoiding the floorboards that groaned and creaked with age—and scanned the living room, checking for anything out of place. A thump from my mother's room propelled me forward, and my eyes narrowed on her partially open door. After my mother passed, despite the protests of my older brothers, I'd locked her room to preserve her things. I stopped at the edge of the doorjamb to listen.

"It's not here!" a man hissed in frustration. *Slam.*

He was trashing my mother's room! I tightened my grip on the gun and rolled my shoulders to stay loose.

"Keep your voice down," a second man pleaded. "Her son will be home soon. Maybe we should have just waited outside."

Another hiss.

As they continued to manhandle my mother's things, I felt really grateful for those anger management classes. Breathing deep kept me from breaking protocol and taking on these two guys without backup. Then again, who follows protocol nowadays? And it was my house, damn it!

"We'll be in trouble if we come back without it," the hisser muttered, heavy footsteps resounding as he bumped into something solid.

I held on to my restraint for a few more moments until I heard glass breaking. *That's it!* I thought, my lip curling back in a snarl as I nudged the door open enough to slip into the room.

You know that feeling you get when you see something that can't possibly be real but your brain tries hard to rationalize it—almost as if time slows down just enough for you to figure out what you probably should be seeing before it starts returning to normal speed? I think my brain derailed a bit when I saw the two lizard-like men hunched over my mother's dresser. Both were facing away from me, giving me a wonderful view of the light reflecting off the scales running along the back of their necks and arms.

Once my brain reconnected with my body, I cleared my throat.

Both jumped, almost spinning into each other to confront me. My stomach quivered a little bit when I got a glimpse of their faces. One of them was still mostly human except for a few scales on his face emphasizing his cheekbones. The other one looked like he stepped out of a Spider-Man comic book. If you gave the guy a white lab coat, he could have posed as Dr. Curt Connors when he first started to transform into The Lizard. His face was morphing quickly, going from comic book mad scientist to science fiction nightmare iguana. The damn thing was turning into a mini Godzilla! What the hell was going on?

"Sorry to interrupt your little party," I said, thankful that my voice held steady, "but I don't think you're supposed to be in my house."

The half-formed iguana flared his cheeks at me, and I caught the flicker of a membrane-like piece of skin extending from underneath his chin. He hissed, opening his mouth enough to show off rows of sharklike teeth.

"Not your house, boy," he hissed. "Your mother's mark is still here."

My blood pressure soared. I hated being short, I hated that I didn't look any older than a teenager on a good day, and I hated it when some complete stranger called me "kid" or "boy." Oh, and being a stranger that just broke into my house didn't help either.

"Her mark? Look, I have no idea what you're talking about," I said, keeping my gun trained on them. "This is my house now. And one of my rules is not having uninvited guests that just happen to be Godzilla in human form."

Lizard-man snarled and took a step forward, stopping short when I squeezed off a shot that was inches from removing one of his still-human ears.

"Don't move or the next one's in your skull," I warned, my eyes flicking between the lizard and the still-human one. "Now what was so important that you couldn't wait for me to come home?"

The two looked at each other for a moment, tongues flicking out every now and then like some kind of code. Just when I was beginning to think that they were ignoring me, the one that was still humanish spoke up.

"You are Valerie DuCourt's son, are you not?" he asked calmly, his voice holding the faintest trace of an accent.

Something about these two knowing my mother's maiden name caused the hair on the back of my neck to stand on end. "If I am?"

Humanish gave me a puzzled look. "If you are her son, you must know about the wards on the house or what your mother really did for a living. She was no simple housewife."

"My mom worked three jobs to pay the bills," I snapped, my hands again tightening around the gun. "She raised four boys on her own and gave up everything for us. You know nothing about her, so I suggest you find another topic to talk about."

"I see," Humanish said gravely and held up his hands. "I do apologize for disturbing you, son of DuCourt. We will leave—"

A roar shook the room, and I almost dropped my gun. Lizard-man apparently didn't like that idea and started to tear at his clothes. "We will not! We will get back what she stole from us!" Then he went full reptile.

Take Godzilla and shrink him down to the size of an average grizzly bear. That's what was now in the room with me. As the transformation took place, all evidence of humanity disappeared. As clothing ripped and fell to the floor, his skin turned dark green and his nails grew into wicked-looking claws. His hair mutated into deadly spines that trailed down his back, meeting the tail that had pushed its way through his shredded jeans and now whipped back and forth in a deadly motion. He bared his teeth before letting out another roar and lunging at me.

I'll be honest with you—I froze. Well, hell, wouldn't you if a guy turned into a lizard in front of you?

Oi! Snap out of it! I told myself as a piece of a lamp flew past my head. *Get your ass in gear!*

And I did move when that tail came around and hit my calf. I let out a startled yell as my knees hit the carpet with enough force that I dropped the gun. I looked up at the sound of a hiss and came face-to-face with the Godgrizzla.

I tried to come up with a witty one-liner—you know, like an action hero in the movies when he confronts the bad guy? But all that came out was "Dude … you have a serious case of dog breath."

Grizzly lizard-man didn't take that too well and used a hand about the size of a dinner plate to pick me up by the hair and hurl me into the far wall.

Pain … everywhere. My head felt like a drum was banging inside my skull, and every time I twitched, a fresh wave of suffering started. Gah, I didn't want to move.

"Miar," a stern voice commanded, "get up!"

I groaned in answer, and my eyes began to water as I tried to focus them. *Who is yelling at me?*

"Damn it, Miar, get up!"

Don't wanna . . .

A gunshot followed by an animallike scream somewhere in the room drowned out the rest of my thought.

"Miar . . . Miar!"

***

First thing I noticed when I woke up wasn't the pain. It was that I was nearly naked and lying on the living room floor. The second thing was the complete stranger sitting on my couch. My eyes took a moment to focus; everything was slightly blurry. The pounding in my skull and the glare from the setting sun didn't help, but my vision finally cleared, and I was able to get a good look at my intruder.

Everything about him screamed *money*. His black jacket and pants had to have been tailor-made for his long, lean frame. Gray pinstripes ran through his black vest, tastefully offset by an olive-green shirt. He didn't seem to be wearing a tie, but that didn't mean that he hadn't been wearing one earlier. When my gaze landed on the stranger's shoes, I felt my mouth go dry. He was wearing Barker Black shoes. Those things were expensive and not just because they were handmade in England. They were the shoes of kings and oligarchs, better suited for red carpets and marbled hallways than my worn living room rug.

"Enjoy your nap?" the man asked, his voice holding the lilting hints of an Irish accent. Turning his head enough to look down at me, he followed my gaze. "If you want to know how to acquire a pair of shoes like this, all you have to do is ask."

I managed not to grimace as I pushed myself up to a sitting position. "They're a bit above my pay grade."

The man shrugged and began inspecting his fingernails. "Suit yourself, Mr. Miar, although I must say you could do with a wardrobe change."

A scowl formed on my face before I could stop it. "Why don't you see yourself out before I shoot you?"

The man paused and studied me. His eyes were like pieces of ice—a cold, almost-translucent blue. I felt a sudden urge to hide.

"Need I remind you that I was the one who rescued you from a rather upset lizard?"

I blinked. "You?"

"Yes."

Silence stretched between us as I tried to process what I'd just heard. The lizards were one thing, but this guy just happened to be nearby? I wasn't buying it. And wasn't that a bit backward? The rich in Waco never got their hands dirty—ever. Trust me, I've met my share of them while acting as security so no one would crash their classy parties.

"You really should get a housekeeper, Mr. Miar. Your home is filthy."

I lifted my head to look at him and found he'd moved over to the bookcase on the far wall. His back was to me, showing me that I was right about the suit being fitted just for him.

When did he move? I wondered, getting to my feet and letting out a hiss as my leg twinged. Realizing how ridiculous I must look to the man in front of me, I began searching for my pants, moving slowly to discourage the loud hammering in my head and the thought of my leg folding under me from the pain.

"Excuse me," I answered, putting a bit of snark into my words, "not all of us have the money you do."

His back stiffened, and he turned halfway to look at me, an eyebrow raised in question. A warning bell went off in my head, but apparently it was hiding under the pounding of my headache, so I pressed forward. "Clearly, you know my name. Yours would be …"

More silence. Those icy eyes sent waves of unease through me. He was completely calm and, from what I could tell, hadn't even broken a sweat. I, on the other hand, was starting to lose what bravado I had. Then again, it's kinda hard to keep hold of it when you're standing in front of a complete stranger wearing only your boxers. Throw in what was probably a very damaged leg, and that spells *vulnerable*, ladies and gentlemen.

"My name," he said, snapping me out of my reverie, "is Riley O'Hare. And you should be thankful I didn't let him eat you."

Huh, he's got me there. "Look, O'Hare," I said as I continued looking for my pants, "I'm grateful for you saving my life and all, but I clearly have some cleaning up to do."

Huzzah! How my pants ended up on the back of the couch was beyond me, but I felt a bit better once I had them on .... But not by much. My leg was in misery, and every time I moved, what remained of my jeans would rub against the open wound. Note to self: Wear shorts for a while.

I started looking for my gun. I know—that should have been the first thing I looked for. Criticize all you want, but pants seemed a tad bit more important at the time.

"How did you know I was in trouble anyway?" I asked, walking stiff-legged around the room looking for the rest of my clothes. I caught movement from the corner of my eye as my guest walked over to the one easy chair in the room. He positioned himself behind the chair, looking eerily like a cat, poised and ready to take a swipe at whatever passed by.

"I was merely passing through the area and heard the most awful sound," O'Hare said.

"So you're a concerned citizen?"

He gave me a toothy smile. "But of course."

I located my shirt, limped over, and casually picked it up. It was covered in what appeared to be blood, only darker. Such a shame; I really liked that shirt.

"Going with that theory," I said, tossing the shirt behind me, "tell me why you failed to notify the police or why there isn't an ambulance at my front door?" O'Hare's grip tightened on the back of my chair, tearing the fabric. "And could you *not* put holes in my furniture?"

O'Hare blinked. He slowly released the chair and flexed his fingers. I'd hate to see what those fingers could do wrapped around someone's neck.

"Mr. Miar, we have business to discuss." He gracefully lowered himself into the chair he'd been violating and preened for a bit—fixing his hair and picking his suit free of invisible dust before looking at me expectantly.

I took a deep breath and counted to ten. The last thing I wanted to do was hit him and get thrown in jail for assault.

"Well?"

Scratch that—hitting this guy was the only thing I wanted to do.

Easy, Allen. He's a rich guy, probably with connections. Oh, and he saved your life, I told myself as I settled on the arm of the love seat.

"Tell me," O'Hare said, "what do you know of your mother's profession?"

I shrugged and adjusted my leg a little. "She worked from home most of the time, some kind of editing job, did auditing for a few smaller businesses, and pulled night shifts at Kim's Diner when we needed the extra cash."

O'Hare's mouth twitched into a smile. "Nothing else?"

I shook my head, eyes starting to narrow. "Look, if she owed you money—"

"And her long trips out of town?"

I shifted again, enough to be able to stand quickly if needed. "What do you mean?"

"Oh my, she was a naughty thing, not telling you," O'Hare said, his face splitting into a wide, secret-knowing grin.

"Look, you can either spill what you know or leave. I'm not in the mood."

"I wouldn't be in the mood either had two giant lizards just attacked me," he said with a shrug, that smug grin never leaving his face.

After a beat, I stood. "Here's what you're gonna do: You are going to tell me what you know about my mother, then you are going to explain why I suddenly had Godzilla's babies in my house."

"If I refuse?"

It was my turn to smirk as I walked over to him, leaning in just enough to invade his personal space. "I will be a good, law-abiding citizen and shoot the intruder who came into my home."

O'Hare's smirk faltered for a moment. "You're bluffing. You're a cop—"

"I'd claim self-defense .... Besides, who said I was one of the good cops?"

Neither one of us was willing to look away first. A few tumbleweeds rolling by with old Wild West music playing in the background would have been perfect. Instead, chirping crickets, the occasional blaring car horn, and insane barking dogs were our soundtrack.

I started to turn and caught O'Hare stirring in his seat. Grinning, I counted to myself. *One ... two ... three ...*

"Fine," O'Hare muttered.

I backed away, giving us some distance, and gestured for him to continue as my leg kept up a steady, throbbing rhythm.

"Your mother was a marvelous woman," O'Hare started. "She also was an incredibly special and very talented hunter—extraordinary, really."

I stared at him and slowly shook my head. "No, my mother wasn't a hunter. She didn't even own a gun."

O'Hare's mouth curled into a smirk. "Oh, I beg to differ. She had a lovely little .38 Special pointed in my direction on more than one occasion. But that truly wasn't her style. No, your mother preferred knives. I've had to repair quite a few holes in my wall, thanks to her."

There had to be a mistake. My mother—a woman who was terrified of June bugs and roaches—owned a gun .... And knives ... that she pointed not at animals but at people who wore expensive suits and shoes and looked like mafia bosses? I didn't know Waco was even mafia material.

"Wouldn't know why she would want to kill you," I murmured. "No, wait, I totally do."

"Foolish boy, I've had about enough of this." O'Hare all but growled at me as he stood, his body vibrating with anger. "You are going to need my help, Mr. Miar."

O'Hare seemed to grow in my presence, his confidence wrapping around him like a fluffy blanket. It gave me the creeps. Most people have confidence in short bursts—a promotion at work, during a sports game, or knowing the right answer. But this guy? This guy wore it like a coat and never saw the need to take it off. And it made him seem ten times the size that he actually was. In all honesty, O'Hare *was* taller than me by about five inches.

My cell phone rang, but I ignored it in favor of our little standoff. The shrill cry stopped after a few moments, only for the landline to start.

"Perhaps you should get that," O'Hare advised, nodding to the phone reverberating on the table. I grimaced, not wanting to get closer to him, but at the same time I needed to answer the phone.

"Stay put," I said, pointing a finger at him, then scooped up the receiver. "Miar."

"It took you long enough."

"Zack, I'm a bit busy—"

"I found out who the victim is," Zack said, running over my protest. "Took a bit of looking though. It was like she was living off the grid or something; name's Meredith Strong."

Why does that sound familiar?

"I also have the crime scene photos for you," Zack added. "Do you want me to put them on your desk?"

"Hmm? No, no. I'll pick them up from you tomorrow," I answered, running a hand through my hair. I settled on the arm of the couch and turned away from O'Hare just enough to keep my conversation private but also enough to make sure I could see the Irishman if he decided to move at all. Zack's voice rattled in my ear, the sound washing over me as I started to feel something pull at the back of my mind.

"Earth to Allen?"

"Hmm?" I asked, snapping out of my daze.

"You didn't hear anything I just told you, did you?"

"No …"

Zack sighed. "I *said*, she lived a pretty mundane life: worked in the records area of the Health District downtown, went to college out of state, high school valedictorian. She managed to take her debate team to state a couple of times …. Nothing here that would send up red flags."

Wait a sec, I thought, getting to my feet and limping hastily to the bookshelf. "Does her name pop up in any old police reports?"

I listened to him tapping away on the keyboard as I searched for the book I hated most besides the family album: my high school yearbook. It's not that I had horrible memories about all four of those years; there were some good ones. But most of the time, it was just hell. I was lucky to go a day without being shoved into a trash can. Don't ask how; just know that it can be done.

Zack sucked in some air. "Two reports were filed," he said as I flipped open the yearbook. "One was a hit-and-run. No one was hurt—"

"And the other one?"

"Would you hang on? Let me see .... Someone filled the inside of her car with flour and cooked noodles her last year of school. Person was never caught, but props to the guys that pulled it off. Flour is hell to get out of carpet."

A wave of dread washed over me when I finally found the face in the book that matched the name. I counted to ten twice before I was able to speak again. "Ridgefield High, class of 2005."

"Yeah," Zack said, a bit surprised. "How did you know?"

I put my forehead against the shelf. "Meredith Strong was in my graduating class."

Chapter Three

"*What?*"

I winced and held the phone away from my ear.

"You *know* our exploded person?"

I jammed the yearbook back onto one of the bookshelves, causing me to wobble dangerously on my feet. "Listen, gimme a minute—I've had a rough afternoon, all right?"

Zack fell silent, and I could feel the pain creeping up my leg. "I know the crime scene was ugly—"

I tightened my grip on the shelf I was holding. "Yeah, and then I came home and got thrown across the room by a Godzilla baby." I would need aspirin soon and probably a good bandage. Just a bandage, I hoped—the last thing I wanted was stitches.

"How—"

"I'll explain later, all right?" I closed my eyes to quash the nausea and dizziness that appeared. Once I knew I wasn't going to fall over if I moved, I turned to check on O'Hare. "Crap."

I slammed my hand down on the shelf. A twinge shot up my arm, and parts of my hand went numb. He was gone; the guy who had saved me from becoming lizard food and dangled information about my mother in front of me was gone. How could he have disappeared without my hearing him leave?

"What was that?" Zack yelled in my ear, reminding me I was still on the phone. "Sounded like something fell."

I had two options. I could come clean—tell him everything and run the risk of his calling me crazy and not talking to me again—or I could delay all of it until I had solid proof, still get called crazy, but have him jump in with me. *I'll go with delay.*

"Pizza guy got my delivery wrong." I felt a tiny pang. I hated lying. I was good at telling little white lies like "I'm fine" and "It doesn't hurt"—things that avoided deeper probing into my well-being—but I still didn't enjoy it. Until I had more facts though, I wasn't telling anyone what I saw.

"I keep telling you to stop ordering from that place," Zack said.

"Yeah, I know." I cleared my throat. "Look, I have to go. I'll be by your office in the morning."

I hobbled over to the couch, sighing as I sank into the cushions. My mind started to race, trying to find the logic behind what I'd seen and heard.

I had a very specific set of beliefs: The sky is blue, fire is hot, water is wet, and lizard-men only exist in science fiction. Yet I'd just encountered lizard-men in my home. If I hadn't just gotten my butt kicked by baby Godzilla, I would assume the whole thing had been an elaborate hoax. The very thought of that thorough butt kicking irked me to no end. Don't get me wrong, I had gotten into my fair share of fights as a kid with my brothers and bullies at school, but none of them had ended with my leg sliced open and me knocked out.

"This makes no sense." I winced at how loud I sounded in the empty house. For a moment, I listened to my voice bouncing off the walls. "Godzilla isn't real, people don't explode, and creepy mob bosses don't just vanish in midair!"

I stared at the ceiling, my leg steadily reminding me that I needed first aid and a change of clothes. After a while, I hoisted myself off the couch and made my way to the kitchen. I rummaged in one of the drawers and came up with a pair of kitchen scissors. Carefully, I cut away the bloodstained leg of my pants and tossed it in the trash. Chucking the scissors into the sink, I grabbed a nearby towel and began cleaning the cut the best I could.

The gash itself isn't that deep, I thought. It ran in a curve from the top of my calf to just above my ankle, making a wonderful J shape. Unease poked at me. That thing could have crippled me if it had sliced through my hamstring or Achilles tendon. Lucky didn't even begin to describe it.

I quickly made a makeshift bandage with what I had on hand and then, with a bit of hesitation, picked up the scissors and cut off the other pant leg. Couldn't go around with just one pant leg cut off, could I? Once I was satisfied that my jorts were somewhat even, I limped my way to the bathroom in my mother's room for some aspirin.

Meredith Strong. I couldn't recall much about her from school except how quiet she'd been. I wanted to find out more, but I needed to look into the initial victim first. All I had to go on were the pictures the chief gave me, and they were all the way back at the office. Why? Because I believe in having a good work-life balance, or trying to.

I grabbed a couple of pain pills and swallowed them on my way out the door. I glanced at my watch as I locked up: 4:30 p.m. If the chief wasn't looking for me, I could get in and out in ten minutes tops. Halfway in the car, it dawned on me that I wasn't wearing my gun. *I'll only be gone for a bit*, I reasoned, pulling out of the drive. *It'll be fine.*

***

When I pulled into the station, it was close to five thirty and the night patrol had already begun their shift. I parked in the lot across the street that was reserved for personal cars and tried to come up with a viable excuse for having a towel duct-taped to my leg, in case someone asked.

"All right," I said aloud. "Get in, get the folder Newburn gave you, and get out. Not that hard, Miar."

Ben was on desk duty. I thanked whatever angel had been listening, because Ben wasn't a man to ask questions. He was one of the few who found it rather amusing that I lived in my office sometimes. He even came by one time with a couple of beers and a bag of food. Ben was awesome.

He glanced up and hit the buzzer to unlock the doors to the main area. I waved, and he nodded before going back to whatever he'd been doing before; probably a crossword puzzle—he seemed like that kind of guy.

A few officers raised a hand in greeting on their way to the briefing room, but most ignored me, which was just fine with me. The bullpen, or main area, was nearly deserted except for two officers sitting at their desks, nearly hidden behind stacks of backlogged paperwork. They were so engrossed with their work and the desire to go home, they didn't even notice me. I remembered those days; they weren't the best. I recalled a plethora of dead pens.

I ducked into my office and closed the door, letting the darkness wash over me for a moment before maneuvering with practiced ease to turn on my desk lamp. After a quick peek inside the file to make sure I hadn't grabbed the wrong one, I made a careful but hasty retreat.

No one stopped me on my way out, and even with my limp, I made it back to the car fairly quickly. Once safely inside, my eyes turned to the folder in the seat beside me. The pictures, the coroner's report, the police report—it was all there in that paper sleeve. Now came the part that, most of the time, got me into trouble. *Worry about that later,* I told myself, turning the engine over.

***

On my way home, I swung by Maggie's Occult Shop. It was a little hole-in-the-wall close to downtown that catered to everyone from the hippies looking for door-hanging beads to the local Wiccan practitioners. And if you looked really hard, you could spot a few churchgoers emerging every once in a while.

A bell jingled above me when I walked into the shop, and the smell of incense and dried herbs hit me. I stood in the doorway for a moment, letting my eyes adjust to the dim lighting before glancing around. Trinkets and general occult paraphernalia decorated displays on either side of the door. Low tables lined the front, leaving enough room for a few statues in front of the windows. Each table held something different. A few harbored artfully carved wooden boxes; others held an array of crystals and stones arranged on plum-colored cloth. A stand that held wind chimes had been set up next to the door. They ranged from carved wooden ones to delicate-looking glass ones that sounded like otherworldly laughter when someone opened the door and let in drafts.

Battered secondhand bookshelves stood back-to-back a little farther in on the right, their wooden dividers stuffed with books on magic spells, druidism, paranormal encounters, and alien visitations. A few shelves on the very last bookcase were sectioned off for historical myths and legends, along with one or two books on deities from different religions. There was even a section dedicated to young adult fantasy in case some bored kid wandered away from their parents, but on occasion you could spot an adult back there too.

I wandered farther in and paused to look at the array of incense on the wall near the counter. The shelving unit was a bit taller than me, but short enough that I could reach up comfortably and inspect the burners and wooden boxes on the top.

"Hey, Allen."

I turned—a hand going for my gun out of reflex before I remembered that I hadn't brought it with me—but it was just Maggie.

Margaret "Maggie" Anderson was my oldest and possibly closest friend. She was among the few people who could stand my bad moods. The first time I yelled at her, she broke my nose, which sealed our friendship in some odd way. I'd spent a lot of time in Maggie's shop and occasionally helped out, either in the store or with research for the blog she wrote on the store's website—only when I was caught up on my work, or the chief decided I needed a change of scenery, or I wanted to see daylight.

Maggie had a fondness for changing her hair color whenever it suited her and making sure her clothes matched her hair. Today, she had her hair in two faded but still bright-green buns and was decked out in black pants and a cut-up Flogging Molly T-shirt, which she filled out rather nicely. Her height was boosted by stiletto boots, giving her at least three more inches to tower over me.

Maggie raised an eyebrow and put her hands on her hips. "What's with the jump-and-shoot treatment?"

I walked over to her—well, limped, but you get the idea. "I've had a very eventful day," I said, slumping against the counter.

Maggie's boots thumped softly on the worn carpeted floor as she took a few steps back to look me over. "You have a kitchen towel taped to your leg."

I blinked, then looked down. The towel was still holding up nicely, though the material was looking a little redder than before. I shuddered. I was not looking forward to unwrapping that later on.

"Um ..."

"What happened now?" Maggie asked, exasperated.

"Tripped down the stairs?"

Maggie's hazel eyes narrowed. She leaned forward until her face was close enough for me to smell her cherry perfume. "Don't lie to me."

Plan B: Say something she'll believe. Quick! Come on, brain, think!

"Yeah," I muttered, my mind still scrambling, "about that ..."

Grabbing my arm, she started dragging me to the back of the shop. "What did you do? I swear, if it involves some kind of experiment or theory, I'll smack you."

No time like the present to tell the truth. "I came home and found two giant lizards in my house and got into a fight."

Maggie stopped walking. Then she lightly smacked me on the side of the head. "That's the most ridiculous thing I've ever heard," she said, pulling me into the break room area.

I rubbed the side of my head and grinned sheepishly. "Most of what I said was true."

"Shut it." She pointed to the far side of the room. "Sit."

I sat—or flopped—onto the couch and studied the ceiling while Maggie rummaged through the cabinets.

Maggie and I met in high school, freshman year. One of the varsity football players had been picking on me (for who knows what that day), until Maggie put him in a headlock—in a skirt and heels no less—and proceeded to educate him on why bullying was very, very wrong. We became good friends after that, and she was the one who made sure I didn't fall to pieces when my mother passed away. She was also deeply knowledgeable about a variety of occult and folklore topics, an encyclopedia on legs so to speak.

"Why don't you believe me?" I asked, starting to unwrap my poor man's bandage as she walked over with a first aid kit.

Maggie wrinkled her nose. "I *believe* you were doing some stupid stunt and oopsed," she said. "You have to be more careful. Lie on your stomach."

"Trust me, it wasn't intentional." As I turned over, I heard her gasp.

"Allen … what the hell?"

I propped myself up enough to watch her glare down at my leg and let out an animallike hiss as she slapped a damp rag onto my cut.

"Does that hurt?"

"Yes!" I squeaked, my leg jerking involuntarily as it tried to escape the torture.

"Good." She began to carefully clean it off. I squirmed a bit at the stinging sensation, then slowly began to relax.

"You should let Zack look at this," Maggie said. "You probably need stitches."

I glanced back at her just in time to get a very nice view down the front of her tank top. I turned away, grinning. Hey, what can I say? I'm only human.

"Were you just looking down my shirt?" Maggie asked.

"I'm human."

"You're a guy."

"Is there a difference?"

She smiled, full and bright. She had a wonderful smile, one that always reached her eyes and created little dimples on her cheeks. Occasionally, it was paired with her laugh, which was pure music.

"Not really," she said.

A swat on my tush let me know Maggie was done wrapping me up, and I waited until she moved out of the way before sitting up. I flexed my ankle and felt a small pulse of pain as my muscles protested being used. Oh, this was going to be fun waking up to in the morning.

"But seriously … was this work related?"

"No. I already told you," I said with a shrug. "Lizard-men … well, more like baby Godzillas."

Maggie rolled her eyes. "If you weren't acting so casual about it—instead, showing me that your whole world view has been challenged—I might believe you. Shape-shifters *are* a thing. Fine, I get it, but if you get hurt again and I have to patch you up, you'd better spill."

I blew out a breath. "I promise to tell you when everything is settled," I said, getting to my feet. "At the moment, there're too many questions and not enough answers."

Maggie took my hand and put two white pills in it. "Aspirin. Don't dry swallow them, all right? And take it easy on your leg. You're lucky you can even walk."

I took the pills from her and popped them in my mouth, grinning a little when I heard Maggie sigh.

"Why do I even bother? You never listen anyway."

"Because I'm fun, charming, and entertaining," I answered, "and your world would be horribly boring without me."

Maggie pretended to look unamused and threw a ketchup packet at me. It bounced off my head and fell to the floor, making us both laugh a little as the air in the room became a bit less stuffy.

"So," Maggie started, "how *is* work? You on a new case?"

I took a few experimental steps and nodded. I filled her in on the morning's activities, leaving out the part about the Dallas file in my front seat. While I traded crazy stories with Maggie all the time, there wasn't a need to tell her everything at the moment—especially since I didn't have much to go on. By the time I was done, Maggie's face was scrunched up in disgust.

"That is just nasty," she said, shuddering and rubbing her arms. "So something blew her up like a balloon and then popped her?"

"A gruesome way to put it, but pretty much," I agreed as my phone buzzed. "Do you think you can do a little digging on what that might be?"

"Maybe," Maggie said, crossing her arms over her chest and smiling when my eyes followed the movement. "If you renounce your accusation from a few weeks ago, when you said that paranormal wasn't real."

My phone buzzed again, and I ignored it. "I didn't say that it wasn't real—"

"I believe the phrase you used was 'hocus-pocus,'" Maggie interrupted, using air quotes on the last two words. "Say it's real, and I'll help you."

"Maggie, now isn't the time …."

The woman in front of me raised an eyebrow and tapped her foot. Who knew little boot taps could be intimidating?

"Fine," I said, reaching into my pocket to grab my phone. "It's real! All of it's real! Bigfoot, the tooth fairy, hell, the damn wolf man is real! Happy now?"

I was rewarded with another full smile and a pat on the head as Maggie made her way to the front of the store. I stood there for a moment, shaking my head. *Did I just admit that all of her crazy theories are real?*

I flipped my phone open without looking at the readout. "Miar."

"Where the hell are you?"

Just what I needed.

"At the occult shop, Chief," I said, heading to the front of the store. "Whatever happened, I didn't do it."

"We've been trying to get ahold of you for the past thirty minutes," Newburn grit out. "Your neighbor called in; said she heard gunshots and an animal roaring."

"I can explain—"

"Yes, you will," Newburn said, his growl making the hairs on my arm stand up. "We're here at your house, but guess who's not?"

"Me. I'm on my way."

***

I have chosen to repress some memories: The fact that I have three older brothers, how my mother died, and a few other dark episodes are safely tucked away in my mental vault. I do, however, like remembering other things, and most of the time they outweigh the bad. But occasionally, those unwanted thoughts creep out, wrap around me like a vise, and start to squeeze until I can barely breathe. Tonight was one of those occasions.

"Allen!"

I turned when I heard my name called.

Newburn emerged from the sea of people that had gathered, his huge mass parting them like Moses and the Red Sea. He was dressed in civvies, a worn but still acceptable T-shirt that barely seemed to hold his muscled chest in and a pair of shorts. He'd been at home when he got the call, apparently, and rushed over to find an empty house. I felt horrible.

"Chief," I sighed, running a hand over my face. "Was all this really necessary?" I nodded to the three squad cars, EMT, and fire truck in my driveway, lights going and everything.

"It is when I get disturbing calls about one of my people and then can't find them," Newburn said. He stopped in front of me and took in my appearance. "You all right?"

"Yeah," I assured him. "I'm fine."

"Your house has been ransacked. And there's quite a bit of blood in the living room."

"Anyone see who trashed my house?"

Newburn pulled a small notepad from the pocket of his shorts and flipped through a couple of pages. "A few witnesses claimed to see two guys leaving, couldn't see them clearly, but they were big and burly. Pro wrestler types. Sound like anyone you know?"

"Not that I can recall," I answered, watching some of the crime scene guys walk around. "Did any of them have a tail?"

"What?! No ..." he answered with a confused look.

"Just checking."

I stepped away, trying not to hobble. If I hobbled, Newburn would ask more questions that I wasn't in the mood to answer.

"Mind telling me what happened?" he asked, falling into step beside me as we made our way to the house.

I shrugged. "There were a few intruders when I got home. I confronted them. And then we got into a bit of a confrontation. Then they left. House was fine."

Newburn nodded and made a small sound, his long legs carrying him to the house a bit faster than my own. When I caught up to him, he was standing at the base of my front steps.

"Doesn't look like your typical gunfight," he said.

I stared at my house in horror. The front door was hanging on a single hinge and was decorated with deep gouges that extended through the doorframe. Part of the frame near the lock was splintered, the wood sticking out in vicious, needlelike teeth. From what I could see, the whole locking mechanism was missing, as if someone or some*thing* had physically ripped it out of the frame.

"Any idea who could have done this?"

Mutely, I shook my head no and walked up the stairs, being careful not to touch anything. Inside, the house was a complete mess. The shelves on my bookcase were splintered, and books were scattered all over the living room in a flurry of black-and-white pages. A few were ripped in half, their pages shredded into confetti.

The furniture was gutted, the stuffing clumped all over the room. A few pieces had landed in my blood near the entertainment center, creating little blossoms of red amid the sea of white. Chairs were broken and thrown around the room; there were dents in my walls. Pictures that hadn't been touched since my parents were alive were shattered on the floor. One or two had been shredded by the same claws that attacked the door. Even my curtains hadn't survived the assault and hung in tatters on their little rungs above the windows.

My face flushed and my heartbeat sped up as adrenaline hit me. This used to be my safe space, my place of peace. The one place that was sacred and secure; where I didn't have to worry about work, my height, or even what my coworkers thought of me; where I could sit in my boxers and watch cheesy movies without worrying. Not even my paranoia about my brother disturbed this place. But now, it had been violated. They had disrupted the balance I'd created painstakingly over the years.

"Ein Stück Dreck," I growled, crouching down to retrieve a surviving picture of my parents.

"Do I want to know what you just said?" Newburn asked, his footsteps stopping nearby.

I shook my head and stood. Of the four of us boys, only I had become fluent in my mother's native tongue, and I sometimes slipped into it without realizing.

"Do you think it's the same people you had trouble with earlier?"

"No," I said as I stood up. "The guys I met earlier were carefully searching, almost like they didn't want to be in the house at all. But whoever did this … they had no problem turning this place inside out."

Newburn grunted, scribbling down some notes as I talked. "They didn't threaten you at all?"

"Nope," I said as one of the paramedics walked over to us. "Like I said earlier, I confronted them, and they left."

"Sir," the officer said, holding up an evidence bag, "we had forensics take a few samples of the blood we spotted earlier. Maybe we can use it to catch the guys that did this."

I really didn't want to give everything up and say a giant lizard attacked me. Oh, and then a mob boss saved my ass. Couldn't forget him, as much as I wanted to. But if I didn't say something now, I'd get thrown into hot water later for wasting the station's time and resources. I decided not to sound crazy and went with a mixture of truth and lie.

"It's mine," I said as casually as I could, pointing to my bandages. "I was moving some stuff around this morning and cut my leg open, blood everywhere. I didn't have a chance to clean it up before I left for work."

The officer raised an eyebrow, and Newburn just stared at me.

"That's a lot of blood."

I shrugged. "I have thin blood." That part wasn't a lie. I did have thin blood.

I took advantage of their silence to look around the living room again. My eyes landed on the yearbook I'd gotten down earlier. It was lying on the floor, its pages ripped and scattered. I crouched down again and fished through the remains for Maggie's picture, along with the comment she'd written in the back of my book.

"Sorry," I apologized, looking back at them. "Long day … bad day."

Newburn grunted. "You aren't kidding, first the hospital and now this. The press is going to start sniffing around soon, and I don't want another incident, so stay away from reporters. Understood?"

I nodded and carefully picked up the pieces of the yearbook I'd been looking for. That was one thing I didn't need to worry about now.

The current circumstances left me with several options. One: Put in more legwork to find out who destroyed my house, work on the Dallas case Newburn dropped into my lap, and take a closer look at the Saint Mary's case. Two: Contact Riley O'Hare somehow and get his help on option one. And finally, three: Hang my neck out there and see how long it took for whoever started all of this to come and kill me. I wasn't too fond of option three, and two was only if I got desperate. That left option one. Damn.

"Are you guys almost done?" I asked the officer.

He nodded and checked the clipboard in his hand. "We'll be out in a few minutes. You have a place to stay for the night?"

"Not really," I answered, running a hand through my hair. "I'd prefer to stay here if they didn't make it to the second floor."

"No," Newburn said as the officer moved off to another part of the house. "Upstairs is clean, for some reason. Must be new to the robbery business."

So that's what they think this is? I almost laughed aloud. How wrong they were.

"Must be," I agreed, letting out a sigh of relief. "Well, at least I only have to clean up one mess."

Newburn stared at me. "Miar, you can't be serious. You don't even have a front door."

"I can manage …."

My boss glared at me, and I gave him the most innocent smile I could manage. He was only trying to help, and I hated being indebted. No door I could deal with. What I couldn't handle would be those things coming back and disabling anyone who thought it would be fun to shoot them. And some of the guys on the force were still a bit green. I also needed to think, and my version of thinking was cleaning. Or in this case, putting up a thing of plywood on my front door so no one could come in and kill me.

"Fine," Newburn relented and tucked the notebook away. "Stay here tonight. I'll put a car out front—"

"Chief..."

Newburn leaned in. "You will take the car out front, Miar, or I can drag you out of here and put you on the couch at my house. Now which is it going to be?"

Chief Newburn had four kids, all girls, and they were loud. Really loud.

"I think I'll take that car."

"You'll call the station if anything happens," Newburn instructed me as the others began to trickle out the door. "Understood?"

"Sure," I said, knowing I wouldn't.

Chapter Four

The next morning, I woke up to every part of my body protesting in some way, shape, or form. I guess I was a bit more bruised than I thought.

I forced myself to a sitting position and just sat there—throbbing. Finally, I rubbed my face and, with a groan, swung my legs over the side of the bed before gingerly sliding off. Agony shot up my leg, setting me down with a short yelp.

"Ow, ow, ow," I chanted, carefully rubbing my wounded appendage. "Aspirin … where's the aspirin?" I looked hopefully at the bathroom door, but no magical plastic bottle danced out to me. I sighed and hoisted myself to my feet again. Oh, this was going to be a fun morning.

Between short breaks and a zombie shuffle, I made it to the bathroom on the second floor. The house originally had four bedrooms on two floors and a huge attic space. But having four boys sharing three rooms wasn't going to happen. So before he died, my dad converted half of the attic into a bedroom, and I claimed it for my own. My brothers lived on the second floor, and Mom and Dad's room was on the main floor along with the other living areas. The only problem with my room was that I had to go down two flights of stairs to reach the front door and one to use the bathroom. Walking downstairs in the dark can be hazardous, and I slipped more than once before I wised up and wrapped Christmas lights around the handrails to light the way. My mother had not been amused but went along with it.

I perched on the toilet lid and started unwrapping my leg, grimacing when I tossed the bandages in the trash can. The wound looked better, but it was still red and a little bit of blood tried to ooze through. Looking at it, I was thankful I hadn't ended up on my face when I was hopping across the second-floor landing. That would have hurt, although I'd wager not as bad as tumbling down the stairs.

"Aspirin," I said, using the edge of the sink to pull me upright, "where are you?"

I rummaged around in the medicine cabinet for a bit before I found the right bottle. I only had a bit of difficulty with the damn childproof container and getting two pills out. I tossed them back and swallowed, making a slight face at the taste. I stood there for a few minutes, my leg slightly bent to keep the weight off of it, and waited for the aspirin to kick in.

Maggie had done a good job of cleaning the cut, but that wouldn't save me from having Zack look at it when I went to see him. He'd probably want to check it for infections and run a few tests. I shuddered at that thought. I was a tough enough guy to take a beating if I needed to and crazy enough to be the front man in a drug raid, but tell me I needed to have blood work done? Nope, no way in hell.

Huffing, I stripped and stepped into the shower. When I was squeaky clean and Irish fresh, I stepped out and wrapped a towel around my waist before starting the trek back up the stairs to my room. Getting dressed was another thing entirely. I couldn't wear my normal attire of jeans and a T-shirt. The jeans would scrape against the bandages, and I would be complaining all day.

I did a mental toss-up and pulled on a pair of black cargo shorts after making sure they didn't harbor any holes, in case I got called into the office. After some digging in my dresser, I came up with a decent shirt that read Give Me Coffee or Give Me Death and yanked it over my head. I ran a brush through my hair and pulled it back into a low ponytail as I limped down the stairs again. I sighed when I arrived on the ground floor and surveyed the disaster that was my living room.

"I'll clean it up when I get home," I said, my voice surprisingly loud in the empty room. I felt a pang of loneliness.

Brushing it off, I continued to the door. I didn't have time to think like that right now. I had no desire at all to get a roommate, mostly because of the hours I worked. But I was also pretty sure that if I brought home any of my work, it would be a huge deal-breaker. Not to mention I was a bit paranoid and very uncomfortable about sharing my personal space with a complete stranger. A pet wouldn't be too bad, but with the repairs that needed to be done on the house now, I knew I wouldn't have the money to take care of it.

The officers guarding my house were gone when I walked outside; probably left to get some breakfast or just to get some sleep. I didn't blame them. It wasn't like I'd begged for the detail anyway.

I shook my head as I turned my engine over. I desperately needed a new life—one that didn't have a slice of weird in it. But weird had been a staple in my life since I was little, at least compared to my brothers and other kids in the neighborhood.

I was never one to play sports or tag or to burn ants with a magnifying glass in the driveway. No, I preferred harmless, solitary pursuits like running around the house pretending to fly, hunting for treasure in the backyard, staging pretend battles with couch cushions, or reading. My mom didn't mind at all, and from what I remember, she encouraged it. I practically begged her to read to me from *Grimms' Fairy Tales* or *The Hobbit*. Occasionally, she would give in and indulge me for hours past my bedtime.

My teachers thought it was amazing that I had such a drive to create and read. Eventually, I started playing *Dungeons and Dragons*, with Mom's permission of course, and it only magnified what was already there and started me on the path of a grade A nerd. Of course, when the kids at school figured this out, I was quickly reminded where people like me resided in the school hierarchy.

The *Cops* theme song began blaring from my cell, bringing me out of my reverie about halfway to the station. I dug the phone out from one of the many pockets on my shorts and flipped it open.

"What's up, Chief?" I asked, holding in a sigh.

"Just calling to see if your intruders came back last night."

"I managed to sleep just fine," I told him as my phone beeped. I glanced at the readout. "And I'll fill out the report, I promise."

Newburn let out a sound of agreement and hung up. Great conversationalist, I tell you.

I switched to the other line.

"Zack, my man," I greeted, stopping for a light. "I was just about to call you."

"I would hope so," Zack said, unamused. "Considering the things I've been hearing this morning."

I blinked. "Uh ..."

"Gunshots? Blood everywhere?" Zack said in my ear. "Your living room looking like drunken frat boys got ahold of it? Ringing any bells?"

Some people really shouldn't miss their morning coffee. I stared into space for a beat and turned down one of the streets nearby and parked so I could talk without the risk of causing an accident.

"Are you talking about the emergency call to my house?"

An exasperated grunt was my answer. Guess I was right.

"What else would I be asking about?" Zack said, his tone making me slide down in my seat. "What did you get yourself into this time?"

I pulled at my seat belt in irritation. No coffee and a scolding, a perfect wake-up call for a nonmorning person.

"Nothing, just a routine case. And while we're on the subject, why is everyone treating me like a four-year-old?"

"Because you tend to act like one. Now get over here and tell me what's going on."

I stared at the phone and, with a few choice words, slipped it back into my pocket before putting the car in drive. It was going to be a long day.

***

The city morgue was housed in what used to be an old printing store. It was a modest building with the basement and first two floors dedicated to the realm of the dead and their paperwork. The other floors had been converted into apartments for people who thought it was cool to live above a bunch of corpses. Of course, the affordable rent might have had something to do with it. And the location in the nicer part of downtown was ideal. It was set just far enough away from the main street that the only complaints called in were about the bars nearby. It also worked out great in hiding the comings and goings of the local meat wagon.

I pulled into the parking lot and sat there for a moment, my head spinning as I tried to come up with a plausible excuse for not letting him know I was okay besides "I got attacked by lizards." Yeah, no pressure at all.

"You're a terrible liar when it comes to keeping your butt out of the fire," I muttered to myself. "On the other hand, if you tell him the truth, he'll think you're lying anyway."

I sighed and made my way across the parking lot, glancing down at the basement windows as I approached the building. The Smash Mouth floating out of a half-open window told me Zack was inside. If I were lucky, he wouldn't throw a medical tray at me this time.

The loading area that led down to the basement looked almost like the entrance to an underground garage. The ground sloped down gently before leveling out near a pair of metal doors. Zack had posted a sign on the doors: Zombies Ahead. Enter at Your Own Risk. The paramedics thought it was amusing. I thought it was ingenious.

I knocked once before entering. The morgue was clean and smelled faintly of disinfectant with a lingering stench of rotted eggs. A dividing wall ran the width of the room, cutting it in half and leaving enough space at either end for entrance or egress. The front was set up as an office, enabling the business of the recently departed. A desk, chairs, small couch, and even a rug had been put on the linoleum floor in an attempt to make the space a bit cozier. The illusion was somewhat ruined by the meat lockers lining the left side of the room and the cargo elevator on the right. The walls had been decorated with medical diagrams and various posters in hopes of drawing attention away from the wall of steel. Several panels of dark-gray curtains stretched across the dividing wall and openings, effectively hiding the contents on the other side.

The sharp scent of formalin invaded my nostrils, and I sneezed before letting the door shut softly behind me. "Zack?"

"Back here."

Smash Mouth faded into some pop song I didn't know as I crossed the room, pausing when I heard the squeak of my friend's sneakers on the shiny floor. I was about to push through one of the curtains when Zack spoke up again.

"If you come back here and puke, I'll hurt you."

A reliable threat mixed with a warning, my favorite kind. I grinned and carefully parted the curtain enough for a quick glance into the back room. No way I was stepping foot beyond the curtain if he was working on someone. I learned my lesson the last time around.

"Ah, good morning to you too," I answered, stepping away from the curtain and leaning against the outer wall, the cool concrete digging into my back. "You have anyone on the table?"

"If I didn't, I would be out there waiting for you," Zack informed me, plopping something into one of the many plastic containers he kept on hand. "Martha Connors, forty years old, died of natural causes."

The plopping sound made my throat constrict, and I was very glad I'd stayed on this side of the curtain. It meant I didn't have to watch him take out poor Martha Connors's insides and put them in plastic containers.

"Oh, that's nice ...."

I listened to Zack walk to another part of the room. "I thought so too. Some days it's nice not having to dig bullets out of people."

The sound of a fridge door opening and closing reached my ears.

"Give me a minute to clean up this mess," Zack said after a few moments.

Fine by me. I wandered away from the wall and slouched into a chair to wait. Before my mother's funeral, the dead hadn't bothered me so much. They looked at peace, almost as if they were sleeping and were going to wake up at any moment. Of course, I was a kid and had seen bodies at funerals after everything had been done, not realizing that the process was gruesome and at times overwhelming. After being the one grieving and settling affairs, I couldn't look at another dead person, which hindered me in my job a bit, but I was learning to control myself.

The curtain moved and Zack walked out in his white lab coat, wiping his hands on a paper towel.

"Shall we talk," he asked, pitching the towel into a wastebasket, "or do I have to call Maggie?"

I shot him a glare. "She's not my handler."

Zack raised an eyebrow. "Really? Because I remember her threatening you at the station when you thought it was a good idea to live off of ramen noodles and ravioli."

I took in Zack's appearance as he seated himself behind the desk. His dark-blond hair bordered on brown, and he kept it short enough to look professional. His clothes were Walmart specials, though, that didn't match. Typical, but Zack always reasoned that the dead didn't care what he wore.

I stretched my leg to gauge my pain level. It was more like an overly sore muscle now—the kind of ache that lets you know that you're healing. My head came up when Zack cleared his throat, and I realized that I must have spaced out for a bit.

"Hmm," I said in a brilliant cover-up attempt.

Zack shook his head.

"Sorry, I was up late last night, and it was a very eventful day."

Zack leaned forward, placing his arms on the desk's cheap pressboard surface. "You're pale."

"I'm always pale," I said, tilting my head enough to rest it on the back of the chair.

"Tell me what's going on."

I squeezed my eyes shut, muttering under my breath. "Can you at least feed me coffee first?"

Something hit my face and bounced to the floor. Another hit me, then another, until eventually I started to develop a twitch in one of my eyes.

"All right!" I yelled. "Fine, I'll tell you. Just stop throwing crap at me."

Zack's mouth turned up in a triumphant smile.

I pulled myself to a sitting position. Despite my situation, I started to grin. My chair was surrounded by a puddle of crumpled white paper. "Is this what you do when you're bored, paper snowballs?" I asked, kicking a few out of my way.

He ignored my question. "The next thing I would have thrown at you would've stung." He held up a seemingly innocent object dangling from his finger: a rubber band attached to a paper clip. Not a big deal to most. It looked like nothing but boredom taking hold of the average worker. But for my old classmates, it was the ultimate projectile. If used right, the wielder could send it across the room with enough force to leave a bruise that would last for days. And speaking as one who had been on the receiving end of those deadly things, I was glad Zack stopped when he did.

I raised an eyebrow.

"Sometimes I get bored," Zack said with a shrug, twirling the device around his finger by the rubber band. "So … Maggie said I might need to do some touch-up work on your leg."

I did my best fish impression. Zack's smile widened. I couldn't believe she'd told him. I mean, it wasn't like I could hide the cut on my leg, or that I wasn't going to eventually tell him what happened—maybe a few days after the case was solved—but come on.

"I … I am not a four-year-old," I protested with a huff. "I don't need a supervisor!"

"Apparently you do," Zack said, walking over. "Go lie down on the couch; it will be easier for me to check that way."

When I didn't move, Zack sighed. A sharp sting hit my leg a second later.

"Ow!" That monkey wrench coworker of mine fired that paper clip thing at me!

Zack chuckled as he disappeared behind the curtain. I made my way to the couch. Pillowing my head with my arms, I let my mind wander. Had the lizard-men come back and ransacked my house, or was it someone else? I shook my head. I'd already told Newburn the truth, that it didn't feel like the first set of guys, which meant someone else had poked around in my house.

"Talk," Zack said, pulling one of the chairs over to me.

I felt the nerve endings in my leg come to life as Zack's gloved fingers pressed into my cut, making me jump and yelp. Well, I tried to jump; Zack's other hand was firmly pressed into the small of my back, keeping me in place.

"This is weird," Zack said, the pressure on my leg getting firmer. "This cut and the bruising around it is consistent with claw marks, both sharp and blunt force, unlike a knife or broken glass, which are just sharp. They're common among people injured by animals …. Tigers … Komodo dragons … iguanas …"

Try Godzilla-sized iguanas, I thought, grimacing.

I wiggled a little, but Zack didn't let up. He just sat there waiting patiently for me to start talking. Normally, I wouldn't mind something like this, and it happened once in a while when I didn't want to tell my friends how dangerous a case was going to be. After a few minutes, they generally let it go and everything was fine.

"If I tell you what happened, will you let me go?"

"Naturally."

The pressure eased just a bit. I waited for the shimmer of panic I was feeling to subside before propping myself up on my elbows to look over my shoulder at Zack. He must have seen something on my face because he let go of my leg completely and moved back a bit more, giving me room to breathe.

"I came home from the crime scene to find lizards the size of grizzly bears with pissy, prom-queen attitudes searching my mother's room," I said. "When I confronted them, one got a bit rough and sliced my leg open."

There was a short pause before Zack started to giggle. Not a manly chuckle, no—a full-blown giggle. I blinked, my mouth slowly turning down in a frown.

"Mind telling me what's so funny?"

Zack calmed down enough to wipe at his face, still smiling, and shook his head.

"Great," he said, putting a hand over his mouth to hide a smile, "now all I'm seeing is dancing, singing cartoon dinosaurs parading through New York City."

"The *We're Back* movie? Well, if you throw in bad clown makeup and a unicycle, it would describe my day."

Zack sighed. "Such a good movie .... And you let the weirdest people through your door."

I smirked against my will, relieved that Zack hadn't called me a liar. "Well, you play with the dead. What's so different between us?"

"The difference is," Zack said, motioning for me to sit up, "that the dead have no desire to kill; only the living do."

The chair squeaked as Zack began to gather his things. He wasn't much taller than me, two inches at most, which was nice considering everyone else looked like a giant. He was close to my age too—either a year ahead or behind; I could never keep him and Maggie straight.

"So am I all set to go, Doc?"

Zack glanced over his shoulder at me. "Yes, I would caution you against running around, but we both know that's not going to happen."

"Pretty much," I agreed. "What about the cut?"

"It's fine," he answered, walking away. "The cut wasn't deep, and if you were dealing with a lizard-man, you're lucky it isn't infected. I would get it looked at by an actual doctor to be sure though."

"Say what?" I blurted out, staring at him. *Didn't Maggie fuss at me over a "deep" cut?*

"Your cut was shallow," Zack said, not turning as he walked. "I think Maggie got a bit concerned when you showed up with a cut like that on your leg. You know she tends to exaggerate when she's upset."

"Yeah ... maybe."

Zack stripped off his gloves and added them to the pile of used equipment. He took off his lab coat next, showing off a three-quarter-sleeved light-blue shirt and dark jeans. Next to me, he looked professional.

"Nice digs," I said, getting to my feet and walking around a bit, getting used to the slight pull the drying glue had on my skin.

"They were on sale," Zack answered. "I assume you haven't eaten yet this morning either?"

I shook my head. I never ate breakfast unless someone else made it. My cooking skills involved reheating things in the microwave; even then, it had a fifty-fifty chance of going up in flames. I could burn water.

Zack heaved a long-suffering sigh and rummaged around in his desk before emerging with his wallet and car keys. "Come on, let's go then."

Score! And if I played it right, I wouldn't have to pay for the food either. The idea must have shown on my face because Zack pointed a finger at me and shook his head.

"I am not paying for yours this time," he said, heading for the big doors. "Forget it."

"I didn't say anything."

"It was written all over your face, Allen."

Zack slid his plastic ID card to set the alarm before leading the way toward the parking lot. I gulped and slowed my walk to a snail pace as I realized he intended to drive.

Zack paused at his car door and raised an eyebrow. "What?"

You know those old pickup trucks that look like more rust than vehicle? That's Zack's truck. Unlike most of the cars and trucks made nowadays, his was a beast of steel. The damn thing had a roar to match too. It still ran, otherwise I wouldn't ride in it, but I always had this small fear that the bottom would fall out of it if we went too fast.

"Is this thing gonna fall apart as we pull out?" I asked, crossing my arms over my chest. "I'm pretty sure I have some chicken wire at the house that we can use to secure everything."

"Are you insulting my truck?"

I put my hand up. "I would never …. I have zip ties in my trunk though."

Zack opened the door and slid inside, reaching over to roll down the window by hand. "Quit being a prima donna and get in."

I climbed in, settling on the towel-covered seat, and said a small prayer as Zack started the engine. Despite my misgivings, or perhaps to distract myself from them, I closed my eyes and let my mind wander back to the case.

When I wanted to sort through the details of a case, I used an active memorization technique called the method of loci, more popularly known as a "mind palace," although mine was more of a vault. I took a deep breath, keeping my eyes closed, and slowly a door started to form. The door was round and painted a bright, cheerful green with a few scratches on the outside, as if an object had been thudded against it one too many times. I took hold of the small golden knob that appeared on the left side and very carefully opened the door.

The inside was spacious. The floor tiles clicked under my shoes as I walked into an entryway and looked around. It had been a while since I'd been in here, but I knew exactly where to go. As I continued to walk, the walls around me turned solid and wooden pillars pushed out from the walls, setting off separate rooms. Each room had a distinct door—wrought iron, shiny stainless steel, rusty and beaten steel, plain wood, intricately carved wood, and so forth. Each material meant something, and each room held something completely different.

I paused at a door about a third of the way down the hall and ran a hand over the plain, unfinished pine door. This one. I pushed the door open and walked in. The inside was blank, nothing on the walls, no previous use, which was perfect.

With practiced ease, I called up a dry-erase board and a marker. Uncapping the marker, I started in the far-left corner and wrote down what I knew about the lizard-men I had encountered—their careful search, how they'd talked to me before one got a bit antsy.

I stepped back briefly before going to the right side and then began with a description of my house after the second search—how the intruders had ransacked the first floor, destroyed my bookshelf, and yet touched nothing on the other floors. Pausing for a brief moment, I looked at the words I'd written.

My books. Why had they attacked the shelves? I circled the word *book* a few times with my marker to make sure I would remember before I moved on.

Another board appeared on my left, and I moved over to it, setting my marker down in its tray. This board had a small table in front of it. A stack of shiny Polaroids sat on top of its beaten surface—crime scene photos from the Dallas case and a few from Saint Mary's. I took a deep breath and began to sort through them. The Saint Mary's incident went on the right; Dallas on the left. As far as memories went, the crime scene I had just been to had the most detail: splatter patterns, range of how far the blood had gone, and even where a few more solid pieces had landed after the blast. It was all there but … but the folder the chief gave me …. I turned to look at the information I had and frowned. The photos and police reports were there, carefully arranged so that everything could be seen, but it wasn't near enough; not like there should have been.

I huffed and stepped back to study both boards. I was missing a vital piece of information, a clue that I needed for the next step in both hospital cases. I would have to go back over everything in the file when I got back to the house. Otherwise, it was going to keep driving me nuts and make me very irritable until I found it.

"Allen!"

I blinked and watched in frustration as my mind vault dropped away, bringing me back to the cab of Zack's truck; his parked truck.

"What? What happened?" I asked, looking around.

Zack was staring at me, his face paler than normal, eyes wide. "You stopped breathing …. I looked over, and I thought you were just sleeping …. Then I tried to wake you …." The grip on his keys tightened, clinking a few together, the sounds bouncing off the inside of the truck's cab.

"Zack—"

"You weren't breathing, Allen!" Zack said. "You scared the hell out of me."

I shifted in my seat. "Sorry. I dunno what happened. I was thinking about the case …. And poking around in my own head."

Zack's head did a jittery up-and-down, side-to-side bob for a minute before he nodded in the direction of the building outside his window—a silent invitation or reminder that we were supposed to be eating; fine by me.

"Feed me, Seymore!" I cried as we got out of his truck and walked up to the doors, my voice pitching to the range of an eleven-year-old. "Feed me!"

"Shut up, you weirdo," Zack said as he lightly shoved me backward.

***

IHOP is a wonderful place. You can walk in at three in the morning in dire need of a steak, and they'll serve it to you without protest. Because of this and its location close to the highway, it was frequented by truckers, travelers, hungover college kids … and me. Their pancakes are to die for—and I don't run the risk of setting my kitchen on fire.

We settled in a corner booth with a good view of the front door and the kitchen before ordering a carafe of coffee. I had a feeling that caffeine would be my best friend throughout the day. I still had to turn in a report about the guys who turned my living room into a war zone. That should be fun to put in the computer under my address.

I took a sip of the dark drink as soon as it arrived and sighed. The warmth spread through me, and the wheels in my head started to turn a bit faster now that they had been metaphorically greased. Autopilot also turned off, and my eyes started taking in details, noticing the exits and any potential threats or problems.

"Hey, space cadet," Zack called, waving a hand in my face.

I smacked his hand away and took another drink—my caffeine love affair was broken only when our waitress came back to take our order: bacon and eggs for Zack; a stack of pancakes and bacon for me; the breakfast of champions, my dear friends.

I turned my gaze to the rest of the customers and staff. It had become a habit and a fun game of trying to figure out who they were or what they'd been doing before coming here. Most of the people this morning were ordinary and easy to dismiss, but a few stuck out, like the guy sitting a few tables down wearing something that belonged in an eighties flashback. Oh, and the woman who seemed to love the back of Zack's head, considering how hard she was staring at him. Then again, both could just be people who enjoyed dressing in really bad clothes and admiring us.

"So," I said softly, refilling my cup with luscious steaming goodness. "My cases, the one from Dallas and the incident at Saint Mary's, have to be related …. Both victims died in the hospital. The only difference is the location. One in the ER waiting room, and one in an examination room."

Zack held up his hand. "Can I just say, I cannot believe the chief is good with you looking into this …. After what happened last time."

I grumbled, my eyes turning to watch one of the employees walk in our direction. "I couldn't just say no."

Zack laughed. "This'll be good for you—you get to join the land of the living—so long as you don't start problems and Robins doesn't find out you were selected for this case. You know how competitive he is."

I ran a hand through my hair, sliding the tie out of it as I did. "Competition is healthy."

"Not for you two."

LeRoy Robins was one of those cops I worked hard to avoid. He was strict and by the book, my exact opposite. He had also lost his funny bone somewhere in the police academy, something I was very fond of reminding him.

"Something about the file is bothering me," I told Zack. "The photos and coroner's report seemed off."

Zack's response was lost as a tingling sensation crawled up my spine and settled at the back of my head. Something was definitely off about the waitress coming at us, enough to set off little alarms in my brain. As gentlemanly as I could, I looked her over, the alarms getting louder the closer she got. Her walk was predatory, like a hunter who had found its prey and wasn't about to let it get away. I had a sudden sinking feeling that I wasn't on top of the food chain, which wouldn't have been too bad if I had been by myself; less chance of casualties. But I had a partially full restaurant and a coworker who thought I was nuts.

"Remember when I told you that I met a giant lizard?" I asked, gauging the distance between us and the front doors.

"Yeah …"

Too far, we'd never make it in time. I huffed and looked over Zack's shoulder at the waitress again; she was getting closer.

"Well, it's about to happen again."

Zack started to turn his head, and I gave him a quick tap on the shin.

"Don't turn around," I told him, glancing toward the kitchen and shifting my coffee closer to the outside edge of the table. "It's not watching you; it's watching me."

"Well, aren't you popular with the reptiles," Zack said, his jaw tightening a bit, his voice wavering just slightly. "You have a plan?"

To be fair, I've never seen Zack upset. Ever. He was always collected and a bit quiet when he was working. But then again, the quiet ones were always the worst when they did decide to show emotions; learned that one the hard way.

"Yeah," I said, tapping the table to get his attention, "you get all these people out of here and to the next parking lot."

"Okay …"

I threw some cash on the table because, for those of you who haven't been in the food service industry, it's grueling work. Forty-plus hours on your feet, and the pay is crap. The customers are horrible, but occasionally you have a decent group or two that know how to tip well and have decent manners. I tip really well.

I grinned at Zack briefly before I swept my arm out, knocking my coffee to the ground, and got to my feet. I stood up as straight as I could manage, scrunching my face up in anger, and pointed a finger at Zack accusingly.

"I thought I told you never to mention my mother and that bastard in the same sentence!" I snarled loud enough for other people to hear. "Don't you ever … ever … talk about her like that again!"

Zack caught on quickly and got to his feet as well, knocking my hand away from him as he rose. His eyes flicked to the syrup containers, then back at me. By this time, our argument had attracted the attention of more than a few diners. Some were watching in amusement, others in distaste, as if we didn't have any manners.

"Get your damn finger out of my face!" Zack snapped. "As for your mother, I only call them as I see them."

I grabbed one of the syrup containers and brought my hand back, as if I was going to strike him with it. Zack ducked. The syrup flew over his head and cracked against the waitress's face, spilling the contents all over her and the floor.

Then all hell broke loose.

Chapter Five

Normally, when people start yelling at each other in a public setting, someone runs to get the manager or some kind of authority figure. They're the smart ones. The others (idiots) will sit there and look on with interest, in the off chance that it breaks into a full-fledged fight. Apparently, the diner was full of idiots this morning, because after all of that yelling, they were still sitting there, hands over their mouths or over their children's ears. A few had even pulled out their cell phones and were recording the entire thing.

The waitress, however, was watching me with an expression that bordered on murderous rage. Guess she didn't like the flavor I threw at her.

"Oh ... crap," I said when she resumed stalking in our direction.

Zack slowly got out of his crouch and glanced up at me. "Did it work?"

"Nope, just made her mad. Time for plan B."

I slipped out of the booth and took a half step forward, then noticed Mr. Eighties blocking the front door. He gave me a smile full of serrated teeth. Not good.

"Zack?"

I really wanted to look behind me and check on him. After all, I did leave him back there with Scary Waitress. But I didn't want to take a chance on Mr. Eighties rushing at me. He was not a small guy by any means.

"Zack, plan B ..."

He didn't answer, and I had a fleeting thought of him being eaten whole. Although he might find it necessary to yell if that happened—at least I hoped he would. I opened my mouth to yell at him again when the fire alarm screamed from above, and I turned to spy Zack near the bathrooms. When had he moved?

"Everyone out!" he yelled. "Now!"

That got everyone moving, right in my direction. I ducked down as the crowd enveloped me, which wasn't very hard considering how short I am. Using the mass of people as cover, I crawled under the table in our booth. If I could shoot these guys before they transformed or whatever, there wouldn't be a problem. My hand moved to my holster, and I blinked as it closed on empty air.

"Blark," I muttered, moving far enough that my back was pressed against the wall. "Can this get any worse?"

I patted my sides and found half a pack of cigarettes and a lighter in my pockets but nothing else. Grumbling, I risked a peek out of my hiding place and felt my skin crawl. Those things were changing. The fire alarm had them hissing, their hands covering their ears, heads swinging from side to side. Mr. Eighties had fallen to his knees and was hunched over, pulling at his hair with semiclawed hands.

As the alarm continued to wail, the woman who had been staring at Zack was halfway to her feet, her mouth opened in a silent scream, which allowed me a view of her serrated teeth. The waitress had started clawing at her ears, a pale-yellow tongue flicking from between her teeth. Wait a second—yellow? Iguana tongues weren't yellow.

Yes, and teeth aren't serrated, lizard-people don't exist, and smart detectives don't forget their guns, I berated myself silently, shifting to see if there was a way through the quickly thinning sea of legs.

I crawled closer to the edge of my hiding spot, making sure not to rattle the table too much, just in time to see plates of grayish armor push their way through the waitress's skin. Her hair began to fall to the floor as her face elongated into a snout. Bile rose in my throat as I watched her eyes slide to the side of her head, widening slightly. She grunted, falling to her knees, her body thickening under the plates to accommodate the weight of them. Muscles shifted and tightened in her legs, making them powerful enough to kick my scrawny ass across the restaurant. Her hands turned skeletal, and I bit my lip to keep from making a sickly noise as her fingernails fell out, replaced with wickedly curved claws. Last to appear was the tail, thick and powerful enough to break my leg instead of just leaving a scar. I'm quite sure I grew more than a few white hairs witnessing that transformation.

"DuCourt," she hissed, tongue flicking the air. "Coward, show yourself!"

Did a lizard roughly the size of a Shetland pony just demand I show myself after calling me a coward? Seriously?

"All I wanted was some damn pancakes and a cup of coffee!" I yelled.

My answer was a roar and the sound of furniture breaking; sounded like a table. Gee, I hope IHOP had insurance.

"Give it to us!" another lizard demanded, as snarls erupted from the others. "Give us the amulet."

Whoa, amulet?

I shifted back from the opening as glass shattered and more tables were smashed. I needed a plan. "Say the magic word," I called out, trying to buy time. Just then my phone erupted into song—of all the luck.

I started to answer it but suddenly had a giant lizard head in my lap, jaws snapping and barely missing vital parts of my anatomy. I let out a startled yelp and tried to scramble away, panic crept in when I felt the wall against my back. The last thing I needed was for a piece of me to go missing.

My reaction was immediate, which is fancy for, I drew back a hand as far as I could and punched that sucker in the nose. It roared and reared back, sending my cover flying and spraying us in coffee-colored water and crockery. The lizard moved away, shaking its head, allowing the other two to move in from either side. They perched atop the booth backrests and looked down at me.

"Whatever it is that you want," I said, carefully shifting into a crouch, "I don't have it."

"Liar!" the one on my left hissed. "DuCourt hid it from us all these years. Now give it to us!"

I glanced around and noticed a small gap between the one on the floor and the edge of the booth. I could make it, but I didn't want to give the other two a reason to try and pull my spine out.

"Look," I said, getting irritated. "I don't know what my mom took from you. But this is not how you get it back."

A deep rumble sounded around me, and I swear it was like being in a movie theater with really good surround sound. The one on the ground started forward again, its yellow tongue flicking in and out of those scaly gray lips. So, in a word, *ew*.

"You will give us the amulet," it hissed, forcing me to stand as it stalked forward, "or we will kill you."

My eyes narrowed. "You did not just threaten me, Leatherface."

Those jaws snapped at my knees, forcing me back against the wall. The two on either side of me joined in on the snapping fest, and I felt a rush of air brush my arms. I suddenly knew what a trapped mouse felt like, a very real Tom and Jerry moment, if you will, with me starring as Jerry.

Suddenly, out of nowhere, a bright-red canister landed on the booth bench to my right—a fire extinguisher! I flicked my eyes to the ceiling, then back to the encircling teeth, wondering where it came from. *Who cares? I'll think more on it later.* I quickly grabbed the extinguisher, teeth barely missing my arm, and pulled the pin. I leveled the hose at the nearest lizard and fired; well, I tried to fire.

"Damn it," I said aloud. "Who keeps an extinguisher with no foam?"

Hissing curled around me as the lizard that had tried to take out my legs stood up. Yes, stood up on its back legs. Now, my five foot five was looking at over six feet of reptile towering over me with claws that were uncomfortably close to my face.

"Okay," I started with a weak laugh, "I know what you're thinking—"

A vicious snarl interrupted me, and I had just enough time to duck before a clawed hand attempted to extract one of my eyes.

"Enough of your games," it hissed, backing up a few steps. "Kill him!"

The other two started climbing down onto the benches. I might have let out a squeak of what most would call fear, but I wasn't afraid. Yeah, and maybe I would turn into a fluffy pink unicorn and dance on rainbows.

The fire extinguisher was still in my hands and my only means of defense. I needed to get out of the middle, but my exit was still blocked. If I stayed there against the wall, I would become an amputee at best. Only one choice then: forward. I let out a yell, taking a knee as I brought the extinguisher down on one creature's foot. Yelling seemed to work as an intimidation tactic in movies, why not now?

"Back up, Bessie!" I called, shifting into a crouch, my legs tensing with sudden adrenaline.

The creature howled in pain, a clawed hand coming down in my direction, and I felt the tips of my hair move. If I hadn't been the height I was, I'd be missing a head. I held the extinguisher in front of me, using it like a shield and sprang up, driving it hard into its stomach. There was a "whoosh" of expelled air at the surprise attack and a sound of annoyance as the thing stumbled sideways.

With snarls and sounds of ripping vinyl and cheap industrial carpet behind me, I kept moving, letting my momentum carry me into the free zone of the restaurant area. I noticed several broken tables and chairs near the front door and winced. That could have been me. My feet carried me to the dividing wall that separated the restrooms from the rest of the dining area. I turned the corner and ducked down to catch my breath, resting my head against the wall. Three of those things were in here. One I could deal with, but three?

"Hanging in there?"

I moved my head to see Zack looking at me from the small niche that led to the men's restroom. His face was flushed, his clothes rumpled from hiding, but other than that he looked fine.

"Some help you are," I answered over the crashing and growls behind me.

"Hey," Zack said as he looked past me to the chaos beyond, "I did my job. I got the people out."

I reached out and grabbed his arm, hauling both of us to our feet. Being a sitting duck was never part of any plan I made. Ever.

"We have to keep moving," I panted, shoving him in front of me and into the kitchen. I paused long enough to grab a bottle of ketchup from one of the register stations and hurried after him. "Crazy-waitress-lizard-thing behind us."

The first part of the kitchen we ran into was the pickup area. It wasn't as big as I'd imagined it would be, maybe because of its galley style—long and narrow with a window and shelf in the center, and entrances into the kitchen on both ends.

Zack stopped just inside the entry. "What in the hell *are* those things?" he asked. He was pretty pale, but I had to give him credit, he hadn't fainted on me yet.

"Giant lizard-people," I answered when nothing else came to mind. "They were formerly people …. Probably still are."

"That's … I mean … you almost got turned into lizard chow, and that's all you have to say?" Zack stammered, his gaze dropping to my hands. "What's with the ketchup bottle and fire extinguisher?"

I looked down briefly at the items I was holding before tossing him the ketchup bottle. "Well, these are what I would like to call weapons."

"And a ketchup bottle helps how?"

I moved around the pickup counter with its stainless-steel countertop and into the actual kitchen area. My mouth watered when the smells hit me: bacon, eggs, ham, toast, and did I mention bacon?

"Damn, I'm hungry," I muttered, pushing quickly invading thoughts of bacon aside, "and to answer your question, yes. Anything right now will help."

I set the extinguisher down on the counter as gently as I could, the sound of metal clinking on metal ringing gently through the kitchen. After making sure that the extinguisher was away from the stovetop, I looked around to see what else could possibly be used to kill those things, or at least lame them enough so Zack and I could run.

The back wall housed the grills, one electric and one gas, with the frying station standing between them. The grills themselves were big enough that two people could stand side by side and still move around without bumping into each other. The frying station was still turned on, the oil bubbling away and baskets poised for deployment on little hooks above the artery-clogging fat.

The sink and dishwasher took up space in the far-left corner, the latter noisily billowing scalding steam against the already warped ceiling tiles. I turned the dishwasher off. The sizzling of the oil, I could deal with, but the noise from the steam-billowing behemoth was too much. I needed to hear the lizards coming.

"This is insane," Zack said. He had taken up a spot by the pickup window.

"Not in the slightest," I said, moving around the prep table in the middle of the room to begin pulling out stacks of dishes. "Now quit whimpering and help me find projectiles."

"No."

I stopped digging around and turned to look at him. He was still standing by the pickup window, holding the ketchup bottle.

"Come again?" I asked, my voice a little heated.

"No," Zack said, his fingers tightening on the bottle. "I said no. This is crazy! Asylum, nuthouse, balls-to-the-wall crazy!"

We heard a roar and a crash—what I could only assume was the sound of giant lizards making their way toward us. The last thing I needed was for Zack to have a full-on panic attack and get one or both of us ripped to shreds. I grabbed his arm and yanked him down into a crouch, so we couldn't be seen through the opening, and put a hand over his mouth.

"Look," I growled, "this wasn't on my agenda for today either, all right? But right now, we have to figure out how to get out of this with all of our limbs!"

He blinked. I took that as a sign that he was listening.

"We need to find a way to keep them in the building. The people outside don't stand a chance if those things get out of here. And as an officer of the law, I'd feel like crap if anyone got hurt." I moved my hand away from Zack's mouth and slowly stood. "Now, I have an idea—"

"I sense a 'but' coming," Zack muttered as he stood and moved around beside me. "And if it involves the freezer, you're a madman."

I glanced at the far side of the room and grinned. I'd forgotten about the freezer. "Nope, can't pull a *Jurassic Park* here; too many, and the kitchen is a bit smaller."

"There were three raptors in that part of the movie, and two kids managed to lock one in the freezer," Zack answered, his voice a bit stronger. "Lame excuse, Miar."

I laughed softly and glanced out the serving window, hoping to catch a glimpse of the lizards. If Zack was cracking jokes at my expense, he was going to be just fine.

"Best excuse ever," I said, dropping my voice a little, "and it does involve explosions."

"Explosions?"

I turned my head, putting a finger to my lips. Besides the constant shriek of the fire alarm, all was quiet. No breaking furniture, no growly, hissy lizard noises. Nothing. That couldn't be good.

Zack looked through the serving window before slowly moving toward one of the kitchen entrances. I shifted and divided my attention between the window and making sure my friend didn't die.

"I think they—" Zack started to say before he yelled and scrambled back as a lizard came around the corner and lunged at him. The other two came from the other side, all teeth and anger—just what we needed.

"Hit it with the extinguisher!" I yelled, frantically looking for something to defend myself with.

A snarl and a snap sounded behind me, closely followed by a yelp. I resisted the urge to make sure Zack was in one piece, although it was cause for concern if the guy watching my back just fainted.

"Get back!" Zack yelled.

I grinned as I rolled under the prep table and hopped to my feet on the other side. Good ol' Zack, not dead or passed out. I tossed a few mugs at one lizard as it came around the prep table.

Gotta make these guys move back, I thought while throwing a few heads of lettuce at them. *Come on, Allen, think ....* And then the light bulb turned on. *Oh, this is going to be messy .... Really messy.*

I hadn't thought of it earlier because I was still in a panic from nearly losing precious limbs. Probably more to it, but that's what I was sticking with for the moment. I grabbed a stack of plates nearby and counted them. Three, I had three plates.

"Zack!" I yelled over the roars and snapping jaws. "On the count of three, run for the exit door on my side!"

"Are you crazy?!" he answered with a grunt.

"Yes, but let's discuss that later," I called, hurling a serving tray.

"I can't make it over there that fast!" he argued.

"Count of three. Ready?"

"No!"

I made sure I heard him backing up before I threw the first plate.

"One."

The plate went wide and hit the counter.

"Two."

I watched the second one go right over one of their heads and heard Zack grunt again as he swung the extinguisher. I chunked the last plate, not bothering to see where it landed, and put both hands on the fryer's handle. The fryer's little hooks released, and I let the basket sink into the hot oil.

"Three!"

I waited until Zack ran past me, dropping the extinguisher on his way, before I lifted the basket from the fryer, sending a thin spray of hot oil over the two lizards coming at me. What I could only interpret as screams came from the creatures in front of me. Gray scales cracked and peeled where the oil made contact, almost like a bad sunburn. Some scales fell to the floor with little wet plops, and—I couldn't help it—I turned my head and emptied my stomach onto the floor.

A warm breeze drifted into the kitchen, letting me know that Zack had made it to the door. I risked a glance over my shoulder and saw him motioning for me to hurry before quickly closing the door.

Dipping the fryer basket in the oil again, I tried to ignore the sour taste filling my mouth and made another arc with the oil. This time I made sure to catch the one that Zack had been beating with the extinguisher. Zack's lizard was bleeding from several cuts on its head; it also seemed to have a few broken teeth and one eye emitting a trail of blood. *Had he punctured its eye? Nice one, Zack!*

I created one last arc before I turned tail and ran for the door. On the way, I snatched up the extinguisher from the floor and turned a few dials on the gas stove as high as they would go. I hoped my plan worked ….

By this time, the lizards were flailing in an attempt to get the oil off of them, which was only making it worse. One of them turned to follow me, jaws snapping close to the fabric of my shorts. I turned and beat it a few times with the extinguisher.

The lizards were all screaming and now looked more like zombies than living creatures. The skin on their faces had started to slide off and hung in gelatinous ribbons. Puddles of grayish goo had pooled around legs or under torsos. If I hadn't emptied my stomach earlier … I felt my throat constrict at the idea as I turned one last dial.

"Hurry up!" Zack yelled, cracking the door a little.

"Yeah, hold your horses!" I snapped as I grabbed a stray frying pan and whacked one of the lizards in the nose when it got a tad too close.

I did my best to jump over the flailing tails and managed to fall on my face. Well, it was more like I met the edge of the door when Zack opened it, but who had to know? Through the pulses of pain in my face, I felt Zack's hand yank me through the door, depositing me in an ungraceful heap on the grass outside before he started to close it.

"Wait!" I hollered, staggering to my feet, fishing around in my pants pocket. "Last part of the plan."

I pushed the door open, kicked one of the lizards in the face, and lobbed my little Bic lighter in the direction of the fryer. I caught a glimpse of it disappearing into the boiling oil and slammed the door shut.

"Fire in the hole!"

For once, I didn't have to tell Zack what to do. We both took off into the undeveloped field behind the IHOP, trying to put as much distance between the building and us as we could. I steered the two of us to a dip in the grass, shoving Zack down as the first explosion boomed, the shock wave throwing me ass over kettle to my back. My ears were ringing as I somehow managed to crawl over to Zack. We huddled there against the ground, hands over our ears, as the second boom rocked the ground around us, raining down pieces of debris and who knows what else.

We waited a few minutes before cautiously sitting up enough to peek over the ditch. The building was on fire—well, what was left of it. I turned and sat, knees bent, and patted my pockets, drawing out a pack of cigarettes. Out of habit, I placed one in my mouth before resting my arms on my knees and then looked over at Zack.

"So … you still hungry?"

***

I pushed my plate away and sighed. We'd ended up at Kim's, a little diner off Waco Drive that served huge homemade breakfasts and mouthwatering hamburgers after noon. My mom used to take my brothers and me there while she was working. If it was an afternoon shift, we would do our homework and sip on shakes. And after she passed away, it had become my go-to place for food near the house.

"So those were the things you were telling me about?"

I looked up at Zack. He sat across from me looking a bit haggard and smoke smudged, smelling just a tiny bit like charred reptile. We were lucky that he'd chosen to park closer to the hotel than the restaurant. Otherwise, we'd have been stranded. His truck escaped with just a few scratches and dents from flying debris and a lingering smell of smoke inside.

"No," I said, leaning forward, my sore muscles protesting. "The Godzillas who came to my house were iguanas, the spines and the tail kind of gave them away. The gray, armored, and yellow-tongued friends we just met were Komodo dragons."

"That's not the point," Zack snapped, glaring at me.

I raised an eyebrow at him and mopped up a bit of my eggs with a piece of toast. "It's completely the point. Two drastically distinct kinds of reptiles, two distinct kinds of temperament … didn't you learn anything in school?"

Zack's face was slowly turning red, his eyes narrowing as he leaned forward. "Are you seriously arguing semantics right now? Is this what you think normal looks like? Because it's not. Normal people don't calmly go out for breakfast after almost being devoured by a vicious mini cow–sized reptile. Normal people don't treat a home invasion like it's nothing to worry about. And normal people would care that they just blew up a damn building."

"Say that last part a little louder. I don't think everyone heard you," I muttered, keeping my voice calm and even.

"Most people, especially you," Zack growled, leaning in a bit more—and I swear I thought I saw the silverware rattle against the plate—"don't just brush off getting attacked in their own home."

"Well, it's a good thing that I'm not most people," I snapped back. "And I told you—I'm fine."

"That is a load, and you know it."

"Excuse me, sirs …"

We both turned to see a rather uneasy waiter standing by our table.

"I'm sorry to interrupt you, but could you please lower your voices?" he asked, swallowing nervously and shifting on his feet. "You're disturbing the other guests."

I glanced around. Our little conversation had gotten the attention of the entire place. A few avoided my gaze when I looked in their direction; others just stared openly. Well, that was just great. Hopefully, they hadn't heard the part about the explosion.

"Sorry," I said to the waiter, getting to my feet and putting a few bills on the table. "Mind if we finish this outside, Zack? I kinda want to smoke."

Zack stalked out of the doors behind me, then stomped to his truck.

"Where are you going?" I called out, still leaning against the side of the building and rolling an unlit cigarette between my fingers.

"Shut up," Zack returned, turning to look at me. "You are so frustrating. Your house was broken into. You're working on cases with bodies that are mostly mulch. Why are you so desperate to run into the danger? Hmm? Why?"

I pushed off the wall and tucked the cigarette behind my ear. "For starters, I would like to find out why reptiles are trying to kill me. It's getting a bit annoying. As for the exploded bodies, well, it's something I've never encountered before …."

"Then what?"

"Then I do what I do best," I said with a grin, walking over to the passenger side. "I bring the dirty little bastard in."

Zack sighed. "Allen, you don't even know where to start looking."

"On the contrary, Watson," I grinned, relaxing into the seat, "I know exactly where to start."

***

When my mother died, only a handful of people were at the funeral: a few friends, some people from the church we had attended, my brothers, and me. I don't remember a whole lot about that day, but I do remember it was springtime. I remember because I had a hard time getting sunflowers for her viewing and had to settle for daisies.

I remember what followed that day though: It was a nightmare, what with how my mother's will was written and my brothers trying to find someone to take care of me until I was of age. They eventually left me with my eldest brother, Ethan. That living arrangement was … bad. Turns out, Ethan wasn't exactly the caring type after he had a few drinks. As a result, I stayed over at Maggie's most of the time. That changed once I turned eighteen. Ethan was forced out the door by the way of an arrest warrant, leaving me to my own devices, and Maggie helped me padlock all three of my brothers' rooms and the attic door, promising to help me with them when I was ready. We also cleaned up my mother's room, something I knew I couldn't do on my own.

"You sure about this?"

I looked over at Zack, then back at the wooden padlocked attic door in front of me.

"Don't really have a choice," I answered with a sigh. "All of the arrows we have are pointing this way."

The house had been empty and secure—as secure as a house with no front door could be. I'd spent the first fifteen minutes walking around the house with my gun before pronouncing it safe for Zack to enter. The two of us had shoved a few heavy bookcases in front of the door before heading up to my room in the attic.

My hand tightened around the key I'd taken from my dresser drawer; the cold metal biting into the flesh of my palm grounded me. I fumbled with the padlock for a moment before it popped open, and I heard Zack mutter something under his breath.

"Here we go," I said and slowly pushed the door open.

Both of us stood in the doorway, not knowing what to expect as the smell of dust and mothballs rolled over us. When nothing jumped out to eat us, I reached inside and flipped on the light.

"Wow, your family was a bunch of pack rats."

I snickered and felt a bit of release at the comment. Who knew there could be so much tension over just opening a door? In the dull glow of the light, I could see brown cardboard boxes covered in inches of dust. Some had clear labels scribbled along the side; others were too faded to make out or had been marked out too many times to decipher the original writing. Then there were some that had Ethan's things in them, and I had no desire to open those.

The floorboards creaked under our feet as we entered the room, little dust clouds poofing up with each step we took. My mother had been compulsively neat, which meant that everything had a proper place and was returned to its spot after use. Her compulsion was reflected in each room of the house, even in the neat stacks of boxes in the dusty attic where Zack and I now stood. They had been arranged just so, with a branching path through the brown cardboard maze.

"Where do we even start?" Zack asked, stopping to read the label on one of the boxes. "Has to be close to fifty boxes up here."

"We just start opening boxes," I answered, flipping open a nearby box labeled Kitchen. "Things have been moved around so much up here, it's hard just going by the labels."

Zack grunted as he pulled a box down. "And if I find anything embarrassing?"

"You keep it to yourself," I grumbled and pawed through the box in front of me. "Let's try to keep it kind of neat though, so we can still move around up here."

It took us several hours to get through one side of the attic. Most of the boxes held clothes and books, but occasionally, we would find something really strange—strange for my family at least. I couldn't remember a single time we had gone canoeing, yet we had a set of paddles.

Occasionally, I had to take a break when a box's contents were a bit more than I could handle. Zack, thankfully, didn't ask any questions. We eventually broke for lunch and tramped downstairs. I checked the makeshift front door before joining Zack in the kitchen.

"So how's the organizing in your office? Still a mess?" he asked, drying his hands off with a worn kitchen towel.

I sighed and washed up quickly. "Slowly. And if no one moves anything, I won't have to start over …. Again. These two cases though … All I have is a body from Saint Mary's and photos of the Dallas one."

"To be clear, you have pieces of sludge from Saint Mary's," Zack pointed out as I pulled tamales from the last department bake sale out of the fridge. "Everything else could fit in a bucket."

"Point is," I said, getting out two plates and putting a few tamales on each, "I have next to nothing to go on except pictures."

I put one of the plates in the microwave and turned around so I could lean on the counter and still talk to Zack. I ran a hand through my hair, yanking out the tie to put it up again. One of these days I'd cut it, but I kinda liked it long.

"You're right though," I told Zack as the timer went off.

He responded only with a chuff that translated to a combination of "duh," "I'm shocked you're acknowledging it," and "right about what?"

I slid the plate in front of him.

A drawer rattled as Zack fished around for a fork. I pushed the buttons again to nuke my share of the food.

"They're connected," I answered, retrieving my food and grabbing a fork. The legs of my chair scraped loudly in the quiet as I sat down. "That much I'm sure of. I haven't figured out the why or how yet."

"Suspects?"

"Only one," I answered. "I'd like to know a bit more about him before I officially say he's on the list. He's a man with money, lots of it, so trying to dig anything incriminating up on him might be a chore. But the way he talked about the iguanas that broke in … it was almost like he knew them? Or knew more than he was letting on? However, it's a mistake to theorize before you have all the data. You do that, and you're twisting facts to suit your theories, instead of theories to suit facts. You should know that."

"Only because of conversations with you," Zack shook his head and finished off his food. "Who made it on your list?"

I gave him the brief version of my encounter with Riley O'Hare and enjoyed my friend's startled reaction at what I guessed was the man's occupation.

When he could speak again, Zack let out a low whistle. "Riley O'Hare? You do know there is a rumor that he has regular lunch dates with the mayor. You sure know how to make people angry, Allen."

"It's a gift," I answered, finishing my food. "What bothers me is how he knew to show up at that exact moment."

"That's what bothers you?" Zack inquired, taking our plates to the sink. "Not that someone who is very wealthy and very influential might be exploding people?"

I leaned back in my chair, my hands automatically taking out the cigarette pack and fingering it. "Exploding people bother me regardless of who's doing it. And O'Hare wasn't alone when he came to my house."

"How could you possibly know that?"

"He was completely relaxed," I answered, my fingers moving over the pack's stiff paper. "No nervous twitches, no shifty sitting, nothing. The only way he would be that relaxed is with reassurance that someone was nearby if things went bad."

"Wait a sec," Zack said, looking back at me. "If he's a professional criminal, isn't relaxed and confident part of the whole gig?"

"If they want to keep their station, yeah. But stay with me," I smirked a little and continued turning the pack over. "The house was quiet when I woke up, meaning that the others had been cleared out. How? By Riley O'Hare. He made them leave. I just haven't figured out how yet. Maybe he has some kind of influence over them or he's their boss. Otherwise, I think they would have continued their search while I was knocked out."

"For the amulet?"

"Correct," I answered, finally taking a cigarette out of the pack and placing the box on the table. "But instead of waking up to a face full of lizard and a ransacked house, I woke up unharmed except for my leg. I doubt I would have been spared if O'Hare hadn't shown up. The one seemed pretty pissed."

Zack frowned as I got to my feet and walked lazily to the back door. "All right," he said, "say this mob guy is involved. How do we know at least one set of lizards isn't working for him, keeping you busy with exploding people while O'Hare and his goons look for the amulet?"

I frowned, stepping out onto the back porch. That was an idea I hadn't entertained, but it was possible.

"If that is true," I said slowly as I settled on the back step, "then how do the lizard-people fit into all of this? Both O'Hare and the lizards want something my mother had. Are they working together, or am I in the middle of a gang rivalry?"

Silence fell around us. How did it all fit together? How had I never noticed lizard-people before? Were they on a distant branch of the werewolf tree or something? Were werewolves real? And even if I knew what the lizard-people were, how would I capture them? A tar pit? *That could work.*

I growled and ran my hands through my hair, messing it up even more. I had more questions than answers, and it made my head hurt. Why didn't my mom tell me about any of this? Was she really a monster hunter?

"Ugh," I growled aloud, glaring out at the yard, "this sucks."

"Yes … yes, it does," Zack said, sitting down beside me.

I frowned at the yard and shook my head. "Two connected cases in separate places, chaos follows. All right, makes sense. But then we have not one but two shifter groups that want something that my mom was holding on to." My eyes slid over to Zack. "It's too many coincidences, and it's all jumbled in my head."

Zack made a sound of acknowledgement and leaned back against the side rail to look around the backyard. I lit my cigarette and sat there smoking and thinking about my next move. I didn't even look up when my phone started ringing. I was thinking, and thinking took precedence to answering the phone.

"Your phone's ringing."

Really? I hadn't noticed. "If it's important, they can leave a voicemail," I said, inhaling another lungful of smoke. "I'm in the middle of something."

The ringing eventually stopped but started up again a few minutes later, much to my displeasure. Zack snickered from his place beside me as I continued to ignore my phone.

"I don't think they're in the mood to leave a message," he said, getting to his feet. "Answer your phone, Allen."

I ground out the cherry on my lit cigarette and dropped the butt into the bucket I kept outside. "Who are you, my mother?"

"On occasion. Now answer your phone."

Grumbling, I dug the device out of my pocket, flipping it open without looking at the display screen.

"What!"

"Such manners," a voice lilted in my ear. "And you call yourself a public servant."

My back straightened as a chill ran down my spine. I knew that voice. "O'Hare."

He chuckled, and I could hear the smirk in it. What did he want? I had already told him to get lost. More importantly, how did he get my number?

"We seem to have a small problem," O'Hare continued, unperturbed by my silence.

"If this is about me telling you to piss off, I'm not sorry," I answered, finally finding my voice, "and I meant it. I don't want your help."

O'Hare laughed again, and it felt like sandpaper against my skin. "Oh no, you will eventually ask for my help, Mr. Miar, and I can't wait for that day."

He did seem overly determined to make me ask him for help, and I had been more than a bit rude in my refusal. I hadn't done anything to him, unless he had stock in IHOP or the lizards were working with him.

"It's Detective Miar. And I'll still tell you to piss off. What's your point?"

I heard a sigh and formed a mental picture of him rubbing his temples as if I gave him a headache.

"If you aren't going to say anything productive, I'm hanging up," I announced and watched Zack's face scrunch in confusion. "I have better things to do."

O'Hare hummed in answer, the sound reminding me of a fly—a really annoying fly.

"Like replacing your door?"

I felt the blood drain from my face, and I put a hand on the porch railing to keep myself steady. What the hell? Was he watching me? My house?

O'Hare's voice was once again in my ear. Buzzing, annoying ... smug.

"You should get that fixed, Mr. Miar. Just anyone could walk in."

I managed to find my voice, the words coming out heated and angry. "I'm hanging up. Call me again, and our next conversation will be about harassment. Got it?"

I shut my phone with a snap. That guy, what is his deal? *He's rich, bored, and has way too much time on his hands.*

I stood there for a few minutes, not moving, the silence vibrating in my skull. All this because I had refused to roll over like a good dog? Denying his offer to help me, insulting him, and threatening him with bodily harm might not have helped either. So he decided to stalk me and scare me into submission? *Pfft*, screw that.

I already didn't trust him. I didn't know what connection he had to my mother. I didn't really care at this point. All I wanted to do was take his head and smash it into the pavement a few hundred times. Wouldn't get me the answers I needed but it would be very therapeutic. My leg flew out, kicking the cigarette bucket nearby and sending it down the length of the porch with a loud clang.

"What was that about?" Zack demanded as my hands found purchase on the porch railing again.

"O'Hare."

"Come again?"

I turned to face him, my hands shaking. "O'Hare just officially made my suspect list."

Zack, with a determined look on his face, marched up to me and began pulling me down the steps, much to my surprise.

"Come on then," he said. "We can't waste time talking."

We? My eyes went wide at his statement. "Wait, what?"

Zack turned to face me, his keys dangling from his hand. "Your car is still at the morgue, and you don't have a computer here."

Grumbling to myself, I locked the back door before skulking over to the truck and planting myself in the passenger seat.

"Fine," I said, looking over at him, "you can drive me back to the morgue."

"And I'll follow you back to the station to help look things up about this creepy stalker you now have."

I glanced over at him. "You aren't going to let me do this by myself, are you?"

Zack turned the ignition over and pulled out of the drive, a small smile on his face. "Not a chance, Sherlock."

Chapter Six

"**H**amsters in hell, your office is a fire hazard," Zack said, weaving through stacks of paper on the floor.

I ignored him.

"If someone wanted to kill you," he continued, picking his way carefully over to the couch, "they could just lob a match in here and be done with it."

"You're hilarious." I began looking for my dry-erase markers. "All the cases that don't make sense to the other officers or are just too weird for them find their way here," I added, moving a few stacks out of the way and placing them carefully on the floor near my desk.

"How many?"

"I lost count .... A hundred fifty or so," I answered, settling in my chair and booting up the computer. "You'll have to grab a laptop from the charging station outside. I just have the one."

Zack gave me a short nod as he started clearing a space so he could work. He knew enough about my routine to read the first few folders before moving them, so I didn't have to worry about anything getting mixed up or misplaced.

As he stepped out, I half-assed my home-invasion report and thought about which programs to plug O'Hare's name into. Was there a chance we'd find nothing on him? Yes, but at this point I would take a damn parking ticket.

"So what exactly are we looking for," Zack asked when he came back into the room, settling in his spot.

"Anything relevant," I answered, my eyes flicking in his direction, "businesses, background check, employment history …"

We lapsed into silence for the next hour or so; the only thing breaking it was the *tap* of fingers on keyboards.

"How is it," I said, letting out a frustrated sound and pushing back from the desk, "that all I keep finding is this guy's smiling mug at public events and that he's trying to apply for a permit for a business downtown."

"I have a little bit more," Zack chimed in, getting up from his seat and walking to my side of the desk. "A permit application like what you found and a title for a chunk of land outside of Waco."

Ugh, I could feel the start of a headache behind my eyes. So I had a little to go on—something to dig deeper into later when my life wasn't in danger.

"Maybe he lied about knowing your mom," Zack suggested as I got to my feet. "Suspects lie all the time."

I shook my head. "I don't think he lied, but he isn't telling the whole truth either." I sighed. "We should probably head back to the house."

"You still think there's something in the attic?" he asked.

"Yeah, I do," I said with a nod. I couldn't help but burst into laughter as Zack stubbed his toe on my desk. He grumbled under his breath and hopped on one foot while I tried to get myself under control.

"Your office is gonna land me in the ER," he griped.

That reminds me …. "Listen, I've gotta make a quick call, then I'll meet you back at my place, okay?"

Zack walked away with a backward wave. I grabbed a pen, found the number, and began dialing.

"Saint Mary's," a bright voice chirped in my ear. "How can I help you?"

I gave my whole detective intro. "I need to talk to someone about the incident that occurred in your emergency room a couple days ago."

"I'll transfer you to our director of emergency medicine," the receptionist said brightly. "One moment please."

I impatiently tapped my pen on the desk, thinking the hospital had to be my missing puzzle piece. Well, one of the many missing pieces in this whole case—and the first step in unraveling the great mystery that was my mother.

"This is Dr. Wright," a deep voice said as the pleasant sound of elevator music dropped away. "How can I help you?"

"Dr. Wright, this is Allen Miar from the Waco PD. I was wondering if I could ask you a few questions?"

"Of course, Detective, but I am on call," Dr. Wright responded after a brief pause.

"I'll make this quick then. Do you remember a patient by the name of Meredith Strong?"

"I can't say that I do, Detective. I see a lot of people during my shift. Are you sure she was a patient here?"

Fair enough, although a girl coming in and then exploding should be a bit more memorable—unless there was a different reason.

"I understand," I said as casually as I could. "She detonated in your ER waiting room …. Has anyone else come in showing the same symptoms?"

The doctor didn't respond right away. Legally, I could go through all the paperwork to get Meredith's records, and *I would* to cover my tail, but sometimes a simple, direct question delivered the necessary information.

"I don't believe so," Dr. Wright said, clearing his throat, "although I'm not up to date on the case histories from all of our facilities."

"I understand. Just a reminder, Doctor, that if you're hiding information, you're impeding my investigation," I told him, scribbling down a little note.

I heard the doctor sniff. He was lying to me. I couldn't see his face, but it was just a gut feeling. Of course, he was well within his legal rights to tell me to shut up and go the hell away. It was always touch and go with doctors, especially the good ones who wanted to help but couldn't because of patient confidentiality. Of course, some set up every type of red tape imaginable just for spite, but half the time someone was pressuring those doctors to keep their mouths shut.

"I assure you that I remember my rights and responsibilities as a doctor," he replied stiffly.

The rest of my questions were standard. How long was Meredith sitting in the waiting room? What symptoms had she presented? What time did she come in? How much time passed before they heard the explosion? You know, the typical questions any officer would ask.

Dr. Wright's answers were short and to the point, showing that he had experience dealing with police. I scratched down his answers as fast as he gave them.

"Is there anything else I can help you with?" Dr. Wright asked when I paused to look over my notes.

"Just one more question," I said, taking a breath. "Has anyone besides the police been around asking questions about Meredith's death?"

The doctor was silent just a beat too long. He was definitely hiding something.

"I'm sorry, Detective," Dr. Wright apologized, and I swore his voice wavered just a tiny bit, "but I must get back to my patients now."

"Sir," I said, putting my pen down, "this is an open investigation. I can have you arrested for withholding information that would lead to the arrest of the person or persons behind this."

A speaker cracked to life on the other end of the line, paging Dr. Wright, drawing a sigh of relief from the doctor.

"Young man," he said, the firmness returning to his voice, "I've answered all of your questions as best I can. Now please—"

"Who was Meredith Strong to you, sir?" I interrupted with a bit of a cringe. All or nothing.

For a moment, I thought he'd hung up. I put a hand over my other ear to hear the call better. I could hear him breathing.

"Sir?"

"What do you mean?"

"Was she previously a patient of yours? Did you know her outside of work?"

I was walking a quickly thinning line with those questions, especially without reading him his Miranda rights. I had to get this guy into an interrogation room and keep my ass out of the fire.

"Look, Mr. Miar," Dr. Wright answered, heat creeping into his voice, "I don't know what you're insinuating. But I had never seen nor heard of Meredith Strong prior to this incident. Have a good evening."

I was losing him. "At least come down—"

He hung up.

"Damn it. I hate it when that happens!"

***

Tossing my keys onto the small kitchen table, I called out to let Zack know I was back, then threw my coat across one of the kitchenette chairs in frustration. I needed to figure out the truth behind these exploding people, and we absolutely had to find that necklace—no, *amulet*.

"If we're going to discover what my mom has to do with all of this," I said when Zack finally walked in, "the amulet has to be somewhere in that attic. My mom put everything up there."

"What about O'Hare? He's still—"

"He will get the hell out of the way, one way or another," I answered over my shoulder. "He's so eager for my attention that he went through all this trouble. It would be rude for us not to return it …. In full."

"You're playing with fire, Allen," Zack warned, following behind me. "What's your next move?"

"Our next move you mean."

"Our?"

"Yes," I answered, not looking back at him. "If O'Hare is watching me, do you think he didn't notice you working with me? If you think you can take on a mob boss and his suits by yourself, by all means …."

We went back up to the cramped but neat attic and resumed our search. I pulled down the first box my hand landed on, glancing briefly through it before setting it aside and getting another. All the while, my mind was running through other places my mother might have hidden something. My mother was great at finding things other people wanted to hide, but I couldn't think of a single place where she would hide her own things, which only proved that I was either stupid or my mother was just a smidge smarter than I gave her credit for. After about thirty minutes, I was frustrated and about to give up when Zack let out a triumphant sound.

"Please tell me you found something," I called, putting down the latest box I was pawing through. I raised an eyebrow at Zack's muffled response. "Say again?"

"I said, I think so," Zack repeated, his voice still a bit muffled. "Come take a look at this."

I worked my way to the far corner, nudging a few boxes out of the way as I went. Zack was tucked away, as close to the wall as he could get, a stack of boxes almost hiding him from view. With a soft grunt, he hoisted himself upright to allow me to see what he'd found.

It was a beaten-up steamer trunk, one that could have been taken from a Gold Rush–era stagecoach. The leather was cracked and frayed in places, and the hinges barely held on. Most of the color had been rubbed away by time and the relentless Texas heat that turned the attic into an oven. Dints and scratches that varied in size and length decorated the sides and lid. I ran my fingers along the gouges, feeling their dips and depth. It looked like maybe an animal had at it, but the attic light was less than stellar, so it was hard to tell. I felt my hand slip into a leather handle and grinned.

"Grab a handle," I told Zack, scooching to give him room. "Let's take this to the dining room where there's better light." Between the two of us, we awkwardly maneuvered the large trunk down the stairs.

"Okay," Zack panted, sitting heavily on one of the chairs, "you do your thing. I'm taking a break."

I yanked open the curtains for more light before I crouched down again to study the trunk. The tarnished brass straps across the domed top were bent and slightly pried away from the wood, as if they had caught the claws of the creature that had certainly attacked the trunk. Carefully, I brushed my fingers over the wounds, feeling the splintered wood prick the pads of my fingers.

"Could it be your mom's?" Zack asked.

I shifted back a little and smiled. "Oh, I think that's a good bet."

Zack moved his chair closer, blinking when I pointed out the brass name-plate screwed into the wood above the lock. In graceful script etching was my mother's name, Valerie L. DuCourt.

Remembering my mother always made me smile, but this time, I felt a pang of uncertainty as well. What if this changed the way I knew her? Would I still remember her as the loving woman who baked amazing cookies? Would it change my life …. And could I handle it?

You have questions that need answering, I reminded myself and gave the trunk a small glare. "Well, shall we?" I asked, glancing back at Zack, who just nodded.

The trunk wasn't locked, but I took care with the leather straps that held the lid shut and took a deep breath before lifting the lid. The smell of gun oil and old newsprint rolled out of the trunk. I carefully propped the lid open against one of the chairs and let my eyes settle on what was inside.

The trunk was divided into two sections, a removable tray at the top designed for smaller items and a spacious area underneath for larger belongings, such as clothes or shoes. The tray held an array of oddities in five sections. I tilted my head in confusion at the first object that caught my eye: a sickle with a wickedly curved, serrated blade attached to a wooden handle wrapped in black leather. I pulled it out and tested its weight, a bit surprised when I strained to hold on to it; a coil of rope had been tucked underneath it.

The next section was home to a box of plain kitchen matches, a tattered leather-bound book held together with a rubber band, as well as pieces of silver tape and candles of different sizes, shapes, and colors. I pulled the book out and caught faint wisps of my mother's rose-scented hand lotion and traces of ink from the pages.

Zack reached over to pull out what looked like a container of salt, then unceremoniously tossed it back in with a huff. "If there's no amulet," he said, "we have nothing to bargain with."

"Don't rush me," I muttered, pulling out a bible and rosary. Zack's phone rang as I pulled the top tray off, but I tuned it out to better concentrate.

I peered into the bottom of the trunk, which had been sectioned off as well, this time into four compartments. My eyebrows rose when I spied three large pickle jars tucked into one of the corners. I picked each jar up by the lid to read the labels a bit better. Graveyard dirt? Brick dust? What was my mom into?

I shook my head and turned to talk to Zack, only to find his chair empty. I figured he was on his phone, so I continued my search, reaching for a bundle of cloth. I grinned when I felt its weight. It was some kind of bulletproof coat. *Don't know why Mom had it, but cool!* I let go of it and moved to a cigar box sitting in another pile of cloth. I flipped the box open with a finger and started laughing. Various lapel clips and lanyards held every kind of ID card imaginable, everything from a CIA badge to a cheap-looking janitorial staff ID.

Setting the box aside, I fished around in the remaining section, almost taking my fingers off on the blade of a small throwing axe. *Don't they make covers for blades like that?* A bit more carefully, I continued my search and soon drew out a sawed-off shotgun. Not the gun my mother had supposedly used on O'Hare, but it might come in handy later. I set the shotgun to the side and felt my face split into a grin when I spied a small box.

"Oh, I bet I know what you are," I said softly, taking the box out and running my fingers over the initials carved into the top. I carefully opened the lid. Inside, wrapped in an oil rag, was a neat and shiny .38 Special. The exact gun that had stared down creatures and people for her secret …. Secret what? Job? Lifestyle? How exactly would this be classified?

After checking the chamber, I started putting things back into the trunk, minus the .38—that was now mine. Moments later, Zack walked back into the room. He looked a bit shifty but more relaxed than he had earlier.

"Maggie's on her way over; said she had something to show us." He put his hands in the air. "And before you say anything, I did try and tell her not to come."

"I doubt that," I said, getting to my feet and dusting myself off. "I just hope she understands what she's getting into."

He moved out of my way as I started into the kitchen. "Meaning what?"

"Meaning that she'll want to help," I said over my shoulder. I grabbed a Coke from the fridge and headed outside to wait for Maggie.

It was getting dark when her headlights turned into my driveway. I was on the front steps working on my third cigarette and letting my thoughts filter through my brain. I knew I'd started something potentially dangerous to my health when I threatened O'Hare. The chief would have my ass if it got back to him, and considering I'd only been at the office a short time, there was a high possibility that I was going to get a phone call later.

On top of that, I now had to decide how much to tell Maggie. I sighed. She was already going to give me an earful when she saw the house, which was still in its ransacked state; might as well fess up and get the rest over with.

"You!" Maggie exclaimed as she got out of the car. "I've been trying to reach you since this afternoon!"

I winced and watched her walk closer to the house. "Sorry, it was probably on silent."

"That's a lame excuse," she snapped, her eyes going wide when she saw the front door. "What the hell happened?"

"Hmm?" I answered, turning casually to study the damage. "Oh, that. It's an interesting story, actually."

"And I cannot wait to hear it," Maggie said, wrinkling her nose as a stream of smoke hit her. "I really wish you wouldn't smoke."

I took one last lungful and snubbed the rest out on the stair. "If wishes were horses …"

Maggie gently kicked my shin. "You don't get to be a smart-mouth."

"It's my house. I can do what I want."

Maggie put her hand on her hip. "And I can just drive away without telling you what I found. So there!"

I grinned as I leaned over, wrapped my arms around her legs, and pressed the side of my face against her thigh—my grin widening when I heard her squeak.

"Allen," Maggie protested, trying to push me off, "get off me."

"No," I said loudly and shook my head. "You'll leave and never come back!"

Maggie let out a soft snort of laughter.

"You know, if I didn't know you two," Zack yelled out a front window, "watching this would be very awkward."

"Don't encourage him, Zack!" Maggie said, making another attempt to untangle herself.

I felt her wobble, then she slowly started to topple. I twisted so she landed on top of me in the grass.

"Idiot … let me up!"

I lifted my head and was rewarded with an awesome view. "I kinda like it here," I said, grinning as Zack broke into a new round of laughter.

Maggie shifted, elbowing me in the ribs as she got to her feet.

"Ow," I muttered.

I took her offered hand and let Maggie drag me to my feet. A smack to the side of the head was my reward.

"That one stung," I whined. With as many rings as Maggie wore, it was a wonder it hadn't hurt more.

"Oh crap," Maggie said, looking concerned. "I didn't mean to hit you that hard."

I waved her off. "I'm fine, Mags, I promise."

We walked around the back of the house, through the kitchen, and into what remained of my living room. Maggie stopped in the doorway, her mouth falling open in shock.

"Sweet lord! What happened?"

Such poetry my friends have.

I surveyed the shambled living room. "Well …"

Maggie grabbed a handful of my shirt. "I swear, if you say something about Godzilla's babies, I'm going to drop you on your butt."

I grabbed her hand and pulled her toward the dining room. "If I tell you what happened, you're gonna want in on this case," I said, my voice seeming overly loud as we entered the room. I gently pushed her into a chair and looked her in the eye. "You can't blog about it or tell anyone. *Anyone.* You hear me?"

Maggie nodded.

"You'll be in danger," I stressed. "And you could be used to get to me."

Zack let out a snort. "We could end up dead."

I rubbed my temples. "All right, you can help, but I call the shots! Got that?"

My answer was two huge grins and a squeal of delight from Maggie right before she launched herself at me. I ended up on my back, with Maggie practically on top of me, and wrapped in a warm, squishy hug. I hugged her back and stared at the ceiling. Maybe this wouldn't be so bad, having a group to help figure out what was happening.

"I hate to interrupt your cuddle," Zack said, his voice a bit dry, "but you mentioned that you had something to show us, Maggie?"

"Oh yeah," Maggie exclaimed, pushing off my chest to propel herself from the table. "It's in the car .... Zack, come help?"

A grunt escaped me as I got up. I went to the living room to retrieve two folders then returned to the dining room to lay out the crime scene photos on the table, face down—mostly for the sake of my stomach but also to ease Maggie into it.

The back door slammed and Maggie and Zack joined me, each carrying a pile of books. I moved a few pictures out of the way as they set their stacks down with a thump.

"I want you to know that this information was crazy hard to dig up," Maggie said. "I was up until four this morning."

I grinned. "I'll make you cookies or something."

"You'll burn them," Maggie said, waving a hand in my direction. "Just get me a bag of Almond Joys, and we'll be good."

"They weren't burnt," I muttered, grabbing a book. "They were crispy."

"I had to soak them in milk to make them edible, Allen. They were burnt."

"They were crispy. *Burnt* indicates completely black and stuck to the pan."

"Now I want a cookie," Zack grumbled, walking back to the kitchen.

I shifted a few books to read the titles, jumping out of my skin when a loud bang shook the table. I glared at Maggie and the heavy book open in front of her. She pretended I wasn't there and began flipping through pages.

"I think I found what could cause your balloon body," she said.

"Really?" I asked as I sat beside her. "Please share with the class."

"I need to find the spot …." Maggie grabbed another thick volume and blew away some dust that clung to its broken leather spine. The pages were yellowed and fragile. From where I was sitting I could see pieces of handwritten notes and a few illustrations. It looked like an old-timey sorcerer's book. Maggie didn't seem to mind the creepy book at all as she searched delicately through it.

"Mags, where did you find that thing?"

She paused to look up at me before she resumed her careful perusal. "It was in the collectors' section of the shop. It's for hardcore practitioners, not research papers."

"Guess I'm special then."

Maggie smiled, and I felt my face heat up just a little. I quickly grabbed a random book from the stack and began looking through it. Being best friends with a girl? Easy. Falling for your best friend who is a girl? Bad, very bad.

A loud crash came from the kitchen, breaking the sudden awkwardness that had settled between us.

"Zack?" I called, getting up from my chair.

A beat of silence, then he answered. "I'm fine, just dropped something."

I started to sit back down when I saw an image that resembled a faceless child reflecting in the glass doors of the china cabinet against the wall. I tilted my head and the reflection shifted, then disappeared.

"What the—" I said in confusion, not taking my eyes off the cabinet. "Did you see that?"

"Allen?"

Someone's hand was on me. I peered down at it, then back up. Maggie was studying my face, her hand not moving from my arm—not that I was complaining.

"I'm good," I said, sitting back down.

Maggie looked over at Zack, who shrugged from the doorway.

"I thought I saw something, but it was …" I rubbed my face, grumbling in German. My brain was short-circuiting with all the information I'd forced into it. I needed to sort through it. I needed peace for a minute—five minutes—that's all I needed. "It was nothing, just overworked nerves." I smiled feebly, then put my head down on the cool table.

"Here."

I blinked as a cigarette slid into my line of vision, then turned my head just enough to see Zack standing beside me, a frown on his face.

"Go smoke," he said and placed the cigarette on the table when I didn't move. "I'll bring Maggie outside in a sec."

"I thought you didn't encourage smoking?" I asked, getting to my feet and tucking the stick behind my ear.

"I don't, but you were going to sneak off for one anyway."

"True," I agreed. "Thanks."

The darkness enveloped me as I rounded the corner of the house. My feet crunched on the gravel as I navigated through the dark to the front porch. I leaned against the railing for a moment, then took a deep breath before settling on the steps to think.

Things were snowballing—exploding people, were-lizards, crime lords, mysterious trunks, and now faceless phantoms. The faceless thing in the glass had rattled me—*badly*. Maybe if I asked nicely Maggie could take a peek in one of those books of hers.

I twirled the cancer stick through my fingers before placing it in my mouth and flicking my lighter to life. A sigh escaped me, along with a thin trail of smoke as the nicotine rush hit me. My nerves settled with each puff I took, and I rested my head back against the handrail. Time to work.

I called up my mind vault and entered the room I'd created for everything I learned about the case so far. I was greeted with a mess. Pictures of the faceless child were scattered across the room—a distraction when I needed answers. With a growl, I swept the pictures of the faceless out of the room, leaving me still with too much information; more questions than answers. I gathered up the new information about my mother and shoved it out the door as well. Then I looked around the room. *Better.*

Still too much information, and as much as I didn't want to, I had no choice but to start over. Focusing on the wall, I stripped it bare. I went with the classic timeline. A black horizontal line appeared on the wall, and I cracked my mental knuckles.

The Dallas case went up on the wall first, along with the date all of this had started and a few observations from my conversation with the chief. Conversations with O'Hare went up next, placed appropriately on the timeline with dates, times, and facts. After a bit of hesitation, notes about my mother's involvement showed up as well. Next came encounters with lizards, which took a bit longer as I worked through facts and observations.

My head was starting to throb by the time I stopped to look at my work. It was still too much. I let out a huff of frustration and began to pull the bare-bones facts off the wall, letting them hang in the air like a wizard's trick. My eyes ran over what I had pulled, which wasn't much: both of the hospital crime scenes, my conversation with Dr. Wright …

"You dropped your cigarette."

I raised my head to see Zack and Maggie standing at the bottom of the porch stairs, their faces lit by the flashlight in Zack's hand. Both looked worried, and I couldn't blame them. I'd been acting weird ever since I landed this case.

"Huh?"

Zack bent and picked up the almost extinguished cancer stick for me to see. The pitiful thing was mostly ash now.

"Thanks," I said, taking it from him to stub it out. "Okay, I think I need to fill you in some more …."

My friends gave me their attention. "Short version," I began, "my mom apparently led a double life as a hunter of some sort. She took or was given an amulet from someone, and now several parties want it."

"But?"

"She's dead," I said simply. "Leaving me to clean up a giant mess. To make matters worse, I think whatever my mother did is connected to the case I have now. Unfortunately, the only way to solve everything is to find that amulet and figure out what's so special about it."

"What happens when we find it?" Maggie asked. "Do we just hand it over?"

"We'll figure that part out later," I told them. I peered around and got to my feet. "Let's bring this inside."

Chapter Seven

For the next few hours, Zack and I disclosed everything we knew. To her credit, Maggie only had to leave the table once. When she sat back down though, her pizza remained untouched.

"Okay," Maggie said, "so my human balloon comment was a mild analogy?"

"Pretty much," Zack agreed as he continued eating, "although it seems whoever did this had practice or was a serious head case."

"How about both?"

"Could be both." I shrugged and finished off the last piece of crust. "Probably both."

Maggie got up from the table again and ran into the dining room. Zack and I looked at each other before following and found her digging through her pile of books, muttering to herself.

"Find something?"

We couldn't make out Maggie's answer among all the thumps and frantic rustling of paper, and after a few moments the two of us started looking through things again ourselves. Zack settled at one end of the table while I went back to the pictures, using the magnifier I'd retrieved from the mess of a living room to look for more details. I almost dropped the glass when Maggie let out a triumphant cry.

"Jeez," Zack grumbled, looking up from the police reports he'd been reading.

Maggie ignored him and set the book down where Zack and I could both see it. "I thought I remembered seeing something .... Legends about a group of stones that cause something like that. You already know that many cultures believe certain things hold power, stones especially. The tales say that these stones formed from the blood of the first fallen angel—"

"The first fallen angel?" I interrupted, holding up a hand. "We're talking Lucifer?"

"Yes."

"The first big bad?"

"Yes, Allen, now shut up."

I opened my mouth for another comment but fell silent at Maggie's withering glare. She held her glare on me for a bit longer before turning back to her book.

"As I was saying, the blood formed into what looked like normal precious stones, which made their way into the human world and were passed down among the nobility and even regular people. And there's a pattern of war and genocide each time one of the stones appears throughout history. It's rumored that both Napolean and Hitler possessed one of these stones, maybe even the same one, even though it looked different. Each stone has different powers, but at least some of them can be used to kill people, even someone far away."

"Meaning?" Zack asked, shifting in his chair.

"Meaning that the stones are alive enough to change their appearance for the person who is wearing them," Maggie explained, looking a bit impressed. "The stone Napolean supposedly had was on his chain of office or on his crown. The gems in the crown were later replaced with colored glass, which is probably when the stone got put back into circulation. For Hitler, occult historians suspect a watch that he wore—it had a tiny diamond on the watch. Although the diamond necklace he gave his wife is still, in my opinion, a more likely candidate."

"Does it say anything on how to find these stones and or destroy them?" Zack muttered, turning his attention back to the report in his hands.

Maggie shook her head, her eyes scanning the pages. "Not really, because they look like regular gemstones most of the time. They do, however, revert back to their original form when no one possesses them—or maybe I should say, when they're not possessing someone."

"Hang on, the stones can take any form?" I asked.

"That's what it says," Maggie said, marking her place with a finger.

Someone having an idea? a voice mused inside my head.

"Like an amulet?" I asked, scrubbing my face with a hand. "What's the original form?"

Maggie read the page in front of her and raised an eyebrow. "According to this? A coal-like lump that pulses a reddish light."

Great, I would not only be chasing random people with pretty jewelry, but also looking for pulsing lumps of coal. This was going to be fun.

Sounds like a bad episode of Buffy, my inner voice said. I didn't disagree. "Anything else?"

Maggie flipped the page and nodded, looking uneasy. "It says here that many of the people rumored to own one of these stones died in mysterious ways."

My head swam a little. "They what now?"

Zack and Maggie studied me, and I watched recognition register on their faces. If my mother or father had died because of those stones, then possessing a stone didn't just kill people with evil intent; it killed innocent people as well.

"Allen, I didn't think—"

I shook my head at the plea. "I'm all right, Maggie. It just makes me want to close this case even more."

I turned my eyes back to the crime scene pictures and stared blankly at the victim from the Dallas case, my hands shaking. Did the amulet my mother was protecting have one of these stones, and did it kill her? Did she have to deal with constant thoughts of dying and leaving her kids behind? If that was the case, why didn't she just quit?

I was so lost in thought, I didn't realize Maggie had moved until her perfume curled around me. Slightly tanned arms encircled my shoulders and squeezed, saying without words that I wasn't alone.

I patted Maggie's arm. "Back to the matter at hand …. So perhaps the Fallen Stones are involved in these deaths, but we still don't really know how or why."

"I might be able to help you with that," Zack said, pushing the coroner's report from the Dallas file across the table to me. "Read the bottom part, and tell me what you see."

Maggie moved as I pulled the report over to me, sitting up straighter to read it. The form seemed to be legit even though it was a copy. Nothing was forged as far as I could tell. I reached for the folder and flipped through the rest of the pages, a slight frown forming on my face when I turned back to the main incident report.

"What is it?" Maggie asked.

Zack, settling back in his chair, answered her. "According to the coroner's report, only bone fragments were found. Thanks to Allen, we found most of a finger at Saint Mary's. The rest of the body is buckets full of goo and bone chips that will take me years to work through."

"And?" Maggie prodded.

"The Dallas coroner's report," I said, putting the paper on the tabletop, "says the victim would have had to jump from a high building for the bones to shatter the way they did. The officers had to write something in their incident report that was more relevant to what they were seeing. So they wrote it off as a violent and very morbid prank by the lady the nurses had escorted into the room. But they're having a hard time explaining the blood everywhere, the splatter pattern, and the amount."

"The lady was Terry Cockrill, right?" Zack asked, glancing at his paperwork.

"That would be the one."

Maggie chewed her lip for a moment, one of those subconscious habits. "If that's true, then couldn't the coroner have made a mistake?"

Zack and I shared a look across the table. We both knew where she was going with this, and it wasn't a line of thinking that I liked.

"If you're going with the assumption that the police wanted to sweep it under the rug, then I agree," I said, ignoring the unhappy expression Zack threw my way. "But if that is the case, then both reports would match. These don't. The incident report would match up more with the coroner's report. Someone must have put the original medical report in the stack to be faxed over before the coroner was told to change it."

"Wait a sec," Maggie said, holding up her hands for us to stop talking. "So the coroner's report is right?"

"Correct," I nodded, pointing to the paper on the table. "I don't have a medical license, but I do know that when bones shatter, they leave fragments."

Maggie moved back to her stack of books, uncertainty etched on her pretty face.

"What are you thinking?"

"Well," she stated, selecting one of the books and flipping it open to a marked page, "if you want to go with the theory of the Fallen Stones ... it would make sense if the stones had the power to shatter bones—or anything for that matter, right?"

I looked at Zack, who shrugged. "Would that even be possible?"

"Speaking from a medical standpoint," Zack said, "no, but then again, until today, I thought lizard-people didn't exist. So my opinion really shouldn't count."

I pinched the bridge of my nose and counted to ten. They both had valid points, even though I hated to admit it. And who knows, maybe it was time to start looking at this from a completely different perspective. Couldn't hurt.

"All right," I finally said, "if we are going with the Fallen Stones theory, we'll need more information—hard evidence that will help us figure out a way to stop this from happening again."

Zack made a displeased sound, and I shared the feeling. I didn't want to rely on something I couldn't control. The occult is entertaining to read about, but proving that it's real? That's a completely different game, not to mention never-ending. People have searched the globe for the ancient knowledge behind myths, only to find layers of twisted evidence and misinformation, their search ending in disappointment. I liked facts that I could see, hear, or touch. Two close encounters with lizard-people proved to me that at least one type of monster does, in fact, exist. Does that mean other things, like the Fallen Stones, were real? Not necessarily, but if they were, did the amulet hold one of these stones? More importantly, where did my mom hide it? The notion that these stones could kill innocent people, from any location that the person chose, made me sick. I didn't like the options I was presented with, and my savior complex wouldn't let me brush it off. It just meant I had to find a way to fix it, and that meant I needed more data. And I needed it fast before I ended up joining my mother in the afterlife.

I looked at the clock. Only ten thirty? I rubbed my eyes and tried to stifle a yawn.

"If it's all right with you two," I said, getting to my feet, "I think we should all get some sleep and then meet back up tomorrow."

Zack nodded, a look of relief on his face. Maggie, on the other hand, wasn't so happy.

"Wait just a damn minute," she fumed, taking a step in my direction, her finger extended in a scolding gesture. "We're not going out there to do something about all of this?!"

"Maggie—"

"People are dying!"

I backed up as she took another step. "You're a police officer! Go out there and arrest somebody!"

I waited as she paused to catch her breath, then carefully put my hands on her shoulders to keep her from walking closer to me. She was shaking, probably from the rush of adrenaline and fear. Her breathing had also turned harsh and heavy.

"Maggie," I said gently, brushing my thumbs against her collarbones, "we need to rest. Our brains are overloaded with information, and Zack and I have been through a lot today. We'll get together tomorrow after we get off work, okay? If we keep going like this, we won't be any good to anyone, especially ourselves."

"I can't help feeling it's going to get worse," Maggie said, sniffing.

"Zack and I blew up IHOP," I said in a last-ditch effort to make her smile, ignoring the glare Zack sent my way. "And whoever I'm tracking has the power to kill people, and if I hand it over to Riley O'Hare, I could end up like the people in those pictures. And I don't photograph well at all."

"You guys blew up IHOP?"

Zack sighed. "To clarify, that was all Allen's fault."

***

Something was ringing in the darkness of my room. Wait, not a ring, I realized, slowly dragging myself from the depths of sleep—more of a whining keen, high-pitched and shrill. I wanted to smash whatever was making that horrid sound. As I opened my eyes, I came face-to-face with the thing I'd seen in the glass downstairs, but it wasn't alone.

Standing around my bed were three faceless kids. The faces were bottomless gaping holes that seemed to ingest the natural darkness that surrounded them. A sense of utter dread penetrated the air around them like some kind of poison. I was afraid that breathing it in would coat my insides with a film of dark emotions.

I tried to sit up but discovered I couldn't move. My heart rate increased, a wave of panic rising with each second that my muscles strained against invisible tethers, and my breaths became labored. The whine seemed to get louder the more I struggled. I wanted that sound to stop. *Someone stop it!* It grated against my nerves, pulling them too tight for me to think. I opened my mouth to scream for help, but no sound came. *Sweet Lord above, I am in hell.*

The mattress shifted, and I let out another soundless scream when I saw the faceless things crawling onto the bed with me. They stopped once they reached my chest, sitting down on either side of my prone body. The sound, apparently coming from them, enveloped me.

Stop! I yelled silently at them. *Stop all of this and let me up!*

Their heads tilted in unison at my soundless words, as if they heard me. Instead of stopping, the numbers one through three appeared in the air above their heads. Then one by one, they began to disappear.

My stomach rolled as the first one vanished in a violent spray of blood. A static noise filtered into the air, coaxing the whine to a new level of agony. I was sure blood was running from my ears in little rivulets.

Another of the faceless children evaporated into thin air. The third leaned in closer to look at my face before the air was split by a scream—one of those screams you only let out when you have nothing left. I'm pretty sure I joined in with the screaming and watched as the third dissolved into thick black rancid smoke that rolled over me, strangling my lungs and making my eyes water.

My stomach was turning, and the stench of blood clogged my nose. My chest tightened in anticipation of whatever came next. Yet try as I might, I couldn't look away from the sight. It was like watching a bad movie where I'd already guessed the ending.

"Allen!"

A voice filtered into my dream, urgent and concerned. The bed shook again, and I shrieked. Dark memories hovered around the edges of my mind, twisting thoughts of terror and the sound of a child in pain.

"Allen, wake up, damn it!"

My eyes snapped open, and I raised my arm to block the blow I was sure was coming. My forearm connected with the side of Zack's face and sent him tumbling backward off the bed onto the floor.

Zack? Why is he here, in my bedroom? I blinked, listening to Zack's curses and mutterings. I took a breath to speak but started coughing instead. My throat was raw and burning.

"Allen," Zack said calmly, pulling himself off the floor and returning to my side. "I need you to look at me for a moment. Can you do that?"

My breaths came in short pants. "Wha …?" I forced out, trying to rise from the bed, but his hand kept me in place.

"Breathe, Allen."

Zack. That's right—our discussion had run late, so he'd camped out on the living room floor. He pushed me down gently and checked my pupils. His face was pale, almost ghostly, and his eyes stood out eerily against his skin. He took my pulse and made me do a few breathing exercises before he bothered answering me.

"You were screaming," he said finally. "I couldn't get the door open, and when I did … Allen, your body was all contorted on the bed …."

I tried to swallow the lump in my throat, wincing a bit at the sandpaper texture. I must have scared him pretty badly.

"I heard you yell for it to stop," Zack said quietly, "for them to let you up. You went quiet for a moment, and then suddenly you were screaming like someone was trying to kill you."

The food from earlier that evening felt like lead in my belly. "Nightmare," I eked out, shifting a bit on the bed. I hadn't told him about the faceless child before and certainly wasn't going to now.

"Must have been one horrible dream," Zack said grimly.

"Killer clowns and strippers," I deadpanned.

That startled a laugh out of him. The panic that had been flitting around me slowly began to evaporate when the *Cops* theme twittered through the room—my ringtone for the station.

I grabbed the phone and flipped it open. "Who died?"

"Funny, I was going to ask you the same question," Chief Newburn's voice rumbled in my ear, and I felt goose bumps break out on my arms. *Uh-oh.*

"Come down to Saint Mary's, and don't take your time," Newburn grumped before I could say anything. "And if you could swing by and pick up Zack on your way, that would be great."

"Chief, wha—"

"You. Here. Now," Newburn snapped and hung up.

I moved the phone away from my ear and stared at it. It was the middle of the night. What the hell was going on?

"I take it you've been summoned?"

I got to my feet and quickly began yanking on some clothes.

"*We* have been summoned," I told him, sliding my gun into my holster and the badge onto the holder at my belt, "which means we have a dead body."

Zack's phone sprang to life as we headed down the stairs. He threw on some clothes while I grabbed my coat and keys, then I switched off the last of the lights before we made a beeline for the back door.

The ride to Saint Mary's was silent. We were both in our separate worlds, mulling over who knows what. I can tell you that mine wasn't full of rainbows and puppies, that's for sure. Mine had dead people, blood, chunks of flesh …. Oh, and faceless kids. Can't forget those little buggers. What morbid daymare is complete without them?

I pulled into the parking lot and was greeted by flashing blue lights and, to my surprise, a crime scene van. Seemed redundant to have Zack come in, but he was the best at his job. I didn't have a good feeling about what we'd find, and my stomach still wasn't settled from the nightmare.

We had just stepped through the sliding doors and into the ER when I heard someone call my name. I straightened up as much as my height would allow and scanned the crowd, my eyes stopping once I found Chief Newburn heading in our direction.

"I don't want to know how many lights you ran to get here," he grumbled, ushering us past the doors that separated the lobby from the waiting room.

Zack hustled ahead once we passed through the heavy security doors to the bustling center of the ER, leaving me alone with the chief and my increasingly upset stomach, little traitor.

"Only two … or three … can't remember," I answered, covering a yawn.

Newburn fixed me with a glare, and I swallowed hard. Sometimes I walked a very fine line.

I followed him through the short maze of offices and private rooms to one in the far back, away from the commotion and beeping monitors. The room was roped off with yellow crime scene tape, and I could make out the quiet little pops as flashbulbs went off. Newburn raised the tape, nodding for me to follow. I took a few steps and immediately put a hand over my mouth as the smell of death washed over me. I didn't want to look. I really didn't.

"Who is it?" I asked.

"Dr. Albert Wright. Age thirty-nine."

Chapter Eight

"What?" I asked, ignoring my discomfort enough to look at him, trying not to give away my shock.

Newburn repeated what he'd said and pointed to the room with a pencil. "Robins was the first one here. Go talk to him and tell him what you find. I'm going to talk to the rest of the staff."

I groaned. Loudly.

Newburn's eyes flashed. "You will behave and do your job like a professional." He stared at me sternly, waiting for a smart-ass retort. When I successfully kept my smart-assery to myself, he nodded and walked back the way we'd come, leaving me in the hall by myself.

Don't get me wrong, Robins and I *could* work together, but the obscenities we end up shouting at each other usually made the other officers nervous. So Chief Newburn kept us on different shifts and cases. Our offices were even on opposite sides of the station. But at times like these, it was all hands on deck.

So Dr. Wright was dead. I thunked my head against a nearby wall. I'd lost my only lead, damn it. *Well, not entirely,* I thought. *There's always O'Hare.*

"Like hell," I said aloud, startling a few passing nurses. "I'm not asking that jack-hat for help."

"Well," a voice beside me said, "if I had known that beforehand, I wouldn't have asked the chief to call you."

I cut my eyes to the office door and found Robins glaring at me. I took a deep breath and forced a smile.

"Robins, didn't see you standing there."

Robins was a bit taller than me and well muscled but not overly so. His short brown hair was held in place with what seemed like a gallon of gel. His clothes were always ironed to perfection, the creases evident long after morning had passed. I think he even ironed his ties, which were always adorned with a shiny gold pin, a gift from his late grandfather for graduating the police academy. His only glaring flaw was a chipped front tooth and, oh, the consequences of mentioning that.

"I'm sure," Robins sniffed, his eyes taking in the state of my clothes. "Just don't mess up my crime scene."

"Sure," I answered, starting to walk past him, "whatever you say."

Robins brought up an arm, blocking my path, and held out a set of gloves and booties. "Put them on or don't come in," he said flatly. "I'm serious. Don't contaminate my crime scene."

I snatched the protective gear from him and leaned against the doorframe to yank on the booties. Once the shoe coverings were on, I marched into the room, grumbling with every step. *Oh, he's serious, huh,* I thought, pushing up the tape to duck underneath. *Where does he get off ordering me around?*

Something wet and stinky landed on my shoulder and soaked right through the material. My stomach turned, and I steadied myself on something solid—a desk, I think. My gut screamed at me not to look up, but since when do I follow good advice?

I was glad for the desk's support when I finally looked up. There, on the ceiling, was a blood mural, like Jackson Pollock had tried defying gravity. A sick feeling washed over me like an angry ocean. I took a knee and put my forehead against the cool wood of the desk, slowly counting to ten.

"Blood too much for you?"

Stupid Robins. I stood slowly and, careful not to look at the bloodstained ceiling, turned my attention to him. *You can't break his nose, at least not in public.*

"It caught me off guard," I lied, moving away from the desk and closer to Robins. "Now if you don't mind, move. I need to work."

I turned away and could feel his icy scowl boring into the back of my head.

Ignore him, I told myself, taking a breath. *Focus on your job. The faster you can get this done, the faster you can get out of this room.*

With my stomach still quivering, I looked up again. It didn't look any better the second time around, but at least I was prepared for it. The blood, I noticed, had a different pattern this time, as if someone had used a wide brush and turned it to taper the ends into thin tendrils. It felt … personal. My eyes followed the strokes to the wall opposite me where they converged into what could only be described as a blood tree, the gruesome branches twisting and clotting the closer they got to the trunk. The trunk was centered with a large wooden desk and one of those comfy executive roller chairs, which was turned toward the wall.

I took in another gulp of air through my mouth and picked my way through the flow of personnel toward the desk, pausing periodically as something plopped onto the ground from above. Zack's familiar mop of hair bobbed behind the desk, and I steered myself to him. He was crouched down examining something. As I rounded the desk and saw what remained of Dr. Wright, I stumbled back a few paces.

Dr. Wright's body had been carefully divided in half. The front of his face, chest, torso, and legs, apparently, now decorated the wall and ceiling, but the back half were perfectly intact. I glimpsed the inner workings of his body: cross sections of his intestines, lungs, spleen, liver … a grotesque dissection.

I stretched out a hand to find the wall. That's when I looked down. Sitting right beside my foot was a human jawbone. I lost the battle with my body and emptied my stomach onto the shiny office floor. I heard cursing and scrambling, and then someone placed a bucket beside me. I waved weakly in thanks and managed to get the next heave into the bucket.

"Damn it all, Miar! You couldn't have tried to miss the evidence?!"

I raised my eyes to Robins's face, which was twisting in anger. Wiping my mouth with a paper towel one of the officers had given me, I took a step in his direction.

"Oh, calm down," I answered around the paper towel. "It was just a jawbone. Hey, those teeth are perfect. Maybe you can figure out who his dentist was and have your chipped tooth fixed."

A few snickers erupted around the room, and Robins's face turned several shades of red. He opened his mouth, and I pretended that I was about to hurl again, this time on his spotless trousers. Robins let out a yowl that sounded like an unhappy cat as he jumped a step away from me and pointed at the door.

"Out!"

I coughed and spat into the bucket. "But I thought you needed my help?"

"I said out!" Robins snapped, his facial color deepening. "Before you contaminate my crime scene more!"

I gave him what I hoped was my most mournful expression and began the slow trek to the door. I wondered what I managed to get his blood pressure up to this time. I sent a text to Zack, asking if he could check on Robins just for fun, grinning at the thought. Putting my phone away, I moved beyond the tape and into the small crowd that had started to gather. It was mostly hospital staff—nurses, a few doctors, a couple of patients—all trying to catch a glimpse of what had happened inside the cordoned-off room. Many had their hands over their mouths, but one nurse looked a tad too comfortable with the entire situation. I paused to watch the woman, and my skin started to crawl. Her face was devoid of thought or emotion—except her eyes. They were alight with some sick satisfaction.

Stripping the plastic booties off, I headed for the nearest bathroom. No way was I making inquiries with vomit-flavored breath. I shoved the booties in the trash, rinsed my mouth out a few times, and then scrubbed my face as if I could wash the image of Dr. Wright away.

"Come on, Allen," I said to my reflection. "Get a grip on yourself and go talk to the creepy nurse." For once, I listened to my own advice and went to find the nurse, popping a piece of gum into my mouth as I exited the bathroom.

The crowd outside Dr. Wright's office had been dispersed, and the creepy nurse was nowhere in sight. I spotted a reception area down the hall and decided to start there. With any luck, I could get the nurse's name and maybe some extra information. I waited patiently for the receptionist to finish speaking with a heavyset man. She looked up and smiled when she noticed I was standing nearby, a very nice smile that formed little crinkles at the corners of her eyes. It was infectious. I returned her smile, giving her a little wave as I held up my badge. Hopefully, her day wouldn't turn sour after I asked her a few questions. Eventually, she sent the man away with what looked like a blanket and turned her attention to me.

"How can I help you, officer?"

I flashed a bit of a smile. "I wanted to say how sorry I am to hear about Dr. Wright. Horrible way to go."

"No one should die that way," the nurse said, wiping at her eyes. "Who or what could have done that?"

"That's what I'm trying to figure out," I answered, leaning against the counter. "I'd like to take a peek at Dr. Wright's files?"

"I don't know how much help I can be," she said. "As I'm sure you remember, I can't give you access to patient or personnel files without the proper paperwork. Do you want the number for our legal department?"

Damn it.

"You're right. I'll get the paperwork," I said, holding my hands up. "By the way, what can you tell me about a nurse here—a bit taller than me, brownish hair, might enjoy the nasty aspects of her job a bit too much?"

The receptionist sighed and reached for a stack of papers. "That sounds like Madison. She's normally at one of the clinics, but she was helping out here today."

I retrieved the small notebook I carried inside my coat as well as a pen. Maybe this wasn't going to be a waste after all.

"Out of curiosity, did she ever work with Dr. Wright?" I asked, scribbling her answers down.

"She did actually. They both worked at the clinic I mentioned earlier for a few months, and then Dr. Wright came here to run the ER. Apparently, he asked for the transfer because of a problem at the clinic. No one gave it a second thought at the time. We needed the help, and he is—was—a great addition to our team," she paused to hand off a stack of papers to a passing nurse. "I'm sorry, Detective, but is there anything else I can do for you?"

And my time was up. I couldn't get mad at the woman for doing her job; doesn't mean I had to be happy with it though. "Any chance you could get me the clinic's business card," I asked, trying to sound hopeful. "I'll get out of your hair after that, I promise."

The receptionist gave me a patient smile and began looking around her desk for the card. I drummed my fingers on the countertop. I needed those files, but I didn't want to scare her off or make a scene. The rational part of my brain followed that line of thought—everything by the book, don't cut corners, do the paperwork. The irrational half wanted to demand what I needed and not give a damn about protocol. Unfortunately, the rational half ran on caffeine, which I was sorely lacking.

I opened my mouth to try a different tack, when a smooth voice purred behind me.

"I'm sure you can bend the rules this one time, especially since Detective Miar is only trying to do his job."

The receptionist blushed a pale shade of red, and I didn't have to turn to see who was behind me. *Riley O'Hare,* I thought. *What is that cocky bastard doing here?*

"Of course," she stammered. "I'll be right back."

I watched her move quickly to a door and swipe a key card before going inside. I ignored O'Hare as best I could, even though I could feel him just behind my shoulder. The hair on the back of my neck started to prickle the longer the receptionist took to find the file. *Where is she?* I thought. *Why is this taking so long?*

"You seem well rested," O'Hare said, moving to lean on the counter beside me.

"That's what happens when I don't have weirdos breaking into my house," I answered.

O'Hare huffed. "All the more reason for you to fix that door."

The receptionist finally returned and set a stack of files down on the counter in front of me, her eyes flicking briefly to the man behind me. "Here you go, sir. I decided to make photocopies for you and Mr. O'Hare. I also pulled a few things that might be of interest to you. You'll still have to go to the clinic for anything on Madison though. Her records aren't here."

I nodded my thanks, hands curling around the edge of the stack before O'Hare could grab it. *What the hell? How powerful is this guy?* I turned away from the desk when an arm came up, blocking my way, and I tensed as O'Hare leaned in. He was close enough for me to smell his cologne, rich and musky, and too far into my personal space.

"I think we need to talk, Mr. Miar," he said, clearly amused at how uncomfortable he was making me.

A nasty comment gathered behind my teeth, but I swallowed it before it could cause trouble. "Oh," I said instead, as calmly and evenly as I could manage, "what about?"

O'Hare was in another tailored suit, his hair neatly combed and styled. He'd brought a cane this time, black with a silver handle formed into an animal of some kind. The smile he wore was unnerving, sharklike, suggesting he wouldn't take no for an answer. He pointed to a nearby exam room. As he turned away from me and walked toward the room, two well-muscled men in casual clothes took positions on either side of the door. O'Hare paid them no mind as he opened the door and slipped inside.

I swallowed hard and glanced around the hall for any sign of backup. I really didn't want to go in there, not because I'd be in a room with O'Hare, but mostly because he had two goons with him and I had no one.

"You're digging a hole, Miar," I grumbled aloud, adjusting my grip on the files and walking to the door O'Hare had disappeared behind.

The goons looked at me briefly, then went back to watching the hallway. Guess they thought I wasn't much of a threat. I gave them both a quick once-over. Now that I was closer, I could tell they were about my age, maybe two or three years older. They were both definitely muscled but not overly so; otherwise, they'd stick out too much. But even in their casual clothes, they still had a deadly air about them, a predatory presence that wouldn't disappear no matter what they were wearing. One of them had dark-tinted sunglasses on that did nothing to soften the intensity of his gaze.

"Can I help you?"

The question came out in a low rumble, and I heard the other guy shift against the wall. Probably making sure he could keep an eye down the hall and watch his buddy in case he needed help. Apparently, not that many people just walked up to them.

"Yes … cake or death?"

Laughter that sounded remarkably close to barking erupted from my right as the other guard understood the reference. The goon in front of me shifted on his feet, and I could see a vein starting to form on his neck. Time to go.

I grabbed the door handle, gave the angry man a bright smile, and said, "Clearly not an Eddie Izzard fan," before pushing my way into the room.

Chapter Nine

The first thing that hit me was the smell; not like the stench of death at a crime scene or the sterile smell of a hospital room. This was bitter—the type of bitter that roused people on cold winter mornings, that fueled humanoid engines around the world. *Oh wonderful black bean, how I love you!*

The room, it turned out, was a makeshift storage and break room. Stacks of chairs and boxes of office supplies were piled everywhere. I raised an eyebrow at the path winding through the mess.

"Come along, Mr. Miar," O'Hare called from somewhere in the back of the room.

I made my way cautiously along the narrow path in the direction of his voice. "You always hang out in hospital storage rooms?"

I found him behind a stack of boxes close to the back, seated at a small table and sipping coffee from a cheap paper cup. With anyone else, the scene would have looked ridiculous. Yet O'Hare made the whole thing seem classy—had to be the suit. Though I tried to keep him in my line of sight, my eyes were drawn to the coffeepot plugged into the wall close by. Damn him for distracting me with that roasted pot of goodness.

"Do sit down," O'Hare said, not looking up from his cup. "We have a few things to discuss, I believe."

"The only thing I want to do," I told him, still standing, "is break your nose."

Those icy eyes looked up, sending a chill through me. This guy scared the hell out of me, and he knew it.

"I admit that keeping an eye on you is a bit extreme," O'Hare said, setting his cup down, "but as you might have guessed, I dislike people getting into my business."

"Didn't you ask me to get into your business?"

O'Hare's mouth twisted into a slightly feral smile. "You, Mr. Miar, are an asset. One that is expendable when you cease to be useful to me."

I frowned. "If that's true," I said, pretending he hadn't just threatened me as I picked up the coffeepot and poured myself a cup, "then why do you keep popping up? You trying to date me or something?"

I flicked my gaze over to him. He was still composed, but his hand was white-knuckling the head of his cane so hard the whole thing vibrated from tension. I kept my face neutral and used my own cup to hide a smile. I'd hit some kind of nerve. He needed me for something, but what—finding the amulet or something else?

"Don't worry, Mr. Miar," O'Hare answered, giving me that smile again, "you aren't my type at all."

I took a swallow of my coffee, feeling my senses wake up a bit more, and leaned against the wall nearby. "Now that we have that out of the way, what did you want to ask me?"

"Have you made any progress on your case?"

So he didn't have anyone at the station on his payroll. At least that was one thing I didn't have to worry about.

"I can't discuss an ongoing investigation," I said, watching him carefully. "Surely you understand that, Mr. O'Hare."

"I'm sure we could work something out," O'Hare said, watching me just as closely.

"I could even ease your struggles in the department—"

"No."

O'Hare was taken aback. "Excuse me?"

I set my now-empty cup down on the table. He was clearly used to getting his way, adept at removing people who prevented him from reaching a goal. That alone made me dislike him. People like him were why I became a police officer in the first place. And despite all of my own setbacks, I liked to think I was doing a good job of keeping my city safe.

"No, I don't want your money or your help." I gave him a polite but deadly grin as I walked to the door. "Now, if you don't have anything else to say, I'll be going. Oh, and thanks for the files."

I didn't have time to waste on him. I needed to close this case before anyone else ended up a bloodstain on the wall. There were already more bodies than I cared to think about, and I had a sinking feeling that the murders were far from over.

O'Hare's voice rang though the room. "I will *burn* you, Miar."

I paused, my hand on the door. "Bring it on."

***

I thunked my head against the steering wheel of my car. Not only had I hurled at a crime scene, which I would never live down, but I also threatened O'Hare …. Again. I was doing amazingly well today. Thankfully, I managed to escape from the hospital unnoticed by Robins and the rest of the patrol staff on scene. I'd probably get a call later to come in and fill out a bunch of paperwork—no big deal. If I was really lucky, the only one who would notice my absence would be the chief. And he didn't really care so long as my work got done. For now, I had a few leads to follow up on.

I glanced at the stack of files in the passenger seat. I'd already flipped through some of it when I got to the car, scanning through the information for anything useful, and discovered that the good doctor had been on call and assigned to see Meredith Strong before she exploded. He was also mentioned in another incident in Baton Rouge, Louisiana, where the patient had died mysteriously before they were seen by the doctor …. The attending nurse? None other than Madison Corvell. Turns out our creepy nurse was popping up everywhere. Since I didn't have enough gas to get to Louisiana, I decided to swing by the clinic. The glowing numbers on my dash told me it was a little past four thirty in the morning. I needed food, coffee, and more gum. It didn't have to be in that order though. Starbucks sounded like a good idea, and by the time I got there, they'd be open for business.

I turned the car in that direction and let recent conversations, facts, and suppositions flow through my mind. My mom supposedly had a powerful amulet hidden away somewhere, and Riley O'Hare and two sets of lizard-people wanted it. People were dying in unusual ways that I didn't have answers for, and O'Hare was interested in that too. What caused their deaths? Was it the amulet? If so, how was it all connected? What was linking them together? My gut said I was on the right track, but I needed a clear connection and hard evidence. I made a face when I remembered one of the faceless kids in my dream had been split in half just like Dr. Wright. Were those little creeps trying to tell me something?

I pulled into the Starbucks parking lot and killed the engine. Hopefully, I was on the verge of a break in the case and could get rid of the bad guy before anyone else ended up as a splatter painting. Climbing out of the car, I pulled the cigarettes from my pocket and positioned myself at one of the outside tables. The staff inside was still bustling around, getting things ready for the early morning rush, so I had a bit of time to think.

The entire case was like a jigsaw puzzle with mismatched and missing pieces. It was frustrating, confusing, and very demanding. The revelations about my mother gave me the hardest time—the notion that I didn't really know her and that she'd hidden this amulet somewhere.

I scratched my head as I tried to think of another hiding place that she might have used for something like that. When she'd passed, I'd found some money and mementos hidden in not-so-secret places: an envelope in her sock drawer, an unused boot beside the fireplace, a jar full of coins on the top shelf of a kitchen cabinet. But none of that had been jewelry. Come to think of it, I never saw her wear anything fancy besides her wedding ring.

I twirled the cigarette between my fingers. There was always the possibility that the amulet had been stolen from the house at some point. Maybe after the house was ransacked? I didn't like that thought at all. I really needed to fix my door.

"Americano black and a blueberry muffin."

Blinking, I looked up as a cup appeared in front of me, along with a blueberry muffin about as big as my head.

"I'm sorry, um …" I stuttered, my eyes glued to the muffin, my mouth watering as the smell of fresh baked goods and coffee wafted in my direction. "I didn't—"

"It's what you always get though, isn't it?" A young guy was standing nervously nearby. His wildly curly hair was deep brown and his skin an unusual shade of bronze. The poor kid looked absolutely terrified of me for some reason and kept moving his weight from foot to foot.

The morning light highlighted the faint shimmer of green scales on his cheekbones, just like one of the guys I'd caught in my house when all of this started. My eyes narrowed. I was almost certain he was the one who'd seemed less eager for confrontation. The kid paled, his whole body shaking as he realized I remembered him.

"Please," he begged quietly, a few scales starting to show on his hands, "let me explain."

I wanted to make some smart-ass comment and put a new level of fear in the guy, but I have a strict rule about punching down, and I was too tired to be mad. I'd used up all of my anger on O'Hare. Instead, I kicked a chair out for him and pointed to it.

"Sit."

"But … I …"

"Kid, I've had a bad morning. Sit your butt down." I took the top off my coffee cup and gulped it.

He fiddled with the edges of his apron for a few seconds before perching on the chair, his eyes wide, like he thought I was going to jump him at any moment.

"Why don't you start by telling me your name?" I said as gently as I could.

"Corbin. Corbin Matthews. And I'm sorry about what happened. I told my brother we shouldn't go in before you got home. He didn't listen."

Brother, hmm? That explained why they were arguing.

"Both of you are lucky I didn't shoot first," I said around a mouthful of muffin, "but we'll get to that later." I dusted off my fingers and pulled a pen out of my pocket, then straightened out one of the napkins he'd brought me. "Tell me why you were in my house, and don't lie to me. Got it?"

Corbin swallowed and managed a nod. "We were sent there, my brother and me, to recover something your mother was keeping safe for us."

"The amulet."

It wasn't a question, just a casual mention to see what he would do. Corbin jumped as if I'd stabbed him with a hot poker, and he looked ready to bolt.

"How—"

"I've had the pleasure of running into more than one party that is eager to find it," I answered, tapping the top of my pen against the table and leaning forward a bit. "What no one will tell me is why my mother had this thing in the first place. And why in the hell everyone wants it back suddenly."

Waiting for his answer, I took another sip of coffee. The silence that stretched between us was so long that I almost repeated my question. Corbin took a deep breath and nodded as if he'd come to some private decision that I was more of a threat than whoever had sent him there in the first place.

"My people aren't from here, Mr. Miar," he said, eyes flicking to the napkin as I started writing again. "We originally came from what is now southern Mexico, but our family decided to move north and settled along what became the southern border of Texas. At one time, we were a proud people, flourishing for millennia, peaceful and plenty. We even managed to avoid human conflicts."

"What changed?"

Corbin looked down at his hands. "A man came to town one day. He was unlike anything we had ever seen before."

"What do you know about the man?"

"I only know what my grandfather told me," Corbin said, his attention returning to me, "that the man seemed cloaked in darkness and shadow, with eyes that burned like the setting sun, and that a feeling of dread followed him through the town. He claimed to have heard about the town's prosperity and wanted to see it for himself. He stayed only a few nights, and before he left, he insisted on giving the mayor a gift—a beautiful golden necklace with one flawless red gem hanging from its cord. When the man left, life went on as usual .... But then it started."

I scooted closer, my pen and napkin abandoned in favor of listening to the story Corbin was spinning. I tried to remind myself that I needed to stay focused on the facts and not get distracted by a fairy tale. But I couldn't help it. Something about Corbin's story rang true.

Corbin remained silent for a moment, his eyes briefly changing colors. "People started to die, Mr. Miar. We didn't know—"

"Corbin! Can you get back to work?"

I won't lie, we both jumped at the intrusion of another employee at the door.

Corbin scrambled to his feet, almost turning the table over in his haste. "I'm sorry," he called, dusting his apron off. "I'll be right there." He looked at me and shrugged.

I sighed as I got to my feet. Digging one of my cards out of my wallet, I held it out to the kid. "Call me if you think of anything else that might help, okay?"

I got a mumbled response, which I took as a yes, as he shoved my card into his apron pocket before hurrying away.

I took a few minutes to finish my coffee and muffin and headed back to my car. Glancing at my watch, I let out a groan. It was only a little past six as I made my way to the clinic. *Gonna be another long day.*

The clinic was in a small brick structure on the north side of Highway 35, close to Walmart and what used to be a Blockbuster video store. Affiliated with the hospital system, it provided care to patients who didn't have enough money or the means to go to the main hospital.

Madison's employment record was waiting for me when I arrived, along with a smiling nurse who practically shoved it at me before closing and locking the door. I would have been annoyed if I wasn't caffeinated and slightly impressed with how big the file was. Instead, I was sitting in my car looking over the file's contents, and oh boy.

Madison had been a great worker both in Baton Rouge and here in Waco, except where Dr. Wright was concerned. She'd worked with him in Baton Rouge until Wright requested a transfer to Waco. No particular reason appeared on his transfer request. Shortly after he'd arrived at the clinic, she transferred too. According to Wright's second transfer request, he had been very concerned about Madison's sudden interest in him.

I stretched in my seat, careful not to drop anything. What had she done in Baton Rouge that spooked him so badly? Stalker maybe? That explanation didn't feel quite right. Maybe he had somehow seen something he couldn't explain?

Like me and my reptilian fan club?

I grimaced, putting a hand over my face. Is that what alerted him? Was Madison one of the lizards? Or did she just have a serial killer vibe? Ugh, there were too many questions again.

I put the file on the dash and pulled out a cigarette. I didn't normally smoke in my car, but I needed a fix. I released a breath of tobacco smoke and rolled three of the windows down—right as a breeze came through. The papers fluttered and lifted into the air. I frantically grabbed the pages before they sailed out the window, then rolled up one of the windows.

"At least no one saw that," I muttered, flicking the ash out the window and smoothing out another report.

It would have been worse if you had to chase the papers across the parking lot.

"True ..." My voice trailed off when my eyes landed on Madison's evaluation report. I had a moment to register what I was looking at before my mind seized up in a sudden panic, and I tossed the report to the passenger-side floorboard like a hot potato. I had caught fragments: part-time ... graduate psychology program ... patient list. But none were more important than the two words at the top of the page: Jefferson Institution—the same place where my personal demon, my oldest brother, was sitting in a padded cell. She'd worked at the Jefferson Institution? Seriously? Had she talked to Ethan? Did he tell her about me?

My chest tightened as fear and anxiety attempted to swallow me. I was vaguely aware of the heat of the cherry burning my fingers as I tossed it out the window and took deep breaths in order to focus. *I don't have time for this!*

My hands went through my hair, fingers gripping the strands hard enough to hurt. *Get your act together.* I closed my eyes for a moment, then nodded. *You're fine. Everything is fine.* I tucked the rest of Madison's papers back into the file and put it with the rest before turning the car over. My next stop was home for a quick shower. I knew I looked horrible and, if I had to guess, smelled bad enough to match. I was going to Meredith Strong's viewing later, so I needed to be presentable—not like a college kid who had pulled an all-nighter to finish a paper.

***

There is a reason I don't wear suits to work. It's not because I don't look good in them. The problem is I look … cute. I'm talking cheek-pinching aunties, sixth-grader-going-to-his-first-dance cute. Of course, it didn't help that when I'd finally made detective and went to my first crime scene, I had bystanders who didn't believe I was an officer. Even the victim's grandmother patted me on the cheek, then handed me a piece of candy. Yeah, that spread through the station like wildfire.

For the longest time though, the chief didn't believe me and demanded that I follow the dress code like everyone else. Until it happened again. He stopped by my desk the next day, handed me a form to fill out, and said, "Lose the suit. Look professional; nothing childish." It's the only argument I ever won without saying a word or throwing a fist.

Going to a victim's viewing called for nice clothes, not necessarily a suit, but nice. I stepped out of my car at Mrs. Strong's address in a light-green button-up shirt, clean pair of dark blue jeans, and black dress coat that only bulged a bit where my gun was safely tucked away out of sight. I knew taking a gun to a wake was probably rude, but with the week I was having, my gut said that going anywhere unarmed was just a stupid idea.

I looked at the house through my aviator shades and frowned a little. It seemed sad. I firmly believed that the exterior of a house tells you something about the people inside. An unkept lawn or peeling paint might reflect lazy, poor, or elderly people inside or people too busy or stressed to worry about the exterior. Similarly, perfectly manicured lawns and gardens reflect residents who value appearances. Maybe they genuinely love gardening and lawn maintenance, or maybe they pay someone to take care of it.

But that's not what I meant by Mrs. Strong's house seeming sad; I was talking about its soul. Most people don't notice a house's soul. A house can look absolutely perfect, yet its soul could be sick from some hidden secret. Or the house could look dilapidated and on the verge of collapse but have a soul bursting with love, a reflection of those who have lived there.

Don't get me wrong—I use both kinds of reflection for information. I don't really have a choice in my line of work. I do, however, reserve judgment until I see everything there is to see.

The Strong house, with its well-maintained lawn and pruned shrubs, was hard not to judge. Everything looked spotless, not a single blade of grass out of place. Maybe it was just me, but it looked staged. Like it was thrown together overnight to create an illusion of normalcy. As if this family had something to hide. The house itself was straining to look happy enough to match the lawn and was failing miserably.

I spied a group of mourners huddled on the porch and was assaulted by the stench of alcohol and expensive cigars as I climbed the stairs. They paused their conversation to look at me with calculating stares. I paid them no mind and walked right in.

The inside of the house was decorated tastefully, professionally if I had to guess, and oozed money. An antique table was positioned near the door and held a vase of wildflowers, along with a mirror that was almost as tall as me. I held in a whistle. Everything in there would cost me two or three paychecks.

I wandered a bit farther in, nodding to anyone who looked in my direction, and let my eyes roam around the room. An uneasy feeling wormed its way into my already occupied thoughts—the feeling growing as I took a closer look at the furniture. It was all brand new. There were even a few with tags or sticky residue from where they had been peeled off. But what bothered me more than the furniture was the lack of family photos. Despite my dislike for my brothers, I did have a few pictures of the four of us before everything went south. Even the pictures of my mom and dad were still up. But this house had nothing that even hinted at what kind of family lived here.

The feeling of sadness clung to me as I made my way toward what I hoped was the kitchen. I needed to find Mrs. Strong, ask my questions, and leave. As I approached the doorway, I spied a group of women huddled around the island, its black marble top strewn with several bottles of wine; not a single cup was dry. I stood there for a few minutes listening to the loud, raucous laughter.

"Mrs. Strong?" I asked, walking into the kitchen as the ladies broke apart enough for me to get a good look at the woman who turned in response. Her hair was a shade of blond that didn't complement her skin tone, but her makeup seemed tastefully done aside from the bright-pink lipstick. She had forgone the traditional black and was instead wearing a powder-blue sundress. Her chocolate-brown eyes spoke volumes as she tried to focus on me.

"Can I help you?" she asked, her hand curling around her wine glass.

I caught the shimmer of a rather large diamond on her finger. "I was wondering if I could ask you a few questions about your daughter."

Mrs. Strong poured herself more wine and set the bottle back down with a loud clank. "What about her?"

"Maybe we can do this in a more secluded setting. I don't want to upset your guests," I said, gesturing to the rest of the ladies who had resumed their wine sipping.

Rule number one that every officer learns: Never ever interview someone in the kitchen. One too many things could be used as a weapon. Knives are the most common concern, although I do know an officer who got a food processor thrown at him.

"You're a naughty boy," Mrs. Strong grinned. "Trying to get me alone …." Her friends twittered around her.

Great, they were all sauced. Just what I needed. If they were guys, I'd have no problem hauling them outside and demanding answers. Doing that to a woman wasn't even on the table. Hell, I didn't even like interrogating females. These women were laughing and giggling, watching me as I stood at the edge of their circle. Damn my moral code.

I took a step back and started to reach for my badge when I noticed something on one lady's hand. I glanced at the others and felt my stomach disappear into my intestines. *Scales.* I could see patches of scales on various pieces of uncovered skin. I'd only met five creatures with scales so far, and they'd tried to kill me. And in my desperate search for answers, I'd walked straight into a nest. Stupid, stupid, stupid!

"Crap," I muttered as their gazes suddenly felt more sinister.

One of the women slid off her stool and stalked toward me, her eyes flashing a deep yellow. Her nails extended to form curved claws, and before I could think to move, three neat slices appeared on the front of my shirt.

"Did you kill her?" she hissed, swaying a bit, and I put a bit of distance between us.

I grimaced as the cuts started to sting—one more thing to replace, one more bandage. "If you're talking about Meredith, no. I was at her crime scene."

A yellow tongue snuck out from between human lips, and I held back a squeak of fear. *Komodo dragons? Why them?*

"Liar, you smell of fear!"

"Lady, you and your friends look hungry," I answered, "and I'm not a piece of meat."

She hissed at me, and the few who hadn't been looking now gave me their undivided attention. Having any group of women look at you with hungry eyes is a bit disturbing, but these women could turn into giant lizards and rip me to pieces. I was terrified.

"Look," I said, the hair on my arms starting to rise, "I'm investigating her death. I knew her in high school, and I want to find out what happened."

A shriek came from Mrs. Strong, and I flinched. That sound reminded me of a rabbit screaming. It was inhuman and just freaked me out to no end. The group moved forward in unison, slowly creeping in my direction. More than one of them stumbled, showing just how much alcohol they had consumed before I'd arrived.

"Who are you to think you could help us?" Mrs. Strong hissed, her carefully manicured nails slowly growing into painted claws.

I calmly pulled my gun, making sure to keep it at my side, and unclipped my badge from my belt. I raised the little golden shield, my back straightening. Please let this work.

"Detective Allen Miar of the Waco PD."

I swear some of the color drained from their faces. The hissing stopped, and they all moved back as if the air around me was poisoned. A few pressed themselves against the far counter, eyes wide and fearful. All, that is, except Mrs. Strong. She stood straight, her eyes narrowed and focused on me. She raised a hand and addressed the group.

"Excuse us, ladies," she said, smiling enough to show serrated teeth. "Mr. DuCourt and I have business to discuss."

Chapter Ten

The kitchen was silent except for the constant drip of the faucet and the occasional tap of Mrs. Strong's Freddy Krueger nails. No one moved, their bodies turning into humanlike statues. Maggie would have called it cool; I called it creepy. I was starting to get goose bumps from all of them staring when Mrs. Strong let out a low growl. Everyone, including me, snapped to attention and the ladies went rushing to the doors as fast as their high-heeled shoes would allow.

I blinked and slowly put my badge away. The gun stayed out until the last one was gone, and then I slid it into its holster.

Mrs. Strong eased into the role of hostess. She retrieved another glass from the cabinet behind her. "Please, sit."

I stared at her from my spot across the room. She was kidding, right?

"You and your friends just tried to skewer me," I blurted out, unable to stop myself. "I think I'm good standing."

"You came to offer condolences and assistance," she said, unperturbed by my outburst. "I acted rashly and violated the laws of hospitality. Saying no is both insulting and enticing to me, Mr. DuCourt, but if you wish to die here, I can happily oblige."

Oh boy. I had no desire to get any closer, not unless I had a cattle prod handy. I already knew what those claws could do to me if she chose to use them. I was more nervous about her teeth, specifically the bacteria in her lizard saliva. Komodo dragons were among the deadliest reptiles on the planet, able to consume 80 percent of their body weight in one sitting. Given the size of the goons at the IHOP, she could swallow me whole.

"One condition," I said, watching her pour wine into the glass, "the name is Miar, not DuCourt."

"Most would ask for protection from the rest of my nest," Mrs. Strong mused, pushing the glass to the edge of the island. "But very well, I accept your condition. Now, please sit."

I walked over to the island and noticed a sliding-glass door. "Do you mind if we take this outside?" I asked, gesturing to the yard. "It's a wonderful day, and this really is a private matter."

Mrs. Strong considered my suggestion, then threw the door open and sauntered out. My chest eased a bit as I followed.

Mrs. Strong chose to recline on one of the lounge chairs, her white pumps discarded, showing off daintily painted toenails.

I cleared my throat and settled on the edge of another lounge chair, leaving enough space between us in case anything got too intense. Without even looking, I fished the crumpled napkin from earlier out of my pocket and found a pen in another. Making sure I could see both her and the back door wasn't easy to do, but I managed.

"How can I help you?" she asked, once I had gotten myself settled. "I'm afraid most of what I know about my daughter you might already know if you were friends at school."

"Normally, people aren't so eager to help the police," I said, watching for her reaction, "but I'm guessing most people aren't you."

She gave me a toothy grin. "Most people, Mr. Miar, don't have the honor of talking to one like yourself."

She was in her element here, a queen among peasants, and she wanted me to remember it. I dutifully averted my eyes when Mrs. Strong stretched, the outline of her body pressing against the fabric of her sundress.

She chuckled. "Don't want a peek?"

"First and foremost, I am a gentleman," I said, turning my eyes back to her, "then a police officer."

She looked a little put out but waved for me to continue.

"Correct me if I'm wrong," I said casually, "but when I'm attacked by one of your people out in public—unprovoked—that's truly *unhelpful*, no? I'm a little rusty on the rules of engagement …."

A deep hiss came from Mrs. Strong as her irises turned yellow. I chose to believe the hiss meant *yes*. "My apologies—"

"It's fine," I said, holding up a hand to stop her. "I dealt with it."

She stared at me as though searching for a lie in my words. Waste of time, considering I'm not a good liar. I prefer honesty anyway, less backlash if something goes wrong.

"Did you kill them?"

"Dunno," I answered. "There was an explosion …."

Her pupils constricted into slits. "If they did violate the laws, they need to be reminded of them," she snapped. "My apologies for their behavior, Detective Miar."

Oh wow, not the reaction I was expecting, much better than her trying to eat me.

"Everything worked out," I told her. "I got the normals out of the restaurant before the fight broke out, Mrs. Strong."

She looked at me for a moment before tilting her head back and laughing. It was full-throated and full of so many promises. I cleared my throat, trying not to notice how well the sundress fit her.

"You may call me Mary."

I nodded. "Mary, as I said before, I knew Meredith in high school. From what I can remember, she mostly kept to herself and didn't cause any kind of trouble."

Mary's shoulders slumped slightly as she nodded. "She was very quiet; that is, until she became comfortable with you. When she did, she'd open up and chatter away. Even so, there are many things she kept private, even from me."

"Maybe Meredith had a friend who might know if she was involved in anything dangerous?"

Mary thought a moment, then gave a helpless shrug.

"Can you think of any changes in your daughter's routine? Any sudden change in behavior? Mention of a boyfriend?" I asked, raising an eyebrow. "That seems to be the one thing all ladies love to talk about."

Mary shook her head slowly. "Not that I am aware. Like I said, she was very private. Her love life in particular was always a great mystery to me."

I ran a hand over my hair and frowned at my notes. My leads were drying up, and here I was with the people who had tried to kill me in a pancake house.

"One last question. May I have a look around Meredith's home? It might give me a few more clues as to what happened to her."

Mary nodded. "Of course, if it will aid you in your investigation, I will be more than happy to help."

"Thank—"

"I do have one condition though," she said, an edge coming into her voice. "We don't want anything precious of hers getting lost before the family is able to go through her belongings. So please refrain from removing anything."

I shook my head. "That's something I can't agree to. If I find something about the investigation, I'm obligated to take it with me. However, I will provide a list of any items removed, and you'll be able to pick them up at the station when the case is closed."

A twitch formed near Mary's eye as she got gracefully to her feet and started back into the house, waving for me to follow her inside. She handed me a shiny silver key from a kitchen drawer. "I trust that will be returned as well?"

I nodded, pocketing the key, and told her I'd be in touch. I didn't look around as I hightailed it out of the house. Once I was safe inside my car with the doors locked, I blew out a breath and yanked the tie off. That whole situation gave me the creeps, the really bad kind that made you think your skin was trying to separate from your body. Switching my now sweat-stained dress shirt out for a T-shirt didn't take long. I pulled the coat back on and felt Meredith's key bite into my skin through the fabric of my jeans. I pulled the key out of my pocket to study it. It was a plain silver house key, no decorations or colored plastic clinging to it; just cold, naked metal. I had the key and permission to enter the home. My day was looking up.

I pulled out my cell. "Hey, got any plans today?"

***

"Why did I agree to do this again?"

I looked over at Zack as we walked up the path to Meredith's home. He had showered and changed but still looked a bit worn from too little sleep and a rough awakening. Maybe I should have asked Maggie to come with me.

"Because you said it was insane of me to do this by myself with some pissed-off mob boss and giant lizard-people gunning for me," I answered, turning back to the door.

Zack grumbled something about sleep.

The neighborhood was composed of nice quiet streets with a few toys in more than one yard. I felt relaxed here. It almost felt like something was radiating calm into the air. I breathed deep—I could use some Zen right about now.

I lightly pressed my fingers against Meredith's wooden door, letting my fingers slide down. "Do you feel that?"

"Feel what?"

"That sense of tranquility," I answered, putting the key into the lock.

"Allen, you're being extra weird," Zack answered, looking around Meredith's small front yard, "but I do feel something."

The door unlocked with a click, and I carefully pushed it open. A small white ball of fluff rushed out and attacked my shoes. "What the—"

The house's defender, a West Highland white terrier, was gnawing on my sneakers in vicious cuteness. The little guy didn't seem starved, so someone must have stopped by to feed him. He just wanted attention. I may seem like a tough guy most of the time, but I could easily fall victim to the cuteness of a ball of fur or feathers. I was the kid whose mother had to worry about what I smuggled into the house next. Once, I snuck a couple of grass snakes into my room and hid them in a shoebox at the back of my closet. They would have been fine, except my mom demanded to know why I'd put frozen mice in the freezer. When I showed her the snakes, she flipped out and knocked over the box, releasing the snakes into the house. I had to ask two of my brothers to help me catch them and turn them loose in the backyard. I was grounded for a week and had my backpack checked on a regular basis whenever I came home after that.

The terrier yapped a few times, its little tail swinging its whole hind end back and forth in happiness. I smiled as it ran away only to turn and make a dive for my shoes again. Zack sighed and walked past me into the kitchen.

The house was small but cozy, and the dining and living spaces ran together, creating a good-sized communal area. I studied one of the walls. It was adorned with awards and achievements and the family photos that had been missing from her parents' home. In a few, Meredith posed with her mother and a man I assumed was her father. The others were frozen moments from girls' nights out, graduation, summer trips, and birthday parties.

The terrier had given up on attacking my shoes and was now sprawled out, relaxed but still listening, its ears twitching every time Zack and I moved.

"Nothing looks out of the norm here," Zack called from the kitchen.

I scratched my head. There had to be something here that would give us a clue. A nagging thought started to form: What if Mrs. Strong already looked here? I mean, someone was clearly feeding the dog because the little thing wasn't skin and bones, but why just leave him here?

The kitchen was cramped but manageable for a single woman and her small dog, with a worn wooden screen door that led out back. A small utility area held the water heater, washer and dryer, and a second fridge or freezer. I couldn't tell without opening it. Unlike the house I'd been to that morning, nothing that inhabited these rooms was brand new—which raised a few more questions I'd file away for later.

I scooted around Zack and peeked into the fridge. Not much by way of food, just some fruit that was turning sour, a few veggies, and one carton of slightly chunky sour cream. Must have been grocery day when she died. A whine brought my attention to the dog who was now pawing at a little plastic dish.

"You want some supper?"

My answer was a bark and a full back-end wag. Viciously cute I tell you. I grinned, moving over to the small pantry at the back of the kitchen in search of dog food.

"Where did you go after the crime scene?" Zack asked.

I gave him the condensed version of my morning as I scooped a bit of food into the dish and watched the dog attack it with glee.

"O'Hare would kill me in a public setting to make an example out of me, but I don't think he's behind Meredith's death," I told him. "Corbin is the nicer of the two Godzilla spawn I met when this whole thing started. Mrs. Strong ... I don't know how to describe it. She wasn't playing the part of the grieving parent, but when I started asking questions, she got a little agitated."

Zack rubbed his eyes; he didn't look pleased.

I started pawing through the kitchen trash, pulling out receipts that might be important and setting them aside. Zack followed my lead, opening cabinets and rattling off what was inside them: flour, sugar, bread, coffee, several selections of cereal. Nothing unusual. I tuned him out as I used a nearby counter to start sorting through the receipts. A lot of them were from the grocery store, gas stations, various shopping stores around town, and a few for the groomers—again, nothing.

"Whoa."

I looked up from my task to see Zack standing in front of the other fridge, one of those fancy stainless-steel double-door models with the ice dispensers on the front that always broke about halfway through the warranty. Like everything else in the house, it was an older model, but not too old either. It wasn't uncommon to have two fridge units, especially if you liked to stock up when you were at the grocery store, so you weren't buying food every week.

"What is it?" I asked, moving over to him. "Oh ..."

Zack had opened one side of the fridge. It was fully loaded. The top two shelves held common foods; most had spoiled or were quickly approaching the "good until" date. Below that was nothing but meat. I don't mean a few T-bones that you could throw on the grill. I'm talking about a stack of thick sirloins, racks of ribs, rump roasts, tubes of ground chuck, and vacuum-sealed packages of what looked like pig's feet.

"Was she planning a party?"

I shook my head, reaching past Zack to pull one of the crisper drawers open and grinned at the amount of sausage and bacon. She had good taste in meat.

"I think she was like her mother," I said, nudging Zack aside so I could coax another drawer open. "We don't know how fast a metabolism these lizard things have, or what their eating habits are for that matter. But from the look of all this protein, they need a lot of calories."

The bottom crispers were stuffed with various chicken parts: legs, breasts, wings, thighs, and something that looked suspiciously like gizzards. How she'd managed to find those, I didn't want to know.

"Hang on. If she was like her mother," Zack said, opening the other side of the fridge as I closed the first, "then shouldn't her mother have come to you about the situation with her daughter, knowing your history, that your mom was the sheriff of weird around here?"

"*Was* being the key word," I pointed out, peering into the fridge over Zack's shoulder, moving away once I saw that it held more of the same. "Mom's been buried quite a long time. Who knows what's happened since then?"

Zack headed toward the back of the house to search Meredith's bedroom. I could hear him rummaging around as I peered into a bathroom, found it lacking, and made my way through the hall to Zack.

"Anything?"

"Nope," Zack answered, closing an end table drawer.

It didn't take us long to go through the bedroom, and like the rest of the house, it told us nothing. Well, we did discover that Meredith had a fondness for torture devices, in the form of high heels of various heights, and that she had one hell of a protein diet.

"Damn it," I swore softly and rubbed my eyes, grimacing at the texture of the rubber gloves against my skin. "There has to be something here."

"We've looked everywhere," Zack said with a shrug from his spot by the dresser. "Under the bed, closet, dresser ... there's nowhere else to look."

I waved a hand at him, glancing around me as I did. Something had to be here; it just had to be. Otherwise, I had risked getting mauled by a bunch of lizards for nothing. I ran a hand through my hair. Where would she hide something that might tell us more about who she was and who would want to kill her? Like a diary maybe ....

That's when the light bulb went off. The bed. We'd checked around and under it, but not in it.

I began removing pillows, shaking them out before tossing them to the floor.

"What are you—"

"Don't just stand there!"

Zack grumbled but complied, helping me yank the sheets off the bed along with the comforter. I felt the space between the headboard and the mattress. Nothing. I pulled the bottom sheet off, then the mattress protector; still nothing.

"When I tell you, raise the mattress as high as you can," I told Zack, pointing to the now undressed bed.

He grunted in response, lifting the mattress enough for me to see under it. Set dead center on top of the box spring was what looked like a photo album. I crawled under to grab it, scooting out of the way as Zack let the mattress fall back into place.

I ran my hand over the faux-leather front and noticed bits of yellow paper sticking out from between the pages. Frowning, I opened it up to a random page and nearly dropped the book. It was a newspaper clipping about an incident between me and an FBI agent a few months back. I let out a low groan.

"Not your best side," Zack commented, looking over my shoulder and grinning at my half-hearted glare.

"You'll never let that go, will you?" I grumbled, flipping through the rest of the pages.

"Let me see: Forget about you hitting a federal agent and getting threatened with suspension?" Zack snickered. "Not a chance."

I mumbled a few not-so-nice words and focused on the book. It was a scrapbook that included articles about every major case I'd handled so far in my career, along with a few clippings that weren't related to me or my cases. News about disappearances, kidnappings, even a few drownings and murders had been clipped. All of them were tidily arranged, some with notes next to them in neat cursive handwriting.

I wasn't sure if this was flattering or creepy. Why would this girl I barely knew from high school have clippings about me? Was she a secret admirer? Keeping tabs on me for some other reason? Did it have anything to do with my mom and her side job? Was she trying to figure out the best way to ask for help?

I closed the book with a sigh and leaned against the wall. *What else could she have hidden?*

"No one ends up dead for no reason," I said matter-of-factly. "Maybe Meredith found something or crossed someone she shouldn't have. Happens to people all the time."

"No chance that she was just caught in the cross fire?"

I paused, thinking before shaking my head. "No, she kept track of me, which I think means she knew about my mom."

Zack was heaping the bedclothes back on the bed. "But someone found out about it and wasn't too thrilled with the idea of you knowing," he stated.

I grinned and tapped the side of my nose. "Bingo."

"So all we have to do is find out how she got tangled up in all of this," Zack said, a grin coming to his face. "Should be a piece of cake for a guy like you."

A chuckle escaped me as I nodded. *If only it were that easy.* A growing feeling of dread crept into my stomach. I wanted to believe that I could close the case without any more problems, but the nagging in the back of my mind didn't give me any comfort.

Zack froze. "Was that your stomach?"

"Maybe ..."

Zack crossed his arms over his chest. "Did you eat today?"

I kept quiet and occupied myself with picking at the book's spine.

"Allen …"

Silence.

"Miar!"

"Yes!" I relented, throwing a hand in the air. "I had a muffin."

"Just a muffin?"

"Someone," I said, giving him a pointed look, "insists that coffee is not considered food. It comes from beans, so I disagree."

Zack shot me a glare and left the room. "Hurry up and finish. You need to eat something if we're going to keep working."

Mumbling as I turned to leave, my knee collided with the bedside table. A loud clatter broke the air as a few odds and ends rolled off the table. I bent to pick up a picture frame and let out a groan; the glass was broken. This just wasn't my week. I crouched to pick up the pieces and glanced at the photo.

"Holy crap!"

Inside the four-by-six frame was a picture of two young women. One was Meredith, her hair pulled back in a messy bun, a few books in her arms. The other was the image of perfection, hair pulled back with a pair of clips, a frozen drink in her hand, and a slightly wild look to her eyes: Madison Corvell. I flipped the frame over, carefully extracting the picture to see if anything was written on the back.

"Maddi and me, Baton Rouge."

Jackpot. I tucked the photo into my back pocket and secured the scrapbook under my arm. Quickly, I picked up the rest of the glass and set the shards and frame on the table.

"Ready to go?" Zack asked as I appeared in the living room.

"Let's make sure the back door is locked, and then we can go," I said, heading for the back door.

The neighborhood wasn't bad but still, never hurts to be careful. A bark brought me out of my thoughts, and I looked down at the white ankle biter that was sitting on my sneaker.

"Need to go outside?"

Another bark and a tiny tail wag. Guess that meant yes. I pushed the door open and watched the little white fluff ball practically fly down the stairs to the sparsely covered lawn. I stayed on the concrete porch and surveyed the yard. Nothing of much interest. Then I noticed the back gate was open, and the dog was nowhere to be seen. I smacked the heel of my hand against my forehead.

"You all right out there?" Zack called, coming to the door behind me. "Allen, where's the dog?"

Silently, I pointed to the open back gate. "He went for a walk."

"You didn't check the yard before you let him out?"

"No …."

Zack shook his head in disbelief.

"Shut up …."

***

We searched for the dog for over an hour before I reluctantly called animal control to report the little bundle of fuzz. Zack leaned against his car after making one too many snide comments. I moved the food and water to the back porch, in case the dog came home, and made a little cardboard box bed.

We were standing by our cars when Maggie called.

"I did more research on these Fallen Stones," she said distantly, letting me know that she'd put me on speaker. "I wasn't able to find any firsthand accounts, probably because whoever handles them ends up dying. I did, however, manage to dig up bits of hearsay."

"Figures," I muttered, holding a hand up when Zack raised an eyebrow. I hit the speaker button.

"So I called a few local churches and got laughed at," Maggie said with a huff, "which was so rude. You think they would be interested in something that dealt with angels."

"What did you expect?" I asked. "The church is so secretive. They have secret archives and denied the rumors of their special paranormal unit, even after people presented the evidence."

Maggie snorted, and I could picture her making a face at the phone. "Allen, I study the occult, and I haven't even heard about that."

"You've been on the wrong websites then."

"Children," Zack interrupted before the conversation turned into an argument, "focus."

I glared at the phone and handed it off to Zack so I could dig through my pockets.

"Besides the wall you ran into with the church," I asked, pulling out my cigarettes, "what else did you find?"

Rustling came through the speaker and, after a few moments, so did Maggie's voice. "After the fourth church called me crazy, I took a different approach."

"And?" I prodded, lighting the cigarette.

"Annnd," Maggie said, "I got a ton of info. I'm talking enough to fill a few notebooks. I swear you'd think this guy was Giles from *Buffy* with the way he wouldn't stop talking."

I released a breath of smoke into the air, but the wind shifted and blew it right into Zack's face. He wrinkled his nose and coughed softly.

"Sorry …."

"Are you smoking?"

I gave Zack a wide-eyed look and feverishly shook my head. Maggie hated it when I smoked, but it was better than drinking when I was at work, and it kept my stress at a manageable level.

"No," Zack answered.

"Where did you find this guy?" I quickly asked.

"Horton University," Maggie said after a beat. "A professor named Norman Quivel. Total nerd, by the way—you'd like him. And he knew a lot about the stones."

The declaration made me grin. There weren't many people Maggie would consider even close to my level of nerd.

"Aw, Maggie, that's so sweet."

"I mean your IQ level alone is insane," she answered, and I could picture her shrugging. "Plus you know more about poisons, fairy tales, conspiracies, and urban legends than anyone, and that's just a few of the random topics stored in your big ol' brain."

Zack glanced over at me. "What exactly is your IQ?"

I took a short pull of the cigarette. "Somewhere in the one-sixties; can't remember the exact number."

"What the hell? Why are you a cop again?"

"Because he gets bored too easily with everything else," Maggie answered before I could. "Happened a lot in school, but he refused to skip grades."

"Maggie, the guy you talked to, what department is he in?" I asked, cutting their conversation off.

There was a pause, and I thought she'd hung up for a moment. I looked at Zack, and he tilted the phone enough to show me the screen. Little white numbers were ticking away the time, and I frowned.

"Maggie?"

"I'm here," she said, her voice barely audible. "Customer came in."

I repeated my question, finishing my smoke while I waited for her answer.

"Occult Studies," Maggie's crackly voice said through the speaker. "It's more of an elective course than mainstream. It's also not in the handbook due to its controversial content."

Zack laughed. "Would you expect anything else from a university in the Bible Belt?"

"Not really," Maggie and I answered in unison.

Zack rolled his eyes, and I took my phone back, laughing. "So what do we do now?"

"If you give me a minute, I'll tell you," Maggie answered. "I mean, most of what he told me we'd already figured out, but he did answer a question that Zack brought up."

There was a thud and the crinkle of what I assumed was paper before Maggie came back on the line. This time her voice was clear, and neither of us had to strain to hear her.

"Besides the fact that he mostly encouraged me to stop looking for the stones," Maggie said, "Professor Quivel claimed that they not only corrupt those who possess them and bring them to an early grave but also have the power to curse bloodlines."

"Great," Zack muttered. "So is Allen safe? I mean, we doubt his mom used the stone or anything."

"Well, that depends on what stone his mom found," Maggie explained, her voice sounding uncertain. "Quivel mentioned the power of each stone is different—just like no demon or angel is exactly alike—so each stone can deliver a different death according to what power it holds. Death, destruction, possession … the list gets worse the deeper you go."

I didn't like the idea I was getting. A quick glance at Zack showed he also was feeling like we had a bigger problem on our hands than we initially thought.

"Basically," Zack said, "you're saying we have no clue which stone we're up against and no clue if Allen is safe."

"That's the short version," she confirmed.

I sighed and settled against the wall. "Maggie, if these things have been this long without wiping out the entire human race, then there has to be a way to contain them, right?"

As I waited for her response, I watched a black car idling down the street. The windows were tinted just enough to keep me from viewing the driver, but I could feel a predatory stare. "Mags, I need to call you back," I said, snapping the phone closed before she could answer.

"What was that about?"

I nodded in the direction of Zack's car. "Meet me back at the office."

***

"We were being watched," I told Zack as soon as we got out of our cars back at the station.

His face darkened a bit as he looked around, checking his surroundings. Poor guy wasn't used to this much excitement. But he and Maggie had both agreed to help me on this case ….

"Chill," I said. "I lost them in traffic along Waco Drive."

He relaxed visibly and joined me in the afternoon sunlight near the front of the car. "You know who it was?"

"Probably O'Hare. I made him mad again."

Zack's mouth slowly set into a hard line as I filled him in. "So you think he's put a tail on you?" he asked. "To monitor your progress in the case?"

"I know, it sounds like a bad cop show," I said, turning my attention to the street between the station and the parking lot. "He wasn't subtle about offering his help or his displeasure when I said no. Putting a tail on me is the only thing he could do."

A few cars raced past, none of them black and none of them imposing. I couldn't have lost them that easily. Even the most skilled idiots could find the downtown area.

"What does putting a tail on you accomplish?"

"In our last conversation, O'Hare said he would 'burn' me," I said. "I stupidly told him to bring it."

Zack full-on glowered at me.

"*Burn* is what spy organizations do when they want to disavow a source; sometimes they erase that individual's whole existence," I continued, ignoring him. "O'Hare sees me as both an asset and a threat."

Zack made a face as we made our way to the sidewalk. "That makes him a new level of dangerous then, right?"

"It's a new level, for sure," I agreed, looking both ways before starting across, "and one I don't think he's afraid to explore if I suddenly turned expendable."

We climbed the stone steps and waved to the secretary as we pushed through the double doors that led to the heart of the station.

"Right now," I said, "whatever or whoever is killing these people bothers me more than what an angry mob boss might do to me in the future."

A noise of disbelief came from Zack's general direction as I led him to my office.

I weaved with practiced ease through the stacks, markers in hand, over to the board. "Call Maggie back. We have a suspicious nurse to find."

Chapter Eleven

For the record, don't ever, ever hang up on a woman. Ever. If you do, prepare to beg for mercy. Zack and I were both severely scolded—so loudly, in fact, that one of the other officers stuck his head in to see what was going on. He left rather quickly when he heard the tone of Maggie's voice. I swear a beast-like growl came out of the phone ....

I looked up at the board where I'd written everything—the facts anyway—on the timeline in black. With a red marker, I started to write everything I knew about Madison. The only thing I had going for me was that I knew where she worked. I could always call the hospital and go see her when she was on duty, but if she wasn't human, that would be a problem. Too many innocent people present. Although, if I could time it just right, and Robins was there, I could see if he screamed like a girl.

My eyes narrowed at the pleasantly smiling young woman's photo that was taped to my board. Where was she now?

"Before I was so rudely hung up on," Maggie said, clearing her throat a bit, "you were asking about containing the stones. I double-checked my notes and found a few suggestions, but I'm not sure they would work."

Zack perched the phone on a stack of files near me before going to my computer. He held up Madison's file before pointing to the device on my desk. Fine by me if he wanted to do part of the digging.

I nodded and faced the board again. "Let's hear them anyway."

"Um … antipossession charms, buried in a mirror-lined box with a hex bag, stored on hallowed ground—"

"Wait a sec," I interrupted, looking at the phone. "Hallowed ground?"

"Yes, blessed ground. You having a brainstorm over there, Sherlock?"

"Indeed, Miss Adler," I responded, my eyes studying the timeline and then drifting over to the small section I'd set aside for my mom. "What exactly is 'hallowed ground'?"

"Hallowed, blessed, and holy ground are the same thing," Zack said from his spot at the desk. "It becomes hallowed through spiritual practices; worship, memorials, and continuous visits renew the blessing. But if people start neglecting the space or just stop showing up? That's when evil can move in."

I turned enough to look at him. He looked rather pleased with himself. "Meaning?"

"Meaning," Zack said, still typing away at my keyboard, "that the divine power, or whatever you want to call it, is there. It just doesn't have the same punch as, say, a church. That's why in the horror movies you see all the ghoulies in the old neglected graveyards. The moment they try to set foot in a church, all kinds of things happen."

He looked up from the computer screen when I started laughing.

"What?"

"You," I said, pointing a finger at him, "can never make fun of me again, you nerd."

Zack shot me a small glare, without any heat behind it, and went back to the computer's screen. I laughed harder and listened to Maggie attempt to smother a giggle.

"He's right though," she pointed out. "They are all considered the same thing, and the more followers or people that visit certain places, the more of a punch the ground is going to have. Come to think of it, that's probably where the myth involving vampires and churches came from."

Made sense to me. Hollywood had a horrible habit of taking anything they could and cranking up the volume on it for public enjoyment. Granted, most of the time it was a hit and a miss, but they do try.

All this talk about hallowed ground got the wheels turning in my head. We still had no idea where my mother had hidden the stone. It wasn't in the house; Zack and I had searched every box in the attic, and I had searched the trunk. She never wore jewelry aside from her wedding ring, and nothing was in her room either. There was one place though that I hadn't thought to look: her coffin.

I picked up a marker and wrote a bright capital *C* and put a question mark beside it.

"I have a hunch, but it'll have to wait until later. Anything else on our stones?"

I could hear Maggie flipping through her papers.

"No," she said after a moment. "That's all I could get out of that guy."

I rubbed my face with a free hand and continued to stare at the board. "All right, it's something to go on. Thanks, Maggie. You did well."

"Yay!" she squealed. "I helped!"

I started laughing again and caught the sound of snickering from the vicinity of my desk. Keep your occult-shop owners happy, involve them in a case with exploding bodies, and tip them well.

"I do have a tiny favor—"

"If it involves exploding another public building," Maggie interrupted, her voice laced with sarcasm, "you can forget it."

"No, nothing like that. And besides," I said, turning to see Zack sinking in the chair, "I have Zack to help with that. I was thinking more along the lines of a cemetery excursion later tonight."

Maggie made a noise of approval. "I'm so in! Which one? What time? Oh, this is going to be so cool!"

"Take it easy, Maggie," I said, dodging a paper ball that flew in my direction. "Saint Catherine's, the one close to the circle. I'll see you there around eight, all right? And don't forget to bring a flashlight."

"Aye, aye, Captain!"

I peered over Zack's shoulder after Maggie hung up. "Find anything, Zackadoodle?"

Zack visibly cringed at the nickname Maggie had stuck him with a few years ago. Poor guy. Of course, mine wasn't much better.

"I told you not to call me that," Zack reminded me.

I noticed a few search programs had been brought up, displaying different information in little boxes on the computer's screen. Everything from missing persons, zoological societies, newspaper articles from Waco and Louisiana, and others I couldn't see because they were covered up by other windows.

"You really think the zoo website was necessary?" I asked as Zack flipped through the windows. "Don't think we're going to find Madison locked in an enclosure." Although it would make my life a bit easier.

"Research on your giant lizards, or did you forget them?"

"I was trying to. Thanks for reminding me."

"What I do have is Madison's life history up to this point," Zack said, "which is as thrilling as watching paint dry."

I grumbled and went back to my file on Madison. I had already read everything once, storing the important parts away in my memory. Going through it again allowed me to make sure I hadn't missed anything.

Madison was one of the puzzle pieces in this case. Terry Cockrill, the victim in Dallas, was another, and then there was the amulet. All of these were connected, but they were disjointed, not fitting for some reason, and it was bugging me. One of them, at least, had a hand in setting it all in motion.

"I did find a few things about her grades and classes from college …. If you're interested, that is."

I leaned in, my eyes going to the two biggest windows on the screen.

"Damn," I whispered.

Zack nodded and made one of the windows bigger before scrolling down. "Those're just a few of her classes. She already had a whole bunch of AP courses in high school, even enrolled in summer classes to make sure she was able to have this many extra credits. Most of these don't even apply to what she was studying."

I felt inadequate. "That's insane. Did she double major?"

Zack moved the mouse and brought up another window. "Seems so. Took her a bit longer to do it though. Let's see … bachelor of science in nursing with a double major in psychology, then a master's in nursing. Now she's working on a doctorate in clinical psychology. This is impressive …."

No kidding. It also explained why she would have been at the Jefferson Institution. I shuddered and looked over the rest of her classes. The poor girl probably had no social life. Every single spot on her schedule was full of some class or activity, and I mean *every* space. It's a wonder how she managed to eat, much less sleep. I felt something in my chest twinge. I knew I was a workaholic and chose to have next to no life, but she might have been worse than me.

"All right, so we know she was a class A nerd," I said aloud, taking control of the mouse, "but where did she meet our victim?"

"Internship?" Zack suggested, shrugging his shoulders. "That's where I met most of the police force."

"That's one option."

We spent a little while longer flipping through Madison's college life before punching Meredith's name into the search engine. As her classes loaded, I moved around my office, stacking and putting away files, and contemplating a wide variety of things. Most of my thoughts were of lizards, exploding bodies, and the occasional thought that I was an idiot for taking these cases in the first place.

I sighed and carefully moved another stack of files. I would have ended up with it anyway. Why? Simple. No one else had enough—for lack of a better word—balls to tackle something like this. It didn't help that I'm overly curious and have a small problem with the word *no*.

"Um …" Zack flicked his eyes up to me. "I think I found something." He motioned to the screen and moved out of the way. It took my mind a few minutes to realize what I was looking at, my happy mood leaking away as a wave of cold crashed into me.

On the screen was a rather bleak-looking brick building enclosed by a high wrought iron fence. Brick columns on either side of the main gate reached toward the heavens like desperate, gnarled fingers. No pretty flowers or trees dotted the desolate yard. I didn't have to look closer to know that there were bars on the windows separating those inside from the rest of the world. Bars that kept my worst nightmare away from me.

Something touched my shoulder and I jumped, instinct taking over as my hand swung out in a blind backhand. I heard a startled yelp, followed by a muffled curse, before I realized I'd just hit Zack in the face again. He was still in the chair, bent at the waist, dripping blood onto the office carpet. I didn't care so much about the carpet; one more stain wasn't going to kill it. Zack, however, gave me an indignant glare and had a hand clamped over his nose.

"Oops …"

"Oops?!" Zack snapped, his voice muffled by his hand. "What was that for?"

I blinked and attempted to look innocent. "Um … reflex?"

I reached into one of the deep desk drawers and pulled out a handful of fast-food napkins. He said his thanks by jerking them out of my hand and placing half of them over his nose.

"That place," I said, hooking a thumb over my shoulder at the screen, "holds one of the worst people I know. I freaked out a little, maybe?"

Zack moved his hand away, taking the bloodstained paper with it, and scrunched up his nose, letting out a hissing sound.

"Anything broken?"

"No," Zack answered, inspecting his shirt for stains, "but you have one hell of a backhand."

"Though she be but little, she is fierce," I responded with a grin.

"Yeah, sure. I'll remember that next time you get queasy at a crime scene."

I grumbled, sliding my hands into the pockets of my jeans as I walked over to the board. I picked up a marker and started to write, adding what we had dug up so far on both girls to my growing list of information. A yawn forced its way out of my mouth. The adrenaline high I'd gotten earlier from meeting Mrs. Strong was wearing off. I needed a few hours of sleep or more coffee. I was leaning toward coffee and debating a fresh cup of mediocre station brew versus another Starbucks run when a paper ball hit the back of my head.

"What?" I whined, turning around to have another paper ball bounce off my forehead.

Zack was still sitting in my chair, a small arsenal of paper balls littering my desk. "I've been trying to get your attention for a few minutes now. Let's go."

"Where are we going?"

"Maggie's," he answered, getting to his feet and checking his nose one more time. "We need a better plan of attack, and I'll check on your leg while we're there."

I opened my mouth to protest and watched Zack disappear around the corner. And here I thought I was running this case.

We ended up taking my car and stopped by Sonic to get four Route 44 strawberry banana shakes. Were these for us? Oh no …. These were peace offerings to Maggie for the hang up earlier.

"We bring tribute," I called as we walked through the shop door.

The few customers turned to give us annoyed looks at being disturbed. My face broke into a grin as Maggie's head appeared from the stacks near the back of the store. Her hair was up in a half bun, pieces escaping to frame her face in an array of neon green and electric blue. She had forgone contacts for the day in favor of a pair of rectangular red plastic lenses, making her look more like a college student than a shop owner.

"Tribute?" she inquired, shelving a few books on her way to meet us. "Didn't know I was worthy of tribute."

I ducked my head when she stopped in front of me and held out the tray. "More of a 'please don't kill me, I'm sorry' type of thing."

"My, my," Maggie said, taking the tray from me, "if I had known chewing you out would get me shakes, I'd have done it more often."

Maggie put one shake on a small table near the counter before heading to the break room, her plaid miniskirt swishing back and forth as she left. She looked really good in that skirt ....

She came back out and handed a spoon to Zack and me. We waited until she had taken the first bite before digging in ourselves.

"So this nighttime adventure?" she asked as we paused with a heavy dose of brain freeze. "What's the equipment list?"

"Nothing big. Flashlights, glow sticks, and whatever else you want to bring. Just make sure it won't attract attention. I may be a detective, but I can still get into trouble for being places without permission."

"When has that ever stopped you?" Zack asked with a snort. "Why the glow sticks?"

"Less light I'm guessing," Maggie answered. "Flashlights are really bright and noticeable; glow sticks, not so much for things like this. That's why they're a favored light source at raves. Also, they're really easy to ditch when the police show up."

Zack raised an eyebrow. "You would know that *how* exactly?"

"One too many parties," I answered for her. "You didn't think she rode the good-girl train all the time, did you?" I asked, taking another spoonful of shake. "She rebelled quite a few times."

Maggie rolled her eyes and pointed her spoon at me. "And you didn't?"

I ignored her and turned to study the books that were stacked on the table nearby. Most of them were on varying types of witchcraft, herbal remedies for when modern medicine didn't quite work, and the uses and meanings of crystals. Her inventory reflected her interests. She was always reading something different or bizarre. As teenagers, she would call and wake me up in the middle of the night to rant and rave about some insane theory or what-if question that entered her head. Combine that with her punk-meets-goth style of dress, and you have Maggie in a nutshell.

My mother was less than thrilled the first time she saw Maggie's hair and clothes and the strange symbols on her jewelry. Mom was brought up in a strict Catholic environment where the mere thought of something other than Christianity got you stuffed in a room to pray and repent. I remember her telling me she was that way until she met my father. He'd gotten my mother to lighten up a bit and to see that "different" didn't mean eternal damnation.

My mom rarely spoke about my dad, and when she did, it left her sad. I was too little when he died to remember much about him. The one thing I faintly remembered was the smell of cigarette smoke and the sound of a guitar. That's probably why I took up smoking. The smell was a small comfort and reminder of him.

"Eh," Maggie said when she saw me checking out the books, "just a refresher course. Thought I might need it if we encounter anything else out of the ordinary."

"Refresher course?"

I moved my head enough to see Maggie swat Zack's hand away from the slowly melting shake.

"If I'm going to help you with creepy cases that involve exploding bodies, Godzuki, and who knows what else, I've got to brush up on my mojo!"

"Let's hope no more cases like this pop up," I said, getting up to stretch and walk around a little bit. They looked at me, then at each other. I felt like a kid again, sitting in the principal's office watching the adults talk. "What?"

"Well," Zack said carefully, "what if something like this does come up again? Not exploding bodies per se, but vampires or aliens? Someone will have to handle it. Why not you?"

I stared at him. "Are you saying that I should be some kind of paranormal sheriff? Have you seen the way I handle stress?"

Maggie's eyes widened in delight. "Oh, that could be so much fun. And it's not like you can't handle stress—you just prefer not to. You could be a mash-up of Buffy, Dylan Dog, and Constantine."

"So a private eye who slays vampires and exorcises demons on the side?"

"I like it," Zack said, chuckling. "Makes you sound like a badass."

He has a point, you know, my inner voice pointed out. *You already get bored so easily with your job. What's the worst that could happen if you decide to become a paranormal sheriff?*

Oh, so many things, I thought back. *But never being bored, never having to listen to Robins complain about me again, it would be worth it …. Wouldn't it?*

Ha, you're thinking about it, aren't you?

I rolled my eyes and looked at my watch. It was two thirty; if I went home now, I could get some sleep before our evening excursion.

"Okay," I said, rubbing my eyes, "bring what you want tonight but keep it light in case we have to make a run for it."

I pushed off the counter, heading to the door.

"Hey, where are you going?" Zack hollered.

"Home. I need sleep."

"Not before I check your leg—and you have to drop me back off at the station!"

***

I finally got to take a nap—this time without being attacked by anything scaly or faceless—and got to the cemetery a little bit before eight.

One of the oldest cemeteries in the city, Saint Catherine's spread over 160 acres. The winding trails that branched off the main road were too narrow for cars, forcing visitors to travel on foot through the grass and gravel-marked paths. The cemetery was open from early morning to sunset for those who wanted to visit their loved ones, one of the many reasons my mother chose this place. Trees dotted the landscape, silent sentries to those buried deep in the soil. Some were so old, their branches threatened to crack under the weight of age and the elements. I wouldn't be surprised if they turned out to be dryads or Ents—those mythical beings of Middle Earth—based on all I'd learned in the last few days. I was weirdly comforted, both body and soul, by their strange majesty.

My hand was going to my pocket for a smoke when the crunch of gravel announced an approaching vehicle. I turned, bringing a hand up to shield my eyes from the headlights, my other drifting to my gun, just in case.

"Allen!"

Zack and Maggie. I blew out a shaky breath and moved my hand away.

Maggie bounced over and threw her arms around me for a hug. She'd changed from her earlier outfit into a black tank top that advertised a local band called Clownfish, purple shorts that showed off a lot of leg, and knee-high boots that added three inches to her height and put my face right in the middle of her very nicely exposed cleavage. I don't think she thought of the extra height when she hugged me, or if she did, she didn't care. Not that I was complaining.

"How long have you been here?" Maggie asked as she continued to hug me.

Seeing as she hadn't moved, her shirt was still obscuring my vision, along with the wonderful things I'd been pressed against.

"Maybe give him some space," Zack said with a grin as my face flushed a wonderful shade of red.

Huffing, Maggie pulled away. "What'd I do?"

"You damn near smothered him," Zack pointed out, placing a black backpack on the ground near my car.

It was Maggie's turn to blush, and I snorted in amusement.

"I can't help it," Maggie muttered, smacking Zack lightly on the arm. "They're just kinda there."

Zack pretended to hold a microphone out to me. "So how did they feel?"

"Squishy," I finally said, going with the safe alternative.

Maggie's head came up, and the look she gave me was murderous. Zack, on the other hand, was laughing so hard I thought he'd have to change his pants. I gave Maggie my best smile as we walked to the entrance.

"Wow ...."

That was an understatement. A few feet into the gravestones facing the entrance was a ten-foot-tall stone angel, wings outstretched in greeting to all who entered. For some reason, the mere presence of that gatekeeper, its weathered gray surface reflecting the light of the moon, was oddly soothing. Rows of graves spread beyond the angel's stone pedestal. Some were moss-ridden and crumbling, names unreadable from years of exposure to the elements. Others were plaques of shining marble, sparkling with the skills of the masons who had crafted them. Where the angel was a soothing presence, the graves were spooky, sending a small chill through my bones.

"I don't know if I should say wow," Zack whispered beside me, "or make like Shaggy and haul butt out of here."

I had the same feeling. But if I was right, the tiny thing that had started all of this was hidden here among these stones. So I ignored the part of my brain that was yelling at me to run.

There weren't many clouds, and the moon was partially full, giving us a bit of light. Just to be on the safe side, I reached into the bag and drew out one of the glow sticks, cracking it a few times and bringing a soft yellow glow around my hand. Turning, I tossed the bag back to Zack and Maggie, waiting until I heard two more cracks behind me. Soon, a green and then a pink light appeared at my side.

"We stay together," I told them as we linked arms. "I don't want you guys getting lost in here."

"And if we do get separated?" Maggie asked as we slowly started forward.

"Find a place to hide and call me," I answered as we moved. "Unless it's a giant lizard, in which case, throw the glow stick away from you and hide until it goes away."

We slowly wound our way down the main trail to the left of the entrance. I knew the way by heart and probably could navigate my way in the dark. I'd come here many nights when I couldn't sleep.

"Where are we going anyway?" Zack asked in a whisper, his arm tightening around mine.

"My mother's grave," I answered in the same hushed tone and stopped walking when a weathered stone structure came into view. In the soft glow of our lights, my mother's mausoleum was a model of creepy. The stately stone was engraved with Latin phrases for blessings and protection. The structure was a standard size for a Roman emperor or a very large family, giving it a presence of importance and respect.

A hand slipped into mine, giving me a small squeeze. "Zack, this better not be you holding my hand," I warned, returning the squeeze, "or we'll need to have a talk."

All of us laughed as we filed one by one into my mother's tomb.

The inside was no less astonishing than the graveyard greeter. My mother had been very specific in her will about what she wanted, and like the devoted son I am, I fulfilled all of her requests. In each corner was a stone angel about five feet high, wings folded back at rest, holding a sword in one hand and an old-fashioned lantern in the other. The center of the floor was sunken, with steps leading down to a pedestal holding a salt-soaked stone sarcophagus covered in engravings. Iron straps held down the stone lid, a great deterrence for thieves and vandals of any kind. Inside the sarcophagus was a regular wooden coffin. Part of the floor around the pedestal was sunken even more to create a small moat, with a small amount of water constantly circulating.

"We can use the flashlights now," I said, moving away and searching for my penlight. "The windows are high enough that no one will see in."

"You aren't completely freaked out by this?" Zack asked as he and Maggie clicked on their flashlights. "We're in a cemetery, in the middle of the night, sneaking around like a group of grave robbers."

"Now that we're here, no," I answered. "Funny story: The owners of the cemetery were definitely a little freaked out when I handed them Mom's detailed instructions for her resting place."

Maggie was in macabre heaven. She flitted from one corner to the next in complete awe. She carefully descended the stairs to the pedestal that held my mother's sarcophagus and examined it in the pale glow of her light.

"Do you have any idea why your mom was so specific about all this?" she asked over her shoulder, then lightly traced a few of the etchings, her purple nails a stark contrast to the gray stone.

I shrugged, letting my light play over a few of the angels. "She never said …. But close to the end, she started getting odd: taught me a few blessings, made me start wearing a cross under my shirt, even taught me a few defensive tricks with everyday objects."

I wandered over to one of the angels, checking to see if the candle I'd placed in the lantern was still there. Thankfully, it was, so I pulled out my lighter and brought the candle to life. I did the same with the other three and made a mental note to bring more candles when I had a chance. Once I was done, I sat on the step above the moat to watch Maggie work. She had pulled a small notepad and pencil from the backpack and was making rubbings of the engravings, occasionally muttering under her breath.

"Do you want more light?" Zack asked, his head peering around the other side of the sarcophagus.

"That would be helpful," Maggie said, sitting back with a small creak from her boots. "What language is this anyway?"

I got up to retrieve more candles from their hiding spots as Zack cracked some more glow sticks. "Latin. She wrote them down ahead of time, so all I had to do was hand the packet of papers to the monument guy. I just assumed they were blessings and things like that."

"Can you read Latin?"

"I'm out of practice," I answered over my shoulder, "but I still know some."

Once the mausoleum was well lit, Zack and I joined Maggie at the center of the moat. The water looked like a unicorn had thrown up in it—pink, aqua, yellow, and green glow sticks illuminating it from within.

Maggie crouched down and pointed to an etching. "This one is different," she said, using her flashlight to show us a few lines of script. "I think it's German."

I crouched down and studied the words, letting the translation run through my mind before I said it aloud. Never had I been so grateful to my mother for teaching me how to read and write in her native language. And never had I felt so stupid for not remembering this phrase from my mother's instructions.

"Hier liegt ein Stein der Hölle. Tod für diefenigen, die ihn von diesem gesegneten Ort entfernen."

Tension crackled through the air as I read the lines aloud, and my friends shivered. I didn't blame them; the German language can sound harsh and aggressive. When I glanced down at my arms, the hair had started to stand. The power of the words spoken aloud was almost hypnotizing.

"What does it mean?" Maggie asked softly.

"Here lies a stone of hell. Death to those who remove it from this blessed place."

Chapter Twelve

The silence in the mausoleum was deafening; the only thing that broke it was the water moving around the little moat.

"You have got to be kidding me!" Zack exclaimed finally. "It's been here the entire time?"

I tried not to wince at his outburst. His words echoed off the walls, bouncing back at an almost painful volume. One thing to remember about places made of stone: They have great acoustics.

"Would you lower your voice?" Maggie hissed. "Have you forgotten we're in here without permission?"

"You want me to lower my voice?" Zack asked, his voice pitching an octave higher than normal. "Allen is being followed by a mob boss because O'Hare wants this thing so badly. I almost died—in an IHOP of all places—because some lizard freaks want it too!"

Tension was growing behind my right eye—from Zack yelling, yes, but also because he was right. All I had wanted to do was make sure the stone was safe …. But disturbing my mom's grave to get to it? Why did it have to be like this? The thought brought a bad taste to my mouth.

I mentioned before that I was raised in a Catholic environment, right? My mother made sure I went to church and knew the prayers, and I even had nuns as teachers for the first few years of my life. I was taught to respect the dead, that they were at peace. And now I was stuck between violating my mother's peace or someone else doing it. Sometimes I hated my job.

"Both of you shut up."

Two sets of eyes turned my way.

"We're not opening the casket," I informed them. "We'll find another way."

Maggie looked relieved; apparently, she wasn't keen on the idea of grave robbing either.

Zack, on the other hand, declared his displeasure with a growl and an attempt to shove me. I dodged his hands but slipped, my foot landing in the moat, my socks and shoe soaking up the flowing water. I'd managed to grab the side of the sarcophagus to keep my balance, but my arm collided painfully with the stone surface. I shook my head and rubbed my arm as I extracted myself from the water.

"Another way?" Zack yelled. "The solution's right in front of you!"

Zack's hands were curled into fists, one white-knuckled around the flash-light. I swallowed hard—at least he hadn't hit me with that.

"And what solution would that be?" I asked, surprised at my own calm as we looked at each other.

Zack swallowed, but to his credit he didn't back down. He'd been there when I'd attempted to beat the hell out of a few bullies in college for ganging up on an older gentleman— well, the end of the fight anyway—and had seen me cut up, bruised, and bloody but still standing. I could only imagine what he was thinking now.

"We get the stone out of the coffin and hand it over to O'Hare. Simple as that," he said, shifting on his feet. "Then we get back to our normal lives—"

"No."

"What did you say?"

"You heard me," I said, dusting my hands off and ignoring the dull throb in my arm. "I said no. One stone is safely interred with my mother. If a stone is being used in these killings, then it isn't this one. How many stones are actually in play? What would handing this stone over to O'Hare accomplish?

Will the killings stop, continue, or get worse? I'm not disturbing that coffin unless we have no other choice. Do you understand?"

Zack bristled. "I understand that we already have no other choices. We nearly got ripped apart by monsters!"

"Look," I said, my voice quiet and even, "I don't like this case any more than you do. It will probably require a ton of paperwork and get me killed in the lamest way. But I signed on to make a difference, to make sure that no other person goes through the abuse I did. I know this might not make any sense to you—I don't expect it to, and honestly right now I don't care. So either get fully on board or get off the fuckin' ship."

I turned away from him and went down to the casket where Maggie was still standing. I sighed, reaching past her to rest a hand on the lid. The coolness of the stone seeped into my hand, driving away the heat of the muggy night outside.

"We aren't opening it," I whispered again.

Maggie nodded but didn't say anything as I started out of the mausoleum. I needed time and space to think, but time was not on my side. I knew it, so did Maggie and Zack, which was probably why the poor guy had snapped.

I made it back to my car when my phone buzzed, startling me. I'd forgotten it was on vibrate. Thankfully, no one was around to see my bad Irish dance as I fumbled and tripped while fishing it from my pocket. I raised an eyebrow at the display screen before flipping it open and placing it against my ear.

"Miar."

"Mr. Miar, it's Corbin Matthews," a nervous voice said. "We met earlier today at Starbucks."

I slid into the driver's seat and cranked the engine, letting the air conditioner cool my face before I answered. "I remember. Thanks again for the coffee."

"Oh, no problem," Corbin said, his voice lightening up just a bit. Poor kid was still nervous talking to me. "I was wondering if I could speak with you again about the incident?"

I perked up a bit. "Sure. We didn't get a chance to finish our conversation, did we?"

"No, sir," Corbin answered. I could feel his tension over the phone. "But there's a small problem."

Of course there was. "Okay …."

"The elders," Corbin said softly, "they want to speak with you as well."

Well, that was a wrench. "Is there any way I could say no?"

There was an audible gulp at the other end. "Not if you want to hear the rest of the story."

Crap. I really, really didn't want to meet another group of lizards that wanted to kill me. But these guys had only tried once, then just destroyed part of my house after breaking into it.

"No one will hurt you," Corbin added quickly. "The elders won't allow it. There was even mention of reimbursing you somehow for the damages to your property. They just want to speak with the one who picked up the star."

Star? I sighed. "How about eight a.m. tomorrow?"

"Great," Corbin said, and I could picture him nodding like an enthusiastic waiter. "We'll send a car for you."

I chuckled despite myself. "See you then, kid."

As I put the phone away, a thought occurred to me: What does one wear to meet tribal elders? Fancy clothes? Casual? Business attire? Fancy seemed a bit over the top, and like I mentioned before, I didn't own a full suit. So that was out. Casual might send an "I don't care about this meeting" message. Definitely didn't want that kind of vibe coming off me when I meet these people. What I normally ended up wearing for work was the best of both worlds. It was also the only choice left. I would need to do laundry. I started laughing. The whole situation was so surreal. I was worried about doing laundry in order to meet lizard royalty. I could mark that off my bingo card now. Was this my life from now on? That thought was sobering.

***

The night was peaceful enough. No phone calls, no one blaring loud music— just blissful silence. Although for some reason, I was now aware of every little sound that occurred in my house. Needless to say, I spent the rest of my night in a state of insomnia.

I have often wondered how the great thinkers throughout time did their brainstorming. I pictured them around a table with friends, or people of the same mindset, tossing around ideas for the next great endeavor. They'd be eating cookies and sipping on tea, or booze—depending on the set of thinkers. Maybe they would go with a classic game of darts, laughing and making bets on the next horse race, or even playing cards. There I was, sitting, or rather lying, on the couch amid my destroyed living room, tossing a crocheted ball into the air and catching it as I pondered these things.

I honestly had no damn clue what I was doing or what needed to happen. Well, let me rephrase that: I knew what needed to happen. Making it happen was a different story, one that held lethal consequences at worst and sticky consequences at best. Was I stuck doing this for the rest of my life? Could I help people who weren't human? More importantly, could I live up to what my mother seemed to have left behind and not get killed?

No, a little voice said from the back of my mind, *not a chance.*

"No to what?" I asked aloud, my agitated voice ringing loudly in the room.

My inner voice was quiet for a moment, as if contemplating what kind of answer to give. *To everything*, it finally answered, and I swore I heard a bit of humor in its tone.

I growled and sat up, propping myself up on the useless back cushions to glare around the room, as if expecting the object of my frustration to appear at any moment; had no clue as to who that might be—the voice, the lizard-people, or O'Hare. Too many options to choose from.

Of course, the little voice was right. There wasn't a foolproof way to solve all of this without changing my life, no matter how much I wanted to. Change wasn't something I was happy with in the slightest, but wasn't this what I wanted to do? Help people in one way or another?

I ran my hands over my face and surveyed the trashed living room with disgust. The place was a mess, and I still needed to fix the door enough so that I didn't worry about burglars. After I moved downstairs, I managed to move a few of the heavier pieces of furniture in front of my almost absent door. It wasn't exactly secure, but it would work until I could get it fixed. Until then, I would use the back door.

I'd already showered and changed clothes, making sure to rewrap my leg even though I hadn't felt much from it yesterday or from the shower. That left me about an hour to finally clean up my living room before Corbin showed up.

Five big trash bags later, my living room looked almost habitable again. I still had to get rid of the couch carcass and take a vacuum to the floors, but other than that, we were good to go. I looked at my watch and decided to wait outside for my ride. I slid my coat on, not bothering to hide the gun I was wearing at my hip. Corbin hadn't said anything about not coming armed. I grabbed as many of the bags as I could and hauled them out to the dumpster before sitting on the porch to wait.

A black Lincoln Town Car came to a stop in front of my house. I shifted the gun as I got to my feet, relaxing only a tiny bit when I saw Corbin get out of the back seat. I didn't fully trust this kid, and I trusted his family even less. With O'Hare, the Komodos, and the mini Godzillas demanding I find and hand over the stone, my trust was running a little thin.

None of them had explained the reason the stone was so special or why they were desperate to get their hands on it. Corbin, on the other hand, told me the truth despite being scared. I liked people who told the truth, and he was the only reason I agreed to meet with his elders. Otherwise, I would have flat-out refused to let an unknown group of people coerce me into meeting them in an unfamiliar location.

Corbin waved as I walked down the path to the street. I returned the greeting with a grin. This kid seemed different from the other lizard-folk I'd met. More relaxed and, if possible, more human. Guess all the snappy animal instincts were of the older generation.

"I could have driven myself you know," I called when I got close enough.

Corbin shrugged, and I raised an eyebrow. Something was off. This wasn't the same nervous, tense guy I met at the coffee shop. He was calmer, more confident; definitely not the same kid.

"It's not a problem," he answered, opening the back door for me. "The elders didn't want you getting lost. They like punctual."

I nodded in agreement but made no move to get in the car. A little warning light was going off in the back of my head, and for once I was trying to listen.

"What changed?" I asked, making a show of leaning on the car, watching him closely. "You were so nervous last time we met."

The supposed Corbin gave a shrug, still holding the door. "Nerves. I mean anyone would be scared around DuCourt's son."

That's when I calmly moved my coat aside to show my mother's gun, the .38 Special from the trunk, and watched his eyes flit from my face to the weapon. His hands went slowly into the air.

"Now, let's try this again," I said, my voice full of fake cheer. "Where's Corbin?"

"I can explain," he said, his face going pale.

"I should hope so." My hand moved to rest on the butt of the gun. "I was hoping to talk to Corbin, not a poor excuse for a double."

Not-Corbin stared at me as the other passenger door opened to reveal another Corbin. What the hell was this? A clone army?

"I told you he would notice," second-Corbin said shakily.

Now that's Corbin, I thought. *Isn't it?* I looked between them and slowly took my hand from the gun. *What is going on here?*

"Guess the rumors are true," not-Corbin said, drawing my eyes back to him. "He can't be fooled."

"Being fooled and being played are two different things," I answered, moving back from the car to give myself room to run if I needed to. "So I'm not going anywhere until someone explains what is going on."

A look of fear passed over second-Corbin's face, and I focused on him. That was Corbin, scared out of his mind by little ol' me. The other one I wouldn't mind shooting.

"We're twins," Corbin said quickly, wincing at his brother's huff. "Please, Mr. Miar …."

I held up a hand and pinched the bridge of my nose as I felt a headache start to form.

"He doesn't look happy."

"Well, Mr. Miar was expecting me not you."

"Aw, I was just—"

"Enough," I said loudly, glaring at both of them. "Either shut up and get in the car so we can go talk to the old people, or I'm going back inside. How's that?"

Corbin perked up, nodded once, and came around to our side of the car. "Right, get in," he said, shoving his twin toward the open door. "We can't keep them waiting."

His twin smirked as he slid into the car, giving me a wink as he did. Oh boy. Thankfully, Corbin got in next, causing a protest from his brother when I slid in and shut the door behind me. The car began to move as soon as the door closed, the locks clicking into place. Good thing I didn't plan on escaping or anything.

I felt a wave of uneasiness spread through my gut when we pulled away from the curb. I took a deep breath. No sense in having a panic attack in the car, much less with people I didn't know. Deep breathing helped, and I focused on the scenery rolling by. Wait a second .... I knew this area. I sat up and twisted, as much as the seat belt would allow, to look behind us. We were only a few blocks from the neighborhood elementary school.

These aren't the ones who tried to kill you, the voice reasoned. *They wouldn't hurt the children.*

"Yeah, and if a frog had wings, it wouldn't bump its ass when it hops," I muttered, settling back in my seat, lapsing into thought.

A potential threat so close to a group that couldn't defend themselves was a big concern. I'd take a stroll later, get a grasp on the atmosphere, maybe chat up a few neighbors. Children are unwavering when it comes to telling who they can trust and who they shouldn't. I nodded, tapping a finger against my chin. The kids would tell me if anything weird was going on in the 'hood.

"Hey, Miar, do you mind?"

I blinked and noticed the car had stopped. Apparently, I'd not only missed the driver parking the car but also opening my door. Both Corbin and his twin were looking over the driver's shoulder at me, one rather amused and the other close to panicked.

"Yeah, yeah," I groused, climbing out of the car and straightening my jacket. I let my gaze drift to the house, and my mouth fell open. The word *house* wasn't even close. Two stories of off-white painted bricks had been constructed in a U shape, creating a courtyard within the three wings. A fountain sat in the center surrounded by flowers, blots of bright color against the blank background of the house. Manicured bushes squatted between the color blotches, breaking up the intense coloration. They even had some of those little spiral trees on either side of the door and spaced out along a smooth, paved path that led down to the sidewalk.

"Welcome to Casa Rodriguez."

Not-Corbin's arms were thrown dramatically wide, like someone who had just flung back the drapes with wild abandon. Corbin, on the other hand, looked like he desperately wanted to sink into the ground from embarrassment on his brother's behalf.

Well, that's interesting, I thought. *Didn't Corbin say his last name was Matthews?*

"Shall we?" his twin asked, not bothering to look back at us, before he hooked his arm around Corbin's neck and started walking. I caught the barest hint of a grin as he dragged his brother up the walk, leaving me to walk by myself.

When my feet started moving, a rather odd thought popped into my head that made me snicker: What do lizard-folk serve at official meetings? Jellied flies on toast with little pieces of fruit? Or would it be something a bit more exotic? Maybe deep-fried spiders on skewers? I grinned. I'd just have to wait and see.

Chapter Thirteen

The courtyard garden was more peaceful than I expected. The path broke into a square big enough for visiting guests to walk around the circular fountain without the fear of getting wet. The spiral trees I'd spied earlier stood on either side of the double wooden doors along with a few more plants that I couldn't identify; probably couldn't even say the names either. Getting closer, I wasn't at all surprised to see that the fountain was shaped like a lizard of some kind. It was posed on a few rocks, as if sunning itself, and looked scarily lifelike. I would have been completely convinced it was alive if water hadn't funneled from the lizard's mouth, cascading down the shiny brass rocks into a little pool at the bottom so that the process could start all over again.

"Is all of your garden art like that?" I asked, making my way over to the twins, who looked up from their conversation as I approached.

"No, but like many people we are proud of our culture," Corbin said softly, leading us into the entryway. "But we should hurry. They don't like to be kept waiting."

The inside of the house was bright and cool, thanks to the many ceiling fans and open windows. The house had a very strong Spanish feel to it. Instead of carpet or wood, they had stone tiles running throughout the entryway and, from what I could tell, throughout the entire first floor. A beautiful staircase curved down to meet us from the second floor, framing a set of impressive French doors that gave me a glimpse of the backyard. The stairs had been crafted out of a dark, almost black wood with a distinctive greenish sheen. Eggshell-colored walls coaxed the iridescent colors from the wood when the light hit the stairs at the right angle.

We turned right down a short hallway that held art probably more expensive than my house, and then stopped at the edge of a large open living room.

"Elders," Corbin said softly when we rounded the corner, "we have brought him."

Toward the end of the room, two sofas faced each other, allowing me a clear view of six older gentlemen. They rose to their feet, and one waved me in. Both twins nudged me forward, making me stumble a bit.

Soft murmurs and a few chuckles went around the half circle, and the one who had motioned me forward grinned at me. They were all Hispanic. Gray painted their beards of various lengths, and their attire ran from business suits to resort clothes. Good thing I went with work clothes ….

"It is an honor to meet you," the greeter said as the group began to sit down. "We have many things to discuss."

There was no chair for me to sit in. Rude—no, a power play. I could play that game. I settled myself on the ground, a vulnerable position in a room full of things that could kill me, but it also let them know that I didn't feel threatened. It was a bit awkward because of the shoulder holster, but I managed and smoothed out a few wrinkles on my jacket. The elders watched me with mixed emotions: Surprise was the most dominant, closely followed by amusement, then distaste. Apparently, they'd never seen someone sit on the floor before.

"I should say," I said, pretending not to notice the looks I was getting, "two of your people broke into my house and then proceeded to toss me around like a rag doll. What's up with that?"

I heard a squeak from behind me and assumed Corbin had a small heart attack at my lack of rules or protocol.

"We do apologize for that," the greeter said, his tone apologetic, as the others nodded in agreement. "I'm sure Corbin has told you about our proposal?"

"That you guys would pay for the damages?" I asked, my eyes not leaving the man's face. "Yeah, he told me. I do appreciate that, less of a strain on my bank account …. So let's talk about the stone."

Tension threaded through the room almost instantaneously. Subtle is not my middle name. Running on a few hours of sleep didn't help either.

"What do you want to know?" one of the men asked, his voice coming out in a deep rumble.

"I know that it's killing people," I said flatly. "And now that I know there's more than one, I'm more than a bit unsettled. Especially since it seems like you guys are inclined to sit back and let everyone die."

The man who had spoken was one of the suits on the couch to my right and had more strands of gray going through his beard than his hair. His eyes were already a lighter shade of brown, and he suddenly had a case of ants in the pants; guess it was the tail.

To some, my presence can feel probing. I notice things that other people don't, and when it suits me, I point them out, which makes people with something to hide very nervous, maybe even aggressive around me. Others perceive me as unpredictable, maybe a little unhinged, like a mad genius. I use it all to my advantage.

"Look," I said as a round of whispers went through the room, "all I want to do is catch the person who is responsible for dumping exploding bodies on my desk."

"What are you willing to do to make all of this stop?" another elder asked, his accent sweet enough to make any woman swoon. "We do not play by your rules, human. We live in a world that is vastly different from yours."

I felt the beginnings of worry ball in my stomach. "I want to bring these people in regardless of what else needs to be done. I took an oath to uphold the law, and I will do my job—with or without your help, got that?"

That got a laugh, and I glanced around at all of them. I took a chance and looked behind me to see if the twins were still there. They weren't, the cowards.

Although I had a feeling that Corbin had been the one to drag his twin away. With the way his brother acted, I wondered if I'd arrested him before.

"What's so funny?" I asked, as I shifted to a better sitting position in the event I needed to make a flying leap out of the nearest window, which would be a mite difficult considering the nearest window was close to where the men were sitting.

"You are nothing like the stories we've heard," one answered, drawing my attention to one of the couches. "They lack the detail and … uniqueness … you carry."

"Really? Most just come right out and say that I'm an ass."

A few men frowned, and I felt my stomach twist a bit. *Stay cool, Allen. Don't rock the boat.* I cleared my throat. "Sorry," I said, dropping my eyes a bit to look respectful, or what I hoped was respectful, but making sure that I could still see them. "I didn't mean to be sarcastic. I only have a small amount of time to spare; I'm a bit busy at the moment."

"We know."

I brought my head up at the statement, my eyes narrowing just a smidge. How the hell did they know? Had they been the ones in the SUV instead of O'Hare? My instinct of needing to run was starting to stir, and for once, I agreed. The only thing stopping me was the glaring fact that I would be torn to bits if I twitched the wrong way.

Why not just hear them out? They might have a few answers, the voice in my head advised. It had a point.

"You seem a bit surprised, Mr. Miar," a man to my left said, his voice sounding like truck hydraulics—loud, hissing, and annoying. "Is it so hard for that small human mind of yours to understand?"

He rose to his feet and sauntered over, his expensive shoes squeaking on the tile floor as he walked. He stopped in front of me, and I tried not to gag on the choking cloud of cologne that rolled off him. I wanted to tell him to move and go take a shower, just to get the guy out of my personal space. I didn't though. I sat there all nice and patient, biting my tongue against every comment that flooded my brain. See, I can exercise self-control.

"You mind backing up?" I said, working on not going into a coughing fit. "You're blocking my light."

The guy crouched down instead, invading more of my space, and leaned in until his face was inches from my own. His eyes were tinged with green, and when he smirked, I could see the beginnings of serrated teeth. Teeth that should never, ever be that close to anyone's face. My gag reflex tried to engage when he let out a short breath in my direction. The stench of rotten vegetation wafted out of his mouth.

"In your light, am I?" he asked, watching me with those beast-like eyes.

"Yep," I managed to answer, breathing through my mouth. "And now you're in my personal space. Think you could move back a couple of feet?"

He leaned in farther instead. The others must have sensed my discomfort because one of them got up to move their compatriot away from me. The guy shrugged his fellow lizard off and leaned in enough that I could see tiny reflections of myself in his eyes.

"I'm not taking orders from a hunter's brat," he growled, setting the hair on my arms on end, "especially one that was a vampire's whore."

My next action surprised us both. As if controlled by some other force, my head reared back and slammed into his, sending a flash of pain through both of our skulls. Good thing the human skull is one of the hardest bones to break; otherwise, my brain would have been all over the floor.

The guy in front of me reeled back, falling on his pompous backside, a startled look on his face that was quickly overtaken by another emotion I'd seen a lot recently—anger. I rolled backward, thankful I had decided to take those martial arts lessons after Ethan left, and got to my feet. I pressed my arm against the shoulder holster, making sure my gun remained with me, and sighed when I felt the hard metal press back. I didn't draw it; the last thing I needed was to give them another reason to kill me. Instead, I backed up a few steps, just in time to dodge a chair that came flying at me.

The rest of the men in the room were on their feet now, two working to restrain the guy I'd just hit, who was doing a good job resisting, while the others began to yell in Spanish. Well, most of them. One man hadn't moved from his spot and was watching the exchange as if it were a soccer match. Now, I didn't take Spanish and can barely understand it, much less speak it, but I can understand gestures and raised voices. Apparently, this wasn't part of the plan. My eyes darted around the room again, looking for an exit that didn't involve my turning my back on a room full of mini cow–sized iguanas. No such luck. The windows were farther away now. The only way I was going through them was if someone flung me, but I wasn't up for a trip to the hospital.

A loud bellow snapped my attention back to the group of men. The guy I'd headbutted broke free of the two holding him and was heading straight for me. He was already partially transformed. Most of his features were still human—face, arms, legs—but he'd had enough time to grow that whiplike tail. I hated that thing. Once he was close enough, I dropped my center of gravity, bending my knees so I wouldn't snap my own back in two. I snagged a handful of the front of his shirt and what remained of his pants, getting a startled grunt in return. Guess he wasn't expecting me to grab him. Using what momentum he'd given me, I lifted him off the ground, turned, and slammed him onto the floor. As the poor guy landed, his sound of surprise turned into a wheeze as air was forced from his lungs. He lay there blinking his big lizard-colored eyes up at me, momentarily immobile. Quickly, before he was able to move again, I put my foot firmly on his sternum and drew my gun.

"Now," I said, panting from the struggle and aiming my gun at his head, "you are going to be very calm, and you will get that way fairly quick, right?"

A growl started to bubble up, and that deadly tail scraped against the tile. I shifted my weight, putting more on the leg that was keeping my opponent down. He stopped growling, but his glare intensified.

"Or so help me," I said, pushing down for emphasis, "if you even so much as twitch and I don't like it, I'll shoot you."

"No, you won't," he croaked out. "You're an officer of the law."

I thumbed the safety off. "Not right now I'm not. I was invited here as me, a civilian, not an officer of the law. You were the genius who came at me. I'm merely defending myself."

He didn't answer, just glared at me. I kept him that way for a few beats until I was certain he wasn't going to try anything else before I eased the pressure on his chest. The room was now quiet. Everyone was watching me or, rather, the gun in my hand. Nothing had been severely damaged, except the chair behind me that was in tiny pieces on the floor.

"Here's what's going to happen," I said, my voice coming out firm and a little irritated. "You're going to tell me the rest of the story of the stones. Then I'm going to walk home and finish patching up my house. Any questions?"

No one answered, other than the harsh breathing of the guy under my foot. Slowly, I moved off my attacker and over to a section of the room where I could see everyone. I watched the guy get up, rubbing his chest where my foot had been, and make his way to one of the couches to sulk. Once he was sitting, I flipped the safety on and slid the gun back into its holster.

"Mr. Miar?"

I turned my head to see the man who had first greeted me a few steps away. I gave him a small smile, and the man seemed to ease a bit.

"Yes, sir?" I asked, not moving from my corner.

"I apologize for José. He's been a bit on edge."

I nodded. I could understand being on edge. I'd been that way ever since this case dropped into my lap.

"Still doesn't give him the excuse to insult my mother," I pointed out, watching José shift in his chair. "The last person who insulted someone I care about ended up with a broken nose and blood all over his nice jacket." I'd process the specific insult—vampire whore—later. My brain just couldn't deal with it in the moment.

He smiled wide at my words. "The federal agent who was on the front page with you a few months back? I remember."

I let out an irritated sigh at the compliment. Did everyone know about that?

"In my defense, he made a rather rude comment," I grumbled. "And not to be rude or anything, but what's your name?"

He stared at me for a moment, then started laughing. The sound was deep and rich, almost primal as it echoed off the walls around us. The others, though, didn't look entirely happy at his reaction; maybe I was supposed to have been eaten versus what happened so far.

"Names have power, Mr. Miar," he answered, once he paused for breath. "My true name is my secret, but you may call me Robert—if that suits you, that is."

I tried not to laugh at the sudden one-eighty the conversation had taken, as if I had stepped into a spy movie. It worked in a way, I guess—the fake names, being asked into an environment that they could control. I wondered if all the monsters used fake names.

"All right, Robert," I said slowly, "one question before anything else happens."

"Of course," Robert encouraged, his dark eyes watching me.

"Should I need to get ahold of you in the near future," I said, choosing my words carefully, "how do I get in touch with you? Assuming you still want anything to do with me after all of this."

Robert winced, almost imperceptibly. I'd put him on the spot, forcing him to give me his contact information or risk my never helping them again when it was needed. Fair decision in my book, but no one was asking me. Something told me that, for them, this wasn't so simple, and in a way, it made sense. Information of any kind, big or small, comes with a price. Even the simple task of getting a person's name has a price tag. Hence, Robert's predicament.

"If I do this," he said, "do you swear that you will never bring harm to this house?"

"And if I have no other choice?" I countered, dreading the answer.

Robert straightened, and the rest of the men behind him mimicked his posture, as if they could feel the shift of the conversation.

"If that is the case, you will tell us, and we will deal with it," Robert said firmly and held his hand out to me. "Agreed?"

I did a fast mental calculation of my options and quickly came to a conclusion: I didn't like it but, unfortunately, had no choice in the matter. This was a lead I had to follow, and it could solve both cases.

"Agreed," I finally said, shaking his hand.

When I took his hand, I swear I heard a soft pop. I looked around the room briefly, wondering where it could have come from. There weren't any speakers of any kind in the room, not even a TV. So what could have made that noise?

"Mr. Miar, while I am thrilled that you liked our agreement, could you let go of my hand?"

I released my grip and heard a few snickers that quickly died away as I looked in the group's direction.

"Sorry," I said, covering my slipup the best I could. "Thought I heard something."

Robert motioned for the rest of the men to leave the room. "Quite all right. This house is old and creaks in the wind, Mr. Miar. It was probably just her settling."

"Probably," I said absentmindedly, looking around the room again for an explanation as to what I'd heard.

When I turned back, the couches and love seat were clear of people, except for one. It was the man who'd sat out the kerfuffle with José. Now that I wasn't kneeling on the floor, I got my first good look at him. Aside from the suit, he had pulled his hair back into a low ponytail and was now reclining against one of the armrests.

"I thought we were going to talk alone?" I asked, following Robert over to the sitting area.

"Forgive me," the man rumbled as we approached, "I do not feel comfortable leaving my father alone with you after the threat you made to José."

Well, that was fair, not that I was going to hurt the old man. But sometimes kids feel the need to protect their parents. Kudos for him.

"If you stay, I need a name to call you," I said, perching myself on the edge of the couch opposite of him. "Unless you prefer to be called Hey You?"

"I am called Raymon."

"All right, Raymon," I said, waiting for Robert to settle on the love seat, "but in my defense, José earned that threat."

Raymon chuckled. "That he did, but forgive me for being overly cautious."

I shrugged, and Robert leaned forward, putting his elbows on his knees.

"How much do you know about the stones?" he asked, his tone serious.

I shifted to mirror Robert's position. With most of the lizard-people out of the room, my little-dog complex came down to a comfortable level, but out of caution or paranoia—maybe both—I remained on the edge of my seat.

"I know that your people received your stone from a stranger," I said, my voice professionally calm. "That's all Corbin managed to tell me before he had to go back to work."

Robert nodded. "A stranger did give our people the stone. It seemed harmless enough. Then one night, something entered our village, something so dark and so evil, Mr. Miar, that it defies words or description. Within the span of an hour, our town was in chaos. Children turned on their parents. Once-loving couples were at the point of killing each other. Race and origin suddenly became something important."

I raised a hand, prompting Robert to pause. "Sorry, but race and origin?"

Raymon chuckled, and Robert's voice took on a parental tone, gentle and patient, but not before I caught a glimpse of something else; pity maybe?

"We are not like you, Mr. Miar," he said as a small sigh escaped him. "You humans break everything down into categories: black and white, right and wrong, male and female. But none of that matters in the end; for in the end, we become food for the earth and, ultimately, for those still living. Before the stone, we lived in harmony with all creatures."

I stared at him for a moment. He had a point; humans did try to separate and box up people according to size, shape, religion, skin color, sex, and half a dozen others I couldn't think of at the moment. Hell, we had more and more people leaving our country for foreign soil because of politics. It never occurred to me that animals and other things wouldn't care about any of that. All they wanted was a peaceful place to live and to be left alone.

"The chaos," I asked, "it broke the town apart, didn't it?"

Robert nodded. "It not only broke us apart but also poisoned our way of thinking."

"How so?"

"We started thinking like humans."

Something close to pain went through my chest. These people were happy and then had it all ripped away. I knew what that was like. My mother was the most important person in my life, and then one day she was gone. I muttered something in German and ran a hand over my face. Rule number one of being a cop, never sympathize with a suspect. Should you do this, they will try their best to twist your sympathy to their advantage.

"What part did my mother have in all of this?" I asked, working to keep the raging smell of empathy away from the two in front of me.

"After many years of hardship … and … an incident, we came to her for help, much like we did with you," Robert said. "We begged her for help with the stone. She finally agreed and took the stone to what she called a safe place. We didn't see or hear anything from her again until we saw her obituary in the paper. Our condolences, Mr. Miar."

I nodded in thanks.

Robert leaned back, looking more worn and tired than he had mere moments ago.

Raymon spoke briefly to him in Spanish, and the old man got to his feet. "I'm just going to stretch my legs, so to say," he said before leaving the room.

I prayed the old guy didn't have a heart attack or something. Last thing I needed was to be blamed for that after threatening to kill someone. My attention went back to Raymon who was watching me with a frown. I crossed my arms over my chest, staring back at him. Our staring contest lasted for about five minutes when I finally snapped under his scrutiny.

"What?"

"You," Raymon said, unperturbed by my outburst.

I felt my shoulders tense. "What about me?"

"I've heard about you from the papers and in stories from people you've helped," he said, shrugging, still looking me over. "I expected you to be …"

"Suave," I supplied, "charismatic, mysterious, full of danger?"

"Taller."

I opened my mouth to make another remark and ended up staring at him, mouth hanging open. Raymon laughed, his deep voice like cannon fire. I'm not saying I jumped, because I didn't, not in the slightest.

"I do not mean to laugh," Raymon said as his laughter dissolved into chuckles, "but your reaction was most amusing."

Despite myself, I felt my own mouth turn up. "Sure, you insult my stature and then laugh at me?"

"Ah," Raymon said, shaking a finger at me, "at least I didn't try to eat you, hmm?"

"Unless you guys suddenly turned carnivore," I said, grinning at him, "I didn't think you ate flesh."

Raymon made a sound of disgust and waved his hand. "Our flesh eating is reserved for other animals, Mr. Miar, not humans, and we are the best example a human parent could want for eating vegetables and fruits."

"So all those times my mom forced me to eat veggies, I can blame you?"

"If you must."

The tension in the air dissipated with the laughter Raymon and I shared. There were still questions that needed answers, ones I'd been dying to know since this whole thing started. Raymon must have sensed that our conversation wasn't over as he settled back on the couch, one arm extended over the back.

"Something else bothering you, Mr. Miar?"

Slowly I nodded, mulling over the right words to use so that I didn't upset the man in front of me and turn into human confetti.

"Was there anyone who wanted the stone before you gave it to my mother?"

Raymon frowned a little as he thought. "There was an incident where knowledge of the stones was passed down, and some children thought the stone would make them stronger, but we took care of it."

"Children?"

"Children to us," Raymon clarified, "but to you, they would be adolescents, preteens."

Kids. They do a lot of stupid things out of anger, pride, depression, and a side of hormones.

"Can I ask how that was handled?"

Raymon sighed. "You must understand, Mr. Miar, that they were just kids."

"Kids throw tantrums," I answered, watching him. "Teens are hormonal, especially when it comes to proving their worth. If it turns out to be something small that led up to what's happening, and you didn't tell me, there won't be much that I can do to keep the press out of this place, much less the rest of the force."

I watched Raymon's mouth set into a firm line, and for a moment, I thought he'd clam up.

"They waited until most of the humans were gone from school and then went behind the gym. They thought it would be a safe place, out of sight. Both sets of children challenged the other—iguana against dragon. It would have been cowardly to refuse." He paused and ran a hand through his hair. "It turned out that a few humans were still left on campus, teachers I believe, and they went to break up the fight."

My stomach did a sick flop, and I dreaded what the next statement would be. Raymon sat back, taking a breath as if to compose himself.

"What happened?" I prompted, making my voice as gentle as I could.

"The stone caused the children to turn on the teachers in the frenzy. When they realized what they had done, the children ran," Raymon said softly. "There wasn't much left for the police to identify."

I was right. My stomach didn't like the idea. I felt the familiar stirrings and counted to ten. I didn't want to embarrass myself again today, especially not in front of someone I just met.

"Damn."

It was all I had. I hadn't expected something as simple as a middle-school brawl to turn into a bloodbath. I had met these things twice, and all I had was a scrape on my leg and a blown-up building. Goose bumps appeared along my arms at the thought of what could have happened if the IHOP incident had turned out differently. I'd be my own case file. "When you said dragons, you meant the Komodo dragons, right?"

"Of course," Raymon assured me with a nod. "They are the only ones in this town besides us."

I breathed a small sigh of relief at that. I doubted I would have been able to keep up with another group of reptiles at the moment. One thing at a time.

"Names?" I asked, pulling my notebook and pen from my pocket.

"Meredith Strong and Terry Cockrill …."

I nearly dropped the pen as my mind whirled. The first two victims—a dragon and an iguana. Could the case be that simple? A childhood rivalry that had been blown out of proportion? I rubbed my eyes and shook my head. I had a feeling the iguanas didn't know I was already investigating Terry's death. Otherwise, they would have led with that.

"Something wrong?"

"No," I lied, hoping my voice was believable enough. "Sorry, you were saying …."

Raymon frowned. "I was telling you where they had gone after the incident. You really should pay more attention, Mr. Miar."

"I blame it on lack of sleep due to a severe lack of door," I snarked back, "and I'm due for lunch and another dose of caffeine. So pardon me for having a space cadet issue."

Raymon held up his hands, a faint grin trying to come to his face. "Forgive me."

"It's fine," I answered, rubbing at my temples, trying to curb the oncoming headache. "Now, you were saying?"

"The girls were separated and sent to different schools to finish their primary education," Raymon said, letting out a huff of air as he stood to pace. "We had no idea where Meredith was placed, not that we particularly cared. Terry, though, was sent to Dallas."

I nodded and scribbled a few notes. I already knew the answer but asked anyway to see what else he might tell me. "Is there any way I could talk to Terry? To get her side of how things happened?"

"I'm afraid not," Raymon said. "She's dead."

Chapter Fourteen

I stared at the man in front of me, the answer hanging in the air between us like fog. "How do you know she's dead?" I asked, mentally kicking myself for how tactless the question sounded. "Not to sound disrespectful—"

"It is a valid question," Raymon said.

"What I meant to ask was, when did you find out she was dead?"

"Several days ago," Raymon answered. "She went to the hospital in Dallas for a medical emergency."

"Was the hospital able to provide her remains?"

The long pause was all I needed. With a small rather intensive word, I pulled out my phone and dialed the station.

"What are you doing?" Raymon asked, sounding panicked.

"My job," I responded as someone picked up at the other end of the line. "This is Miar, badge number thirteen. I need an address for a Madison Corvell. Also, pull any documents on an incident that involved the deaths of several teachers behind a gym at a local middle school."

I glanced back at Raymon to see him glaring. I put my hand over the mouthpiece. "Is there anything else you can think of regarding what happened?"

"No," Raymon said, shaking his head.

"Just those," I told the officer at the other end. "Yeah, just put them on my desk. I'll be there in a bit."

I disconnected and turned to leave, only to find a wall of flesh in my way. Craning my neck, I could see Raymon's face at the top. The expression he wore was something close to unhappy.

"Yes, Goliath, can I help you?"

He didn't answer, but the intense expression on his face didn't lessen either. *Oh, someone isn't pleased with you.*

My fingers twitched as I saw Raymon reach slowly into his jacket.

"Raymon," I said, my voice slow and careful as the faint sound of crinkling reached my ears, "I'm doing my job, remember? I'm trying to figure out what happened. If you kill me, I can't help you."

That made him pause, and I glanced quickly over my shoulder. After gauging the distance between me and freedom, I turned my gaze back to Raymon. Even though his eyes still held the heat of displeasure, he made no move to remove my head from my shoulders. Instead, he'd extended a business card in my direction, damn near touching my nose.

"I think we'd better say goodbye, Mr. Miar," Raymon said, his voice coming out as a sharp hiss. "I trust that you can find your way out?"

Mutely, I took the card and let my ecstatic feet carry me out the front door. I only looked back once my feet hit the curb, and I was surprised when I didn't see a horde of giant lizards gallivanting after me.

I started walking down the street in the direction of my house, whistling while I walked. The street was fairly busy, cars passing by every few minutes from the four-way stop a little way down the road. The lawns around me would put mine to shame, perfectly manicured and green even in the vicious summer. It looked like the cover of a *Better Homes* magazine. My own was green when it wanted, but the closer it got to summer or winter, it transformed into a small hay field with patches of ground that worked wonderfully well for mud puddles.

It didn't take me long to realize that I was being followed. When you're the only one walking, a blue Cadillac crawling along behind you is a bit noticeable.

When the car didn't speed up and go past me, I started to get an itch between my shoulders. Pushing the itchy feeling away, I calmly cut through a lawn and turned down an alley that ran between the backyards of the houses. I knew this one would take me right to my own backyard. I'd used it more than once in elementary school when I wanted to get home before my brothers. I should have been more on edge that a car was following me, but I had bigger things to mull over. O'Hare sending another goon to keep an eye on me was the least of my worries.

I put my feet on autopilot and started filing away information for later. The first thing I mentally grabbed hold of was the incident between Meredith and Terry. To me, it didn't make sense that Meredith would get into any kind of altercation with anyone. She was always so quiet in school and went out of her way to avoid any kind of confrontation. But if she had helped murder those teachers at her old school, maybe her mother had threatened her, or maybe she just wanted to finish school without anything else happening. I shook my head and frowned. Neither explanation felt compelling enough for an old tiger to change her stripes.

I paused for a moment and brought Terry forward. She was my first victim and apparently my missing link. But a link to whom? Madison? The iguana family?

I needed to get these cases closed and fast, which meant I needed to have a chat with O'Hare. I would rather close my hand in a car door, but disliking him didn't change the facts.

"Hold on," I said aloud, startling a few birds into flight with my sudden outburst, "one thing at a time. Focus on the important stuff first."

Isn't saving people important?

I growled and stalked farther into the alley. "Stupid voice, your timing sucks. Shut up."

Here's a fun question, it continued, pretending I hadn't spoken. *Why would an influential person continue to follow you? Especially when you threatened him …. Twice for that matter?*

"He needs me," I snapped, noticing the change in housing structures as I entered my neighborhood. "It's not like he could just go get the stone himself."

The little voice was quiet, and I stopped walking, a tremor of recognition going through me.

Ooh, someone is getting a tingling feeling.

"He could have gotten the stone himself anytime he wanted. Why didn't he?"

Good question. Here's a better one, the voice mused, and I felt its smile rub against my skull. *What creatures can't go into graveyards?*

"Wait a sec …. If he were a vampire, he wouldn't be able to get to the tomb, much less into it. But he could send some other type of supernatural goon after it."

Unless?

"Unless my mother really was a hunter and covered her tomb with every ward known to hunter-kind. So maybe he already has one of the stones and needs me to get another. Maggie did say that there were multiple stones and that the stone itself could change to fit the wearer. That's why they're so hard to find. Son of a—"

There goes the light bulb.

I didn't bother to answer; smug inner me didn't need the ego boost. If there was a chance we were dealing with more than one stone, we were in trouble, serious trouble. We still had no idea how to stop anyone from using the stone aside from getting the stone away from them; even that was risky.

My legs stretched as I took off at a dead sprint for my house. I ducked into a different alley and kept running, vaulting, and dodging various pieces of debris that had escaped my neighbors' trash cans. My lungs were burning by the time I saw the familiar rooftop ahead, my pace slowing despite the urgency in my head to get to the house.

I had slowed to a jog when a bone-rattling roar sounded behind me. Ignoring all of the instincts that were screaming at me to run, I came to a stop as another of those roars split the air. Behind me, about forty feet away, were two barely recognizable creatures. Their skin was blistered black, with cracks in their charred flesh producing a clear stringy liquid, almost like mucus, that hung in thick strips off their bodies. One's face looked like it had been boiled half away. Strips of the mucus-like liquid hung off its skull, like something from a nightmare. In the afternoon sun, I could see the layers of skin, tissue, and bone as one swung its head, sending a spray of the liquid onto the cans and fences nearby. Tiny wisps of smoke drifted into the air from where the goo landed and left the smell of sun-kissed fish in the air. Not a few-hours-old smell either, more of a month-in-the-sun type of smell—one that would make your stomach turn, and I was grateful for once that I hadn't had breakfast.

I gagged anyway though and felt the bile tickle the back of my throat, causing my face to scrunch up in distaste. That's when I noticed they were heading straight for me. My brain was babbling hysterically at me to run, dance, something, to get me out of harm's way. But some part of me was fascinated by those creatures, a part that wanted to reach out and touch that slime-like substance. It wanted to know if it was thick and sticky like corn syrup or if it was a liquid coat of armor.

Another one of those roars broke my trancelike state, barely giving me enough time to throw myself to the side as a paw the size of a baseball glove whizzed through the air. Claws the size of paring knives cut into one of the big metal dumpsters, catching a few plastic bags with enough force to fling pieces of their contents in my direction.

"Give it to us!" they hissed as they swept their heads back and forth. "Give it to us!"

A yellow tongue flickered between cracked, slime-coated lips and curled to touch the inside of its nose.

Hold on, yellow tongue?

"That's impossible," I stammered, getting to my feet as the things turned in my direction, giving me a glimpse of clouded gray eyes. "You should be dead! Both of you."

It was the Komodo dragons Zack and I faced in IHOP before I sent all the pancakes up to heaven. Nothing should have been able to survive that blast. Zack and I had been lucky that the building's debris didn't land on us, even more so that we managed to escape the scene itself. Now that they were closer,

I saw the legs, sides, tail, everything that wasn't covered in blackened skin had a layer of gooey stuff, which in my opinion made them more dangerous than the first time I'd met them. The only thing tugging at the back of my mind was the number. I counted only two, not three—meaning the other was possibly very close by.

The dragons hadn't moved since I stopped talking, their heads weaving back and forth as if pulled by some master puppeteer. They couldn't see me, but they were listening. That's how they must have followed me into the alley, my footsteps ringing like church bells.

Very carefully, trying to make as little noise as possible, I leaned back to look behind the dumpster. It wasn't uncommon on my street for the garbage people not to put the dumpsters back against the fence like they should. That left a bit of a gap between the fence and the brown metal dumpster, a gap I bet I could fit through if push came to shove. I counted houses, grimacing a little when I realized that my house was farther away than I thought. If I managed to get to the other side of the dumpster and make a run for it, I'd only get a few minutes of a head start. I could run; I just didn't know how fast my pursuers would be in their zombielike state.

"Allen?"

The creatures swiveled their heads in the direction of Maggie's voice. Crap, crap, and double crap. I didn't have a choice now; I had to move. I scrambled behind the dumpster and out the other side at a decent run. Still winded from my sprint earlier, my pace was less than adequate for my current predicament. The zombie creature closest to the dumpster let out a bellowing hiss and slammed its head into the container with enough force to leave a large cranium-sized dent in the heavy steel.

"Allen? Hello? Where are you?"

Two houses away, getting chased by a zombie lizard, I mentally answered as sounds of a very large, lumbering mass behind me began to get louder. I moved my feet just a tiny bit quicker.

I almost let out a strained sound of relief when my yard came into view. What came out instead was something akin to the laugh of a madman. But hey, I don't think anyone would have blamed me in my current state. And for anyone that would? Well, shame on them.

"Hey, Maggie," I called, plowing past her to the small toolshed, "what's up?"

Maggie whirled around in order to keep me in sight, a look of confusion washing over her face. "Well, I was going to see if you needed any help cleaning the house, but ... what are you doing?"

I pulled an old sledgehammer out of the shed and hefted it. "Um, what if I told you that I was getting ready to bash a zombie's head in?"

Maggie stared at me, and I shrugged. Tell the girl you want to go to a graveyard in the middle of the night? She's all over it. But tell her you're about to kill a zombie? No, that can't happen. Must be a Tuesday. I didn't get a chance to explain as the zombie lizards rounded the corner, oozy stuff slinging in every direction.

"Holy Mary on a pogo stick," Maggie breathed as I stepped out in front of her. "What is that?"

"Zombie lizard," I answered, perching the business end of the sledgehammer on my shoulder for easy access, "or whatever you would call undead lizards."

Maggie jumped as the things roared and reared up on their back legs, swiping at the air in frustration as they tried to find our direction.

"All right!" I called with all the bravado I could summon. "Bring it on, you slime-sucking fiends. You wanna eat me? Come on!"

There was a pause, and I thought I'd won a battle I didn't have to fight. That thought evaporated when one of the creatures dropped down on all fours and charged me, its lumbering gait turning into a weight-swinging gallop. I gulped and could almost imagine Maggie's expression as I stepped forward to meet the oncoming beast.

Turning my body sideways, I slid into a batter's stance and made sure my feet were planted before I bent my knees. I swung the sledgehammer, connecting with the creature's jaw with a loud crack. The sudden impact was enough to make it stumble sideways, but it was still moving, and I wanted it not to be. I reversed my swing as the other one came up behind me. It missed entirely, and I did a bit of a dance to avoid teeth and deadly goo.

"Give it to us!" the dragon warbled as I untangled myself and got clear of them.

I snatched the steel lid off the trash can that I put recyclables in and held it in front of me as a makeshift shield. A few maniacal giggles escaped me when I realized how ridiculous I must look—less of the twenty-something years I was and more of the twelve-year-old nerd I looked like on most days. Put a metal pot on my head, and I was a knight. I would have, but my neighbors already thought I was a new level of weird; no reason to give them more things to talk about at the neighborhood watch meetings.

Of course, my inner kid didn't give a flying monkey's butt about what anyone thought about me. I was having fun. Screw them if they didn't have a sense of humor. One lizard reared up again while its companion stayed on all fours and forced me to divide my attention between keeping my head and my kneecaps. I didn't like where this plan was going. Then again, I didn't get a choice in the matter.

"Are you talking about the stone?" I asked, taking a gamble. "Is that what you want?"

The reaction was immediate. Both lizards let out bellows that I'm sure rattled the windows of my house. The one on all fours charged me, snapping a maw full of broken yellow teeth at me. I responded like any warrior would—I slammed the sledgehammer into its face with a yell of my own. It recoiled with a snarl, letting the other take its place in front of me.

I heard the distant sounds of rummaging in the shed and said a tiny prayer that it was distant enough that the lizards didn't hear it. But the zombie lizard now in front of me turned its head toward the shed, goopy strings falling onto my poor excuse for a lawn. I shoved my sledgehammer into its midsection, causing it to stumble and turn back to me. Then it decided to bring one of its goo-covered paw-like hands down on top of me and my shield with another roar.

I staggered under the sudden weight and grunted. My feet started to slip and give ground. Stubbornly, I pushed back, brandishing my sledgehammer like a dwarf would a battle-ax. My grunts turned into what I hoped sounded like a frightening battle cry just as a motor kicked to life. The noise startled my opponents enough that they turned their attention from me to the shed. With another motor rev and a cry of her own, Maggie came charging out of the shed, swinging the only chain saw I owned.

She looked a bit murdery, well more than a bit, due to the metal appendage she was waving around, her green-and-blue hair flying out behind her as she ran. Her face was contorted with anger, fear, and maybe a bit of excitement.

Maggie revved the motor, and I realized that she was running right at me. I dodged out of the way, and I swear strands of my hair fell to the ground as Maggie brought that deadly device just past my head. She swung the chain saw in a vicious arc and buried it in the lizard in front of me. I cringed as it let out a shriek of pain and fell back, the rivets in the blade cutting through what was left of its shoulder and biting into bone.

The other lizard let out a low hiss, baring its serrated teeth in a silent snarl. Before I could move, it reared up and lifted a clawed hand covered in goo, flinging that deadly stuff at Maggie's head. A glob landed on her shoulder, ripping a scream from her as it ate through the straps of her tank top and bra, which I knew I'd be replacing in the near future. The wound began to smoke as it reached her skin. She jerked away, her hands releasing the trigger of the saw, and barely missed the claws that came down not long after. The claws caught shirt instead of skin, ripping away a good chunk of cloth as she scrambled away. Being the chivalrous guy that I am, I set myself between the remaining lizard and her.

"Believe me now?" I asked, raising my shield as the lizard brought down another set of claws. I felt the lid buckle and swallowed a squeak as the claws punctured the steel. My arm erupted with pain as the claws found my arm this time, but I didn't let go. If I did, Maggie and I both would be sitting ducks.

Maggie didn't answer my question, and as much as I wanted to turn, I was a good friend and kept my eyes forward. The sound of tearing fabric a few minutes later made my face flush red, and I almost looked.

Don't you turn around, I told myself. *Good people don't ogle their best friend, who is a girl, when they have no shirt.*

The lizard that Maggie had hit with the chain saw was twitching and flailing in an attempt to dislodge the chain saw from its shoulder. It only succeeded in slinging goo and something dark, what I could only assume was blood, over the shield. The other one opened its mouth and began to lean down for a bite. I braced for it, except there was none.

I lowered my shield in time to see a stream of water dousing the creature's hide. The lizard was screaming and jerking, trying to get away from the offending liquid. Apparently, if you spray an acidic-goo zombie with water, it melts. Not an insta-melt type of situation, more of a hissing and boiling exothermic reaction that sloughs off skin and tissue, like the Nazis in *Raiders of the Lost Ark*. Where the water hit, both goo and flesh were blasted away, almost in slow motion, sending chunks of lizard—falling with plops—onto the mostly dirt backyard.

I peeked over my shoulder and nearly dropped my makeshift shield. Maggie was standing there in a pair of cutoff shorts, no shirt, and a lime-green bra. Her face creased with pain as she wielded the garden hose.

"Spit goo on me, will you?!" Maggie yelled, taking a few steps forward. "Huh? You ugly undead circus freak! Eat water, asshat!"

The lizard turned tail and ran back into the alley, bucking the entire time to get rid of the water. Once it had disappeared around the corner, Maggie turned the hose on the lizard she'd hit with the chain saw and gave it a face full of water. It emitted a squeal akin to nails on a chalkboard, swallowing more water each time it opened its mouth.

I moved back from the lizard and over to Maggie, trying not to admire how nice she looked without a shirt. She always looked good—don't get me wrong—but I tried not to notice. Back in high school, any time a guy got the courage to ask her out, all they got was a black eye for their troubles. Since I liked my face without bruises, I didn't say a word.

I tried to wrestle the hose away from Maggie, who gave me a withering look. I promptly let go and stepped away, sputtering for a moment as she gave me a face full of water. Then she proceeded to spray the remaining lizard in my yard with a vengeance.

"Get yeself gone, asshat," I growled, watching the chain saw fall free from the thing's shoulder. "And the next time I catch you in my house or in my yard, I'm going to make sure you don't get up ever again."

For once, something went right. The lizard turned away from the spray, more skin falling to the ground as it started toward the alley. It was wobbling pretty bad, almost falling at one point before straightening enough to hobble out of sight. As soon as the lizard was gone, I turned to check on Maggie.

"Mags!" I asked, watching her throw the hose aside. "You all right?"

Maggie sank to the ground, long legs pulled up against her chest, one hand hovering above her shoulder where the goo had scorched her. She seemed frozen for a moment before her other hand reached for the water hose again. She turned it on her injured shoulder with a hiss. Red blisters bubbled up on her skin as the water washed away the remaining acid, leaving the smell of burning meat lingering in the air.

Little whimpers came from her as she rocked back and forth, and I could see tiny rivers making their way down her cheeks.

Way to go, Miar, your best friend gets hurt saving your sorry butt. What if she can't use her arm again?

"Hey," I said softly, pushing the negative thoughts away, and crouched down in front of her, lightly resting my hands on her knees, the water soaking us both, "you want me to call Zack?"

Maggie just nodded.

I dug my cell phone out of my coat pocket, a bit surprised that it was still in one piece, and called Zack. It was a short conversation: "Maggie's hurt."

"I'll be there in five minutes."

I shook my head a little as I put the phone away. Poor guy was just as smitten with Maggie as the rest of us. He just didn't know how to come out and tell her. I directed my attention back to the lovely lady still sitting in the middle of my backyard, soaking wet. I turned off the water and took off my jacket to drape it as carefully as I could across her front.

Maggie flinched as the material rubbed against her wound, and my guilt grew.

"Sorry," I said quietly, taking up my spot in front of her again, "but we need to get you inside, all right? Don't need my neighbors thinking I'm a perv."

That got a small smile from her and a nod. "Can't have them calling the cops on you, can we?"

"They could," I said, resting my chin on her knees. "Wouldn't do them any good."

Maggie's smile grew despite the obvious discomfort she was in, one of her hands finding mine to hold. My thumb gently brushed the back of her hand for a minute before she let me help her up. We managed to get into the house without any trouble—aside from my wet shoes losing traction on the tile floor for a moment.

Zack came in just behind us, medical bag swinging.

"You all right?" he asked, rushing over to Maggie, immediately checking her vitals. "What happened?"

I took a step back to give him room to work, stepping briefly into my mother's room. I grabbed a shirt that would probably fit and several towels, then made my way back over to my friends. I perched on the arm of the dead couch and watched in silence as Zack inspected the burn. He comforted Maggie whenever she flinched or a small whimper escaped, and then used some sort of cream on it. I had to look away when he brought out the bandages and began wrapping her upper arm and shoulder. He continued to speak quietly to Maggie as he did. I couldn't make out the conversation, but I assumed he was giving instructions about the burn.

"Anyone want to explain what happened?" he said, his eyes resting on me.

Maggie had turned her back to me and was curled into the chair. She was either upset with me or scared; maybe it was both. I wouldn't blame her if it was.

"I was heading home from a meeting," I said finally when she didn't turn, "when I got ambushed in the alley by a pair of lizards."

"Lizards?"

"Zombie lizards to be more exact."

He stared at me, his eyes narrowing, and I watched his face pale.

"Are they the same ones that we ..."

"Blew up?" I supplied, nodding my head. "Probably."

A tiny part of me was glad he was so freaked out. Too bad he hadn't gotten the pleasure of meeting them with the new facelift.

"Those things," Maggie said, her voice barely audible as she turned around enough to see us, "they were the ones you blew up?"

"Technically speaking, yes," I ventured.

"Technically?"

Zack had crossed his arms over his chest in a way that screamed annoyed. I'd gotten Maggie's attention as well, so now they were both staring at me. Neither of them said it aloud—they didn't have to—I knew what they wanted. Same thing I did: answers.

"They were definitely of the undead variety," I said, sitting up a bit straighter. "The point is that they left, so they will be back at some point. Hopefully, not today. If they had stayed, Maggie and I would be dead."

Zack let out a hurt sound, and Maggie put a hand over her mouth.

"What are we going to do?" Maggie asked.

That was a loaded question, and one I had no idea how to answer. The cop part of me wanted to tell them to go home, that everything would be fine, that I'd put a bullet in the undead lizards' skulls. But the other part of me, the part that wanted to run and hide, wouldn't let me lie. My tongue felt stuck to the roof of my mouth, and I hated the thought of going up against those things again.

"Allen?"

"Hmm?" I said softly, my stomach twisting painfully at the matching looks of terror on their faces.

"What do we do?" Zack asked again, a bit slower this time.

Damn, they were asking me to fight these things. I'm not Superman, not in the slightest. I sighed and started walking to the dining room where I had placed the Dallas case file.

"Allen, what are you—"

"I'm doing what everyone is asking me to do," I called over my shoulder and tossed Maggie the shirt. "I'm going to stop the big bad monster."

Chapter Fifteen

Madison Corvell. Terry Cockrill. Meredith Strong. All three were a part of this, and somehow, I had to connect the dots before another person got hurt, or dead. I spread the pictures out on the table again, taking a closer look at them. Pictures and the coroner's report mentioning the bone fragments were the only evidence I had on Terry, and if I called her family to find out more about her, I'd stir up problems like I did earlier. Although, I could give the Dallas Police a ring and see what they had to say. That could be fun. But with my luck they'd try to claim credit for solving the case. I'm not one to share.

"Terry Cockrill was the first one to explode," I said softly as light footsteps came into the room, "then Meredith …."

"So?"

"So these two are the ones who started this whole thing."

Zack and Maggie blinked at me, and I quickly brought them up to speed, pausing every now and then when Maggie dug deeper for details. From the look on her face, she'd be holed up in her shop doing research for a while.

I didn't hold anything back this time. Well, almost … I omitted the part about my nightmare and seeing the faceless kids die around my bed. One less thing to freak them out at the moment. By the time I was done, Maggie's face was a bit green. Zack remained pale, but then again, he was always pale.

"Those two killed those teachers?" Zack asked. "Why?"

"For the same reason kids pick fights," I answered, looking back at the photos.

"Which is?"

I slid the pictures around, trying to find another clue. "Pride, bravado, showing how big your balls are to make other kids respect you. Shall I go on?"

"Speaking from experience?"

"A bit, but mostly from watching it happen to other people," I answered, looking up as a sharp tap vibrated the table.

Maggie's now-chipped, purple nails tapped the table's surface impatiently. "Kids fight because they want to, not just to show how tough they are."

I stared at her. "And how many girls did you get into fights with?"

Maggie wrinkled her nose and let out a playful huff. "That is a personal tally, thank you."

Zack watched the exchange with a snicker. "What did they do? Try to tell you the right way to dress or something?"

"It was a bit more than that," I answered, watching Zack cower a little under the glare that Maggie was aiming at him. "She refused to bow to social norms, so the 'popular girls' felt it necessary to explain how things were done. Maggie spent most of fifth period in the office."

Maggie turned those eyes on me, and I quickly put up my hands to ward her off.

"I never said that you started them," I said, smirking a little, "just that you finished them."

Zack gave me a thumbs-up, grinning like a madman. Well, that is, until Maggie kicked him under the table.

"I can see you," she growled, watching Zack rub his leg. "I'm not blind, you—"

"Maggie," I interrupted, "why did you really come over? Was it just to help me clean?"

Maggie leaned forward, her hands shaking a little, and she bit her lip for a moment before speaking. "I was coming to see if you had an idea for wrapping this up," she said uncertainly, glancing in the direction Zack had just gone. "You left the cemetery in such a hurry last night."

My eyes flicked over to Zack when he walked back in carrying three glasses. He was back to not looking at me after I'd spilled the details of the case; guess he was still upset about our disagreement.

"Yeah," I said slowly, reaching out to take a glass. "I didn't mean to lose my temper, but I'm not apologizing for what I said. I meant it. I'm not handing the stone to O'Hare, and we aren't disturbing my mother's grave."

"I know," Zack said softly, watching me. "I forget sometimes that you don't think like everyone else. And I'm sorry …."

I sniffed the glass's contents and sighed. Plain water. Why couldn't it be stronger? Because drinking on the job is bad, I reminded myself, taking a large swallow.

"Did you figure out something else?"

I peered over the rim at Zack. "Besides that I'm a jerk, and we're in over our heads? Not much."

Maggie snorted her agreement.

"We already knew you were a jerk, Allen," Zack said, "but that's not the point."

Ouch.

"You're right," I said, holding my hands up in surrender. "And I'm sorry about how I acted. But that doesn't change what I said about the case. You guys said you wanted to help—"

"With looking up leads and stitching you up," Zack interjected. "That part I'm good at."

It was my turn to frown. "If I had known that's all you wanted to do … I mean, all you had to do was say something."

Zack gave me a look of disbelief. "There's a reason I deal with the dead! Because I don't have to be involved in investigations!"

"You were the one who wanted to come with me!"

A loud bang made us both jump and look over at Maggie. She was sitting as straight as her arm would allow, her eyes bright with anger.

"Both of you sit down and shut up," she said, her voice calm.

We sat.

"Yes, Allen, you're a jerk. That's a given."

"Hey!"

She pointed a finger at me, and I fell silent. I couldn't fault her for telling the truth.

"But," Maggie said slowly, her eyes going between the two of us, "if you had told us everything up front, regardless of how dangerous it was—and don't try to feed me the whole 'ongoing investigation' line. If I had known from the start, I may not have been so quick to get involved! Or at least I would have let you know how involved I wanted to be. Okay, yeah, I admit that the first time all three of us met up to look through the books was fun ...."

She paused for a breath as I shifted in my seat. It was true. Telling them would have been the right thing to do—the faceless kid standing over Maggie, the nightmare I had, O'Hare having dealings with my mother, O'Hare tailing me, my visit to Casa Iguana, and the growing dread that the end of this case was going to be bloody. But I'd thought distancing them from all the details also distanced them from danger. Maybe I had been selfish. They were grown adults, not kids, and could decide for themselves if they wanted to take the risk. Was I holding on so tightly because they were all I had, no one else I could confide in? I had no intention of contacting any blood relatives, not even if hell froze over. I lived in a huge house all by myself and had more issues than a magazine rack.

"Hey, I told you things about the case that I shouldn't have," I muttered, the excuse sounding lame even to me.

"I'm not done," Maggie snapped. "Zack works with you, he gets to know everything when a case is going on. I don't. If you want us to help you, keeping us out of the loop isn't going to work. I know you aren't used to having a partner, but if you trust me enough to look up all your freaky theories and

Zack enough to go explode restaurants with, then I hate to break it to you: Congrats! You now have two crime-fighting partners!"

I managed to keep a straight face at her declaration. Zack, however, put a hand over his face in exasperation.

She didn't seem amused. "Plus, I knew something was bothering you when you asked me to research the balloon body theory. Researching things for your cases, at least this one, was weird and fun, but what's happening now is insane—and I've read some pretty out-there shit .... This is a whole new level of odd, and to be honest, it's a bit unnerving."

Try living with it, I thought ruefully.

"On the other hand," Maggie continued, attempting to fix her ponytail, "we did say that we would help you, and running out on you would be the biggest mistake ever. So I'm staying."

I grinned and felt a wave of relief roll through me.

Apparently, Zack still thought I was a few crayons short of a full box and would take a bit more convincing. "Maggie!" he exclaimed, pointing accusingly at me. "You almost had third-degree burns because those—"

"Zombie lizards."

"Those things," he said, raising his voice to cover my interruption, "attacked you because you decided to help him! You could have just run away."

Ouch. Thanks, Zack.

"Yes, I know," Maggie said quietly, settling back in the chair. "I'll put it this way: I'd rather help him in some way than find out he's dead from an explosion of blood and brain matter."

I flinched. I took a few more gulps of water, relishing the coolness on my dry mouth and throat. "I won't hold anything against you if you walk out of here right now, Zack. Neither of us will."

He grumbled something about us ending up in his freezer unit.

"Sooooo," I asked, "are you staying?"

"What do you think?"

"I was thinking, we need to figure out if anything in that steamer trunk will help us," I said, getting to my feet.

***

Maggie practically vibrated with excitement as she took the top tray to look through. "How did your mom get her hands on some of this stuff?" she asked, inspecting the throwing axe. "Some of these look like antiques—or they belong in a curio cabinet—trust me, I've seen quite a few to know."

I picked up the coat and draped it over the back of a dining room chair with a clunk. "I have no idea. I didn't get a look at her credit statements until after she passed. I know she got packages from Rome, but she was Catholic, so I thought she just wanted a few things blessed by the Vatican."

Silence fell as we continued sorting through the trunk. I carefully removed the rubber band that was wrapped around the tattered black journal. Opening the book earned me a crack from the aged, heat-damaged leather binding. There, on the first page, was my mother's neat handwriting and a bookmark made of faded blue construction paper with Number One Mom spelled out in crayon. I had made it for Mother's Day one year during elementary school. Blue was her favorite color. It even had those little gold stars stuck on it still. I grinned a bit at the memory.

I turned the book's pages carefully and was a bit surprised with what I found: information on every kind of monster you thought only existed in the movies—Bigfoot, werewolves, fairies, vampires—all of it written in Mom's neat scrawl in black ink. She even included details on how to catch and kill a few of them, along with weaknesses that she had discovered. Occasionally, notes in various colors were added to diagrams or maps of places around town where certain monsters were known to be seen. There were even pages devoted to theories on mysterious events that had happened or tips on how to use everyday objects for defense. Some of the pages weren't about mythical creatures at all but about not-so-ordinary humans—serial killers, sociopaths, homicidal maniacs.

I flipped a few more pages, pausing when I spied big block lettering: THE RULES. The page was only partly readable, the wording washed out or faded due to the time spent in the attic.

Oh, this looks promising.

Will you shut up? I answered, making a face.

So you weren't going to read what's on the page?

I didn't have an answer for that. The book, just flipping through it, held more questions about my mother than I wanted to admit. The main one being "Who was she?" Was she a person who went out and hunted monsters, or was she the person who made cookies and helped her kids with their homework? Everyone I had talked to so far mentioned her with awe and respect. I always wondered why everyone sang her praises to me—showing me all the good she did—while she was alive. Were they expecting me to continue it? I rubbed my temples as my head slowly started to throb.

"Hey."

I looked up and found both of my friends studying me with critical eyes, one probably wondering about my mental health and the other ... who knows.

"What?" I asked, my eyes darting between them. "What did I do?"

"You didn't do anything," Maggie said, watching me in amusement, "but you were standing there with this goofy look on your face. Then it looked like you had a headache."

I held up the bookmark by way of explanation and was rewarded with a chorus of "awws." I shoved the bookmark back in its home, muttering about sentimental value.

"I think it's cute," Maggie said. "What's the book though?"

"It's Mom's," I said, opening it up again to a random page, "and it's full of monsters."

Zack didn't look too thrilled at my declaration, but Maggie did. Then again, she was also the only girl I knew who had skipped class to see the carnival freak show when it came to town.

"What do you mean, 'full of monsters'?" Zack asked, moving closer to see the book. "Whoa ...."

"Yeah." Maggie came to look over my shoulder too. "It's a whoa-worthy thing, and I have no idea if we should use it or pack it safely away."

"Idiot," Maggie grumbled. "The book might have something we could use—like how to stop these lizards or info on the stones."

Right! I was supposed to be looking for a solution, wasn't I? This, children, is why you need to have a proper breakfast in the morning—that or coffee. Your brain must function at the proper speed, so your peers don't have to do the thinking for you. If they do, never agree to anything. Now, I don't eat breakfast due to the simple fact that I have the artful skill of burning water, but I do eat cereal, yogurt, fruit …. You know, things that don't involve a stove. I also pour caffeine down my throat like gasoline to keep me going. This small action keeps me from turning nasty at work and allows me to have productive conversations.

"Give me a break," I murmured. "I didn't get my daily dose of caffeine."

Maggie rolled her eyes. Zack reached for the book and began flipping through the pages.

"It looks like a more gruesome version of a Dungeons & Dragons monster manual, doesn't it?" I said. "But if you give me a few hours, I'm sure I can find something to help us …."

"Don't want to leave it alone, I take it?"

"More along the lines of I don't want it to disappear," I said, grimacing when Zack turned to a particularly gory picture.

"Wait a second," Zack said, pushing the book back to me, "if people wanted to make this book disappear, they would have already done it. I mean, it has been in your attic for some-odd years now. Why would they come after it now?"

Good question. Why hadn't they come after the amulet sooner? I mean, it's not like there weren't any opportunities. I worked crazy hours, and my brothers skipped out just after high school, so it had just been me for the longest time. Why now? And why not the book as well? Unless they didn't know my mom had created the book to help her with whatever she was doing.

I rubbed my face as my phone started buzzing. Nothing made sense anymore, and at that moment I needed something that made sense; solid, unmoving reason—not theories, not a string of what-ifs, but a fact that I could hold on to and have no doubt.

The phone continued its annoying buzz, and I felt my eye twitch. Sometimes I hated that glorified contraption. "Can someone grab that?" I muttered. "I'm trying to think."

I looked at the book as one would a snake. It couldn't bite me, couldn't give me a nasty version of herpes, or anything like that. But somewhere, some person or a creature might do just about anything to get their hands on it.

"It's the chief," Zack said.

Not what I wanted to hear. I snatched the phone out of Zack's offered hand with a muttered apology before holding it up to my ear. My greeting must have come out harsher than I thought because Newburn cleared his throat. I took a deep breath, counted to ten and tried again.

"Yes, sir, what can I do for you?"

"I need you to come in," Newburn said.

"I can't, sir. I'm in the middle of something at the m—"

"I know, I know, the Saint Mary's case," Newburn quietly interrupted, "but you still have to pick up the files you asked for and ..."

I blinked and moved the phone far enough away from my face to stare at it. The chief was being nice, not touchy-feely nice, because that would be a tiny bit awkward, but a shade of nice that looked good on him. I guess I shouldn't be surprised. "Normal" didn't mean anything anymore.

"... an incident at IHOP" Newburn was saying when I put the phone back to my ear. "We're stretched a bit thin, so I need you to come in and interview a witness; says she knows who caused the restaurant to burn down."

Technically, it had exploded.

"Did she get a good look at them?"

"Says she remembers everything," Newburn answered, and I listened to drawers sliding back and forth, "even what the person looked like ...."

My heart dropped somewhere around the vicinity of my knees. Double crap.

"Really?" I said, sounding as casual as I could.

"She said he looked like you."

I almost dropped the phone. I summoned up what I hoped was a believable laugh and tried not to make it sound too forced.

"Me? I love IHOP. Why would I blow up the only breakfast place that makes decent bacon?"

"So you weren't there at all?"

I forged straight ahead. "I was at the meat locker with Zack. We might have driven past, but we didn't stop. We went to Kim's instead."

Newburn was quiet for a beat, his harsh breathing in my ear. "You sayin' she's lying?"

I shook my head, realized he couldn't see it, and spoke into the phone. "Not at all. I'll talk to her, Chief. Just give me a minute to put on some pants, and I'll be on my way."

Newburn grunted an affirmative, and I hung up. I was going to hell in little pieces if my boss found out I'd just lied to him.

"Think you guys are good for a bit?" I asked. "I need to go downtown."

"To cover up the small adventure we had a few days ago?" Zack inquired, glancing over at me.

I grinned, downing the rest of my water. "More or less. I also have to pick up a bit of paperwork I had people pull this morning."

"More or less," Zack snorted.

I snatched my keys off the table when I passed through the kitchen, trusting Maggie to lock up if they left before I returned. Out of habit, I glanced around my backyard, half expecting to see more zombie lizards come out of nowhere. At this point, I would take seeing O'Hare and all his smugness over those things.

I unlocked my car door and was about to slide in when I spotted old Ms. Cambrey peering over the fence at me. She wasn't the nicest lady in the world and rode the gossip train every day. The entire neighborhood was her newsstand, and if she hadn't heard anything that day that suited her fancy, she'd make it up.

"Hey, Ms. Cambrey," I called with a wave.

Ms. Cambrey gave me a short nod and tried to look inconspicuous as she craned her neck for another look around the yard.

"I heard a cat," she said, her voice high and whiny. "You don't have a cat."

"It was a fairly big cat," I said, trying not to rub at my ears. "Think it was part bobcat or something."

I choked back a laugh as Ms. Cambrey gave me a disbelieving look, her eyes lighting up like a kid at Christmas. Oh, I couldn't wait to hear what she came up with this time.

"Really?"

"Yeah," I said, fighting to keep a straight face. "Might want to keep an eye on your trash cans. It could come back."

I climbed into the car on that note, cutting off any further remarks from my nosy neighbor. I watched her dart back inside; no doubt to call animal control to report a wild cat in the area, then call the first person on her gossip chain. By the end of the day, the story would be as inflated as a hot-air balloon.

I made it to the driveway before I started to giggle. Those poor, poor animal control guys would brown their pants if they knew what actually had been making the noise. I entertained myself with a few scenarios, and by the time the station was in view, I was laughing so hard my cheeks hurt.

Was I a horrible person? Maybe, but at least I didn't have to worry about Ms. Cambrey getting into my business for a while. She would be delightfully occupied for days, which in the long run, just might keep her safe.

**

I swiped my ID card to get in the back door and headed for one of the two sets of stairs in the building. The first set was at the front in the booking area and led down to the rooms we used for questioning. You could get there through the back, too, but it was easier to take suspects through the front. And occasionally there would be a show from the unfortunate souls who were a little too drunk in public areas. There were even holding cells for them to sober up in. We also had the occasional homeless person; most of them just got arrested to have a warm place to sleep for the night.

I used the stairs near the back door, which were preferred by most of the officers and staff. I slipped through the door to the second floor and leaned against the wall studying the rows of desks housed in the bullpen. Not many people were at their desks; they were probably out on patrol. Good, fewer people to hold me up with questions I didn't want to answer, like why I hadn't been in much the last few days.

No one noticed me walk into the room. They were all too busy looking at their computer screens or filling out paperwork to care. Careless, very careless, but I couldn't criticize them too much. I was the same way, even more so, when I was working on something. Work goes smoother and faster when you don't have distractions.

As the desks thinned, I saw a woman who must have been the witness sitting in one of the chairs outside my office door. She was wearing a modest shirt with dress pants, nothing too flashy. Considering most of the people who willingly showed up at the station were people with money or little old ladies, it was nice to see someone a bit more reserved sitting in that chair.

The thing that made me a tiny bit nervous was that I couldn't see her eyes. She was wearing a pair of shades that effectively hid them. Most people, trained killers, con artists, even politicians, could train their bodies to project the emotion they wanted for the situation they were in—or in some cases, show none at all—but they couldn't train their eyes. The eyes always give people away. Every single time. That's one reason I never wear shades when talking to people. I preferred the honesty of eye contact.

"Excuse me, Miss," I asked when I arrived at my door, "is there something I can help you with?"

The woman tilted her head up to look at me, and I felt a kind of unease skitter across my skin.

"Are you Allen Miar?" she asked, getting to her feet.

I nodded and pointed to the sign on my door. "That's what they call me."

She smiled, and it was unnerving—a cold, controlled, and slightly crazed look. I had seen that look before; very recently, in fact, on a certain nurse I was trying to find.

"What's the matter?" the woman asked, her lips pulling back to show slightly pointed teeth. "Don't like what you see?"

"If you're talking about those pearly whites," I said carefully, "the answer is no."

Her smile got wider, and I shuddered.

Don't let her see you panic, I told myself. I'd faced the head of the Komodo dragon clan and managed to survive.

I gave her a closed smile, one that I knew didn't reach my eyes. "Hello, Ms. Corvell."

Chapter Sixteen

Madison Corvell was standing right in front of me, in a police station of all places. Not that I was complaining. I actually preferred it when people brought themselves in. If she hadn't shown up soon, I would have ended up going back to the hospital. And that was if nothing in her file gave me a direction to go in. Yet here she was—surrounded by cops—and all just to talk to me.

"I thought you'd be taller."

Her words snapped me out of the daze I'd been in, and I gave her a confused look. "Excuse me?"

She gave me an amused look, raising an arm to show the height she'd expected. "Taller."

Can't yell, I reminded myself. She's a giant iguana who can eat you. I feigned boredom and leaned against the door. "What do you want, Ms. Corvell? I'm very busy."

"I believe you have been looking for me," she said, reaching up to move her shades just enough for me to catch a glimpse of reptilian eyes. "Isn't that right, Mr. Miar?"

I nodded my head slowly. "Lucky me, you came in all on your own. Less paperwork."

She chuckled. "Don't flatter yourself, Mr. Miar. You wouldn't have found me otherwise."

I watched her for a moment, gesturing to the set of stairs nearby. "Let's go downstairs. Less noise." Not to mention interrogation rooms where we could talk and not be disturbed.

"Of course."

I led her to the belly of the station. Most of the poor souls who got dragged downtown didn't get to see what was downstairs, technically the basement. They could be questioned up top, but a select few required a little extra security.

Being the gentleman that I am, I let Madison go down the rubber-edged tile stairs first, then took the lead once we reached the bottom. But I made sure to keep her in sight in case she felt the sudden need to eat me. The walk down the hall was short and quiet as we passed the evidence lockup and record storage.

I paused at interrogation room number four, turning the lights on and swinging the door open for her. "Make yourself comfortable. I'll be with you in just one second."

Madison sashayed into the room, and I shut the door behind her. Damn, that woman gave me the creeps. I debated hitting the button to activate the camera inside the room and decided against it. Our department had spent the extra money to have them installed after one woman declared she had been molested by the officer questioning her. Turned out the lady had been lying, but still. Personally, I liked the extra security. Not that I couldn't take care of myself, but it helped cut out the drama and bullshit that was thrown around on a regular basis. I got myself into enough trouble on my own—I didn't need help. But in the current situation, I had no clue what Madison was going to say, or do. If she decided to shed her human skin and everyone saw, I was going to have more paperwork and one hell of a debrief.

"All right, Ms. Corvell," I said, walking back into the room, "I understand you have information on an incident for us."

"Yes, I do," Madison said. "I know who exploded the restaurant a few days ago."

Well, she didn't waste any time getting to the point, that's for sure.

"Really?" I asked, settling into the chair across from her. "Any reason why you didn't come forward sooner?"

"I heard that a few of my family members had been a bit naughty and that you'd been asking questions about Meredith. I came to help."

Yeah, and I'm a purple octopus.

My eye twitched as I stared hard at the woman across from me. She was so cool and confident, too comfortable with her story, and way too cavalier.

"It doesn't bother you," I asked, leaning forward in my chair, "that I could have you arrested for not coming forward?"

Madison gave me that smile again, and I fought off a shiver as she delicately removed her shades, placing them on the table.

"Now, Mr. Miar, I don't think you'll do that," she said, delight dancing in her eyes. "After all, you don't want me telling your chief what you've been up to, do you?"

She had me there. No amount of pleading would get me out of the hot water or mounds of paperwork if the chief had proof I caused all that destruction. Plus, if I even tried to explain, they'd throw me in the nuthouse. With my luck, I'd end up being bunkmates with my brother. Hell no.

I angled my head to crack my neck, and her grin widened before her gaze went to the camera. "Turn that vile thing off."

I shook my head. "That stays on," I bluffed. "Call it insurance so you don't grow scales on me."

Madison's mouth turned down in a frown. "That's hardly fair, Mr. Miar."

"It's plenty fair. I got tossed around like a rag doll—in my own home, I might add—and had to subdue three others at the expense of a restaurant," I answered, crossing my arms. "So the camera stays on."

The sour look Madison gave me would have made a lemon proud, but she complied and relaxed back in her chair. "That doesn't matter. I could tear you apart in a matter of minutes."

"Actually," I said, taking a stab in the dark and bluffing some more, "I think it does. I had the privilege of a nice little chat with your cousins. They let me in on a little secret. You see, apparently you aren't supposed to break this whole charade of being human. You do, and normal people get involved—people like me—and they don't want that .... Am I wrong?"

The muscles in Madison's face were getting a workout. She walked in with the confidence and swagger of a big fish, with the intention of blackmailing me to get her way. But even the cleverest plan can unravel. History proved that ten times over.

"No" came the stiff reply. "You aren't wrong."

It was almost creepy the way her emotions disappeared underneath a calm mask. I pretended to inspect my cuticles, not reacting, just waiting for her to continue.

Madison sighed. "You should know that I wasn't the only one who liked to kill things .... Meredith killed too."

Well, that was unexpected. I held up a hand to stop her. "Don't start in the middle. Start at the beginning."

Madison gave me that sharklike smile again. "Oh, Mr. Miar, that is the beginning."

"All right," I said with a shrug, "you and Meredith enjoyed killing things. Guess that's that then."

I got to my feet and turned toward the door, ignoring the startled look that briefly crossed Madison's face when she realized I was leaving.

"What do you mean?" Madison called, her voice ringing through the room, a tinge of panic coating her words. "What do you mean, 'that's that'?"

I paused, my hand on the door, and glanced back at her. She seemed rattled. She'd wanted to be in control, but I didn't fit into her little plan. I was supposed to be scared, desperate. Yeah, not exactly my style. I don't get scared that often anymore; I'd had my share of terror earlier in life. Startled, yes. Cautious, yes. But down-to-my-bones terror? Not anymore. I know what's a real threat and what isn't.

"You just confessed that you like to kill people," I pointed out. "And here I thought you were smarter than the average bear."

Madison's eyes flashed with anger. "And you assume this is all you need to convict me? What kind of officer are you?"

"A detective," I said, pointing to the reflective lens in the corner of the room, "the kind who gets the job done. You said it all on camera, Ms. Corvell. Plus, what we've already found in your background jumps you to the top of the list of suspects."

I grinned as Madison sat there, fuming at her predicament. She didn't like her options, and I couldn't blame her. When a suspect sits down in that chair, their whole life gets put under a microscope, rifled through for even the slightest bit of evidence. And if we find something, the only thing that will save them is a really good lawyer.

Madison could let me help, if she would stop trying to power play me, or she could continue and I could risk her blabbing to the whole station that I was a potential nutcase.

The thought of concrete walls, bars, and faded orange jumpsuits must have coaxed her to see reason, or at least some form of it. She crossed her arms with a huff. "Fine."

I feigned surprise. "Ma'am?"

"I said fine," Madison snapped, her voice coming out in a hiss. "I'll play nice."

"I'll listen to what you have to say," I said, sitting back down. "If it's something I can use, then we'll talk. However, you will drop the blackmail angle. I don't like being threatened."

All I got in response was a short nod, which was good enough for me.

"This is what I already know," I said, getting comfortable. "You met Meredith in college in Louisiana. You got pretty close, and maybe one night you ladies found out you have something in common—that you're both pony-sized lizards with a knack for causing harm to others. Am I missing anything so far?"

Madison didn't answer, her gaze firmly set on the table.

"You two got to be really close, best friends if I had to guess," I pressed. "But soon talking about your hunts wasn't enough. So the two of you went out, found some poor schmuck, and turned him into meat paste—"

"No."

"—all to satisfy some sick urge."

"That's not what happened!"

Madison Corvell, who had been so calm and composed, was now slowly coming undone. Her entire body was tense, as if she wanted desperately to lash out and rip my face off. Only a thin thread of self-control was keeping her from going full beast and turning me into sliced cheese.

"Then how did it happen?" I asked, my voice calm and level. "Tell me, and I'll see what I can do to protect you."

Madison went still, her shoulders sagging, although her knuckles were white from clutching the arms of her chair. I shuddered as I wondered what those hands could do if they found my neck. I didn't want to find out, that's for sure.

"It's true," Madison said in a voice so soft I almost missed it. "Meredith and I did meet in college. We had a few classes together."

"How did the killings get brought up?" I asked, not taking my eyes off her. "I'm assuming there wasn't a class for that subject."

Madison's tongue flicked out before she answered. "No, actually it came up through a group project we did for psychology."

"Did she bring it up first or did you?"

"She did. Well, it came up as a topic when we were discussing the project, and it just blossomed from there." She crossed her legs. "It was the start of a beautiful friendship."

"You mean partnership?" I corrected.

Madison laughed, the sound bouncing off the walls and grating against my eardrums. It would have been a sweet sound if it hadn't been overrun with malice.

"Mr. Miar," she chided, "we were merely friends. And even if we were more … that's not for you to know."

My face burned in embarrassment. I deserved that one. Not saying that I was wrong in asking it, just that my delivery could have been better. Thankfully, I was saved by the bell—my phone. I was careful not to answer it too quickly. Just for show, I opened the device slowly, holding up a finger for Madison to give me a moment.

A smooth, lilting voice purred in my ear. "Mr. Miar …."

"What the hell?" O'Hare had the worst timing.

I got to my feet so fast that a sharp pain came to life in the general area of my knee as it connected with the underside of the table.

O'Hare's voice curled around my eardrum. "Now, now, calm down. After all, you need those knees."

My eyes went to the hidden recorder. It wasn't on, so how in the hell can he see me? How does he even know we're down here? I pressed my hand against the mouthpiece and excused myself from the room.

"All right," I growled, leaning my back against the door, "what do you want?"

"I just wanted to see how you were do—"

"Oh no," I interrupted, my voice coming out with more bite than I intended, "you invited yourself into my house and threatened me; you tried to bribe me into working for you; you send your goons to follow me everywhere. This is getting a little old, O'Hare."

O'Hare huffed. "*My* goons?" he asked, his voice curious.

"No, the other guy who has a fleet of black cars at his disposal," I growled. "Of course, you."

"I assure you, Mr. Miar," O'Hare said, his words frosty, "that if my people were following you, you would never know."

Hmm, maybe that was true, but I wasn't going to tell him that. That would be like giving a mouse a cookie. You just don't do things like that.

"Right," I said, my eyes drifting up and down the hall. "And I suppose the next thing you're gonna tell me is that you had nothing to do with the deaths I'm investigating?"

There was a pause, and after a few beats, I thought O'Hare had hung up. When he spoke again, his voice held the faintest trace of unease.

"What do you mean?"

"Meredith Strong, Terry Cockrill, Dr. Wright," I said, listing them off, "all exploded in one grisly way or another. And right now, I have another suspect that could end up the same way. I was finally getting some answers, but then someone had to call in the middle of my interrogation."

"Mr. Miar, I didn't know—"

I couldn't hear the rest of O'Hare's statement because that's when the screaming started. Long, high, agonizing screams. I ended the call as my brain tried to rationalize the noise; tried to convince me that it was one of the drunks upstairs in the holding cells. I mean, that could have been possible if not for a few feet of concrete, rebar, and cheap ceiling tile between me and the floor above. Even if I could hear them yelling, it wouldn't be that clear, that sharp.

I moved stiffly away from the door and didn't turn around to look until I was on the other side of the hall. Only then did I turn to look at the door between me and Madison Corvell.

The human brain is a fascinating piece of work. It's the most complex organ in the human body, controlling billions of nerve cells in a precise network of communication highways that control everything we see, hear, feel, smell, taste, think, and do, including our automatic functions like breathing and how we respond to fear. But just so we're clear, fear reactions are different for everyone. Our nervous systems decide whether we fight, flee, freeze, or fawn in response to fear. Normally, I was all fight; I would run to that door, yank it open, and run in to save the person inside without ever thinking about it. But with everything I had seen in the past few days, there was no way I wanted to open that door. I froze.

She needs help, I told myself as another muffled scream came from behind the door. After a few moments of internal debate, I crossed the hall and pushed the door open. Madison's name was on my lips, ready to call out to her. Instead, I snapped my mouth shut and counted to ten to calm my startled heart.

Madison had fallen to the ground in what seemed like some kind of seizure. As much as I wanted to believe that, in the back of my mind, I knew it was something else. I pushed the table and chairs out of the way before kneeling beside her.

"Madison," I said, trying to find a pulse in her jerking limbs, "can you hear me?"

She responded with another scream and a flailing limb that hit me with enough force to knock me on my keister. I watched with a mixture of fascination and horror as Madison's body twisted and contorted. Then it looked like an invisible rope hoisted her up and left her there, her back bent so much that she was almost folded in half. Her arms were scrambling on either side of her, trying to find something, anything to hold on to to keep herself from folding. Her shirt had ridden up, and I saw the skin along her belly stretched tight enough to see quivering muscle underneath, along with something else. It was about two inches long, dark, and making its way leisurely in between muscle layers and skin.

"Madison." I tried again when there was a pause in her screaming. "Madison!"

An incredibly soft whimper trickled from Madison's mouth, and her eyes turned toward me.

"Help … me."

Something in my chest twisted. No matter what she'd done, no one deserved this kind of pain, and I don't think she had a clue what she'd walked into. Monster or not, she was still human. Kinda.

"I will," I said, taking one of her hands away from its frantic search, "but you have to help me too."

There was a cracking sound as Madison folded a few more inches. The hand I was holding clamped down on mine, the grip getting dangerously close to breaking my hand.

"Hurts," Madison whimpered.

No kidding?

"I know it hurts," I said softly, shoving the queasy part of me to the back of my head, "and I'll try to make it stop, but you have to tell me who has the other stones. How many are there?"

Madison's eyes were glazed over from the pain, her breath coming out in pants. I was surprised she was able to breathe at all with the way she was contorted.

"They do," she grunted as her insides squirmed against her skin. "Won't stop … have them all."

"Who are 'they'?" I demanded. "Give me a name!"

She opened her mouth, but I never got my answer. Instead, her midsection burst apart, showering me and the entire room with a fine spray of blood and mulched stomach muscle and innards. It wasn't like Maggie had described when all of this started. Not like a human balloon that someone had popped with a needle or the sharp corner of a table. The pop that caused her to explode came from inside her, and that's what really rattled me.

After a few tries, I managed to get my feet under me, one hand bracing against the wall as I shuffled to the door. When I reached the door, I fumbled clumsily with the handle until I noticed something was dangling from my other hand. Bile rose in my throat when I realized that it was an arm, a feminine arm, its hand still firmly gripping mine.

A sound I wasn't expecting came out of my mouth, one that could only be compared to a very young girl in hysterics. Give me a break—I was covered in blood and who knows what else. Between Madison's screams and my own, a good crowd of dispatchers and officers had gathered by the time I stumbled into the hallway. Judging by the gasps and curses, I knew I must look like hell. I felt like it too.

Someone yelled for an EMT as they maneuvered me a little way down the hall. To be truthful, I zoned out once I was away from the scene. What I've learned through experience is that when faced with intense trauma, my brain will do a reboot of sorts, like when your computer freezes and you're forced to restart it. During this reboot, I can still hear everything, see people moving, all of it—it's just fuzzy, fogged over if you will. And when I go back later to remember, I have to match figures with voices. I end up with insomnia for a few days while I connect the dots. Coffee helps. Lots and lots of coffee.

I remember someone making me sit down in a chair, telling me to breathe, and putting a trash can between my feet. I was dimly aware of Zack checking my vitals and shining his cursed penlight into my eyes. By the time I came out of the fog, the crime scene had been secured, there wasn't an arm hanging off of me, I had a huge headache, and someone was attempting to ask me questions.

"What part of 'he's in shock' did you not understand?"

Zack, good ol' Zack.

"He was with the victim when the incident occurred. I'd like to know why."

Robins. Damn it. Of all the people who could have questioned me, why did it have to be him?

I rested my head against the wall behind me. "Can you keep it down? The drunks are trying to sleep, and I have a headache."

To their credit, they did quiet down, but that didn't stop the bickering. Zack wanted Robins to wait until I was fully recovered. Robins wasn't having it. He claimed that if I was well enough to be a smart-mouth, then I could answer his questions. Man, this guy was a pain in my ass.

"Hey," I grumbled slowly, opening an eye to look around, "you guys are still loud."

"Mr. Medical Examiner here," Robins said, jabbing an accusing finger at Zack, "seems to have forgotten protocol."

"I didn't forget, Detective," Zack answered with just a little bit of venom. "I may work with the dead, but I'm still a doctor! At least let me finish examining him before you get him riled up again."

"You don't—"

"Oi! McCoy, Spock," I interrupted, "shut up!"

The entire hallway quieted rather quickly. Zack's mouth twitched. Robins, however, looked like he'd just swallowed a lemon.

"I can answer your stupid questions," I said, pointing at Robins, "while the good doctor makes sure I'm fit to leave."

Robins's triumphant mood deflated just a tad, and I didn't miss the smug smirk that flickered over Zack's face as he moved closer to do his doctor thing. Hey, if it meant I could get out of the basement and back out looking for whoever did this, I'd be a happy camper. I was getting rather irked that my promising leads kept exploding.

"What were you two talking about?" Robins asked. "And why did you talk down here instead of in your office?"

"Lollipops and candy canes," I answered, my eyes following Zack's finger, "and I'd rather not show a lady the mess in my office."

"She wasn't even a suspect—"

"No, but she was a witness," I fired back with a slight glare as the pounding in my head intensified. "I wanted her to remember what she saw, undistracted by the stacks of cases people keep claiming they can't solve."

Robins stiffened, his mouth twisting into a sneer. "Maybe she'd still be alive if she'd talked to an officer who wasn't rash and incompetent."

I made an awkward attempt to get to my feet. Zack was a bit faster and shoved me back down, his hand on my shoulder pinning me to my seat. The best I could do from my position was spit a few creative German insults at Robins, which he seemed to understand since his face turned a rather amusing shade of red.

"Enough!" a deep voice boomed, making all three of us freeze.

The remainder of the crowd shifted and parted as Chief Newburn made his way down the hall. He didn't look very happy. He was in his dress uniform, hat tucked carefully under one arm, meaning one of two things: He'd been pulled away from either a press meeting or lunch with the mayor and other goody-goods of the city. My money was on the food.

"Sir," Robins said, making a show of brushing himself off, "I was just questioning Miar about his conversation with the victim—"

"Madison Corvell," I said.

Newburn looked between us.

"The victim," I continued, getting successfully to my feet this time, "was Madison Corvell. And I already told you why I was down here talking to her."

"Don't keep me in suspense," Newburn grunted, shifting his bulk in my direction, and I watched Robins's face sour. "Make it quick."

I repeated the day's events, the part with Madison at least, making sure not to leave out anything. The chief nodded when I finished. Robins looked as if he were fighting off a round of constipation.

"Those are evidence now," Newburn said, gesturing to my clothes.

"Yep." I frowned. I didn't care about the clothes, but the Converse? They took me forever to find, and they were actually comfortable and fit well. It's not that I'm particularly picky about my footwear. No, like many people, I went by feel—and I hadn't had to buy shoes in a year due to how the current ones felt. Then again, they were covered in blood and hell knows what else. "But I'm not walking out of here barefoot," I announced.

"I can put some plastic bags over his shoes, so he can drive home," Zack offered, getting to his feet, tucking the last of his things back into his kit. "I'll follow him home and bag all his clothes there."

Newburn waved a hand, and Robins let out a small squeak as the chief turned to leave.

"Sir ..." he protested, turning to follow him.

"Don't you have a crime scene to get back to?" Newburn said. "Miar, go home and get cleaned up. I expect a report about this incident on my desk in the morning."

"Sure thing, Chief," I answered, not bothering to keep the smile off my face.

A grunt drifted back to me as the chief disappeared down the hall. Zack was biting his lip, and Robins was practically fuming.

"Well," I sighed, clapping Robins on the shoulder with a still-bloody hand, "guess I'll be going now, and you should get back to work." I watched his eyes widen as it dawned on him that he now had a bloody handprint on his shirt.

"Don't forget to put that in a bag," I called over my shoulder. "It's evidence now.

***

I drove home with Zack following close behind me. He tried to get me to let him drive, but I needed time to think. That wasn't a complete lie—I did need to think. And all of Zack's mother hen-ing would have added to the pounding in my head.

Why had Madison been killed? Because she was on the verge of giving me a vital clue? A name maybe? Either way, I had lost another lead, and I was not happy.

My house, thankfully, was still in one piece and reptile-free, from what I could tell. I didn't think I could take another round with any of those guys in the condition I was in.

"All right," Zack said once we made it into the little mudroom near the back door, "what really happened?"

I toed off my shoes, careful not to disturb the plastic bags too much, making a face when I discovered that my socks were soaked too. I set the shoes on the washer along with the socks, motioning for my companion to get one of the big trash bags nearby. Zack complied and waited patiently for me to answer, although I wasn't ready to relive what happened.

"Allen."

Then again, if I didn't tell him, he'd just sic Maggie on me. Lesser of the two evils, right?

"Can I get ungrossed first?" I asked. "I'll give you more details then, all right?"

Zack shook the bag open, held it out, and stared pointedly at me.

I shook my head a bit, my blood-caked hair swinging stiffly back and forth in random clumps. The ride home involved a lot of towels and plastic to keep my seat dry and gunk-free. I suspected Zack would need to collect them too. Once I extracted the notebook and pen from my coat pocket, I shucked it off and chucked it into the open bag. No way my notes were going into evidence. I didn't need to roll out a welcome mat for Robins to put me in a nuthouse. My shirt quickly followed, and then I dumped my still plastic-covered shoes in with a heavy heart. I really liked those shoes.

I paused when it came to my jeans and gave Zack a sideways glance. It wasn't that I was shy about changing in front of guys, I didn't like changing in front of anyone.

"You mind turning around?"

Zack gave me an indignant look. "We both have the same parts."

"Would you just turn the hell around!" I snapped, not missing the grin that went over Zack's face as he did as I requested.

"Bit self-conscious?"

"Shut up."

He laughed, and I toyed with the idea of hitting him with my jeans. As entertaining as that would have been, my room and the rest of my clothes were all the way upstairs. Better not tempt karma. I threw my jeans in the bag and grabbed a towel from the hamper to wrap around my waist before telling him I was done. I looked like I was wearing a skirt, but cover was cover. Zack turned around, snickers worming their way out of his mouth when he saw how I was dressed. I gave him a glare and started into the house. I didn't stop to see if he was following me. All I wanted to do was get clean—clean and rid of the smell of death.

I went to the ground-floor bathroom in my mother's room. I got the shower running and dropped the towel before getting in. I scrubbed my skin and washed my hair countless times before the water running down the drain was clear.

Muttering an apology to my mother, I rifled through her clothes until I found the largest shirt she had and put it on. My mother and I were close enough in height and build that I could borrow a few things without it being too awkward. I made the trek up to my room and grabbed a pair of lounge pants and new boxers. I quickly dressed and walked back down to the living room, my hair still wet from the shower and soaking my shirt.

"So much better," I sighed, flopping down onto my dismantled couch. "I don't feel like a zombie victim anymore. Still have a headache though."

A glass of water and a couple of aspirins waited for me on the coffee table. Good ol' Zack. I turned my head to look at him. He'd looked mildly surprised when I'd flopped onto the couch but only shook his head and leaned his head back in the chair. He looked tired. Not just the kind that others see on the surface—bags under bloodshot eyes, spacing out, irritability. No, this was a bones-deep kind of tired, the kind that makes you want to crawl into bed and not move for days. I knew that kind of tired.

"Hey," I said, focusing on Zack instead of the messy room, "you been sleeping all right?"

"Yeah," Zack answered, stretching a bit before looking over at me. "This case is just so intense."

"Yeah," I agreed, leaning forward to pick up the glass and pills, "and I think before the end, we'll find ourselves stretched to the breaking point."

"Really?"

I felt a bit bad for Zack. His life had been painfully simple before this case: home, work, and back home. It's not like he'd wanted to be dragged along on a wild adventure into the unknown. Zack could have left me on my own. I was grateful he was around to help keep my head above water.

"In for a penny," I said softly, putting my head on the armrest, "in for a pound."

Zack gave a rueful laugh. "Yeah, something like that."

A comfortable silence settled between us, allowing my pounding headache to ease to a more manageable level. I allowed my thoughts to resurface and began sorting through them. One of my suspects-turned-witness had gone from a solid to a liquid in a matter of minutes, leaving me once again with more questions than answers. I thought about Madison's body language, completely relaxed and confident that everything would go her way. That is, until I began questioning her about Meredith. Then I got the phone call from O'Hare and went out to the hall. While his reaction to the car tailing me was odd, the tone of his voice completely changed when I mentioned the other victims. I'd rattled his gilded cage a bit. Maybe he realized that he was just as vulnerable as anyone else.

"What are we going to do?"

I blinked, gently putting my thoughts away at the sound of Zack's voice. "We go back to square one," I answered. "Look through all the evidence again and see if we missed anything."

Neither one of us wanted to hear that, much less think about slogging through all our theories and little pieces of evidence again. I know I didn't, but first things first.

"Before we get all mopey," I said, holding up a hand, "I need to fill out all that stupid paperwork I'm going to get hit with."

"You think that's a good idea?" Zack asked, watching me get up. "Robins will find you the minute he hears you're back in the station."

I sighed and looked down at my damp shirt. Deeming it worthy enough to wear in public, I started searching for shoes.

Zack was right: The moment I walked in, Robins would start his winged monkey impression and make my life a living hell, which, depending on what we talked about, could take hours—time I didn't have.

"I'll take care of Robins," I told Zack, slipping on a worn pair of Vans. "You get that stuff in my laundry room into evidence."

The chair creaked as Zack stood. He walked over to me and gave me a hard shove in the chest, forcing me to sit down on the dead couch.

"No."

That stopped me long enough to blink up at him in sudden confusion. Did he just tell me no?

"Come again?"

"I said no," Zack repeated, crossing his arms. "You were in shock when I got to you, so you should be crashing any moment now. The last place you need to be is at the station."

"But—"

"No buts," he interrupted, checking his pockets for his keys, then headed to the back door. "I'll be back in a little bit. In the meantime, try to eat something and hydrate yourself with something that isn't coffee."

My eyes followed him from my sprawled position on the couch. "Sure thing there, Mom. Anything else you want me to do?"

"Yeah," Zack's voice drifted from the kitchen, "see what that damn book says about giant lizards."

And just like that, he was gone. I got up and started for the kitchen, grabbing my keys from … Where were my keys? I stopped and looked down at my hand where the keys should have been, then back at the table where I'd put them earlier. They weren't there. Quickly, I checked around. Nothing. Then I looked at the back door.

"He wouldn't," I said aloud.

Wouldn't have what?

I frowned at my inner voice. "Don't you ever sleep?" I snapped. "Leave me alone."

Sure, the voice said sarcastically, *that works out so well for you.*

I muttered a few words about ice pick lobotomies and stalked out of the kitchen. I was already pissed that my witness had exploded, and now I couldn't check any other leads because Zack had taken my keys. I walked to the dining table and looked down at the photos and various papers the three of us had left scattered.

While I didn't have my whiteboard to rethink my theories, I did have pictures from the first two crime scenes and a wall. With a bit of grumbling, I cleared the remaining framed photos off the wall that separated the kitchen and dining room. Once it was blank, I taped the crime scene photos to it one by one. Soon, I had the pictures organized in little groups along with notes about more recent events. I frowned as I stepped back to admire my handiwork. There wasn't much to go on, no matter which way I looked at it.

I had lined the groups up in chronological order: Terry Cockrill, Meredith Strong, Dr. Wright, and finally Madison Corvell. Each had a different lifestyle and ethnicity; even the ages were different. Whoever was pulling the strings and causing these deaths wasn't following any kind of pattern, almost like an angry child lashing out and knocking over random things in its path. This thought not only was greatly disturbing but also came dangerously close to an idea that I didn't want to entertain: A Fallen Stone was out there host hopping, which in turn was the cause of all of this havoc.

I rubbed my eyes, the first indication that I was coming down from the earlier shock, and looked at the wall again. Why did they kill Madison and the doctor? What information did they have that was so important to keep quiet? Terry and Meredith were easier to understand. They had pushed the boundaries of their people's laws. But their elders had reprimanded and separated them. Terry was sentenced to stay within the Dallas Fort Worth city limits, and Meredith was forced to move to another district. Presumably, that was the end of their punishment.

A sound of frustration escaped me as I ruffled my hair, making it stick out in all directions. Too much information was clogging my head, blocking facts that the evidence was showing me, along with the stress of the past few days, the building paranoia that I was next to die, and the knowledge that I was constantly putting friends in harm's way.

I know what might help.

"What?"

Stop whining. You don't have too much. It's too little.

"Your point?"

My point is to look in the book, stupid.

Have I mentioned how much I hate that little inner voice?

Despite my grumbling, I retrieved the black book. To be honest, it creeped me out a tiny bit. That simple black book felt like the barrier between a normal, safe life and the madness slithering underneath the happy facade of my town. It could give me the power to do what I couldn't within the limits of a police detective. I could save people, just like my mother apparently.

You're already saving people like your mother did. You could also end up dead, just saying.

True. This book—the contents of this book—was also what put my mother in the ground; it was danger, adventure, and the possibility of dismemberment. This wasn't a whim I could fly off on. I had already toed the line by blowing up a building to keep myself alive and by talking to the iguana clan. What would be so bad about using what was in the book to help people? To save them? Strapping on a shield to protect the people in this town when they couldn't do so for themselves. Would it be so bad just to jump in, to continue what my mother started?

"Saving people, hunting things … protecting those who can't do it them-selves …" I took a deep breath and felt the voice in my head smile as I moved over to the table. "I already stepped into this mess; time to clean up."

Oh, this is going to be fun.

Without another word, I settled in one of the chairs and began to read.

Chapter Seventeen

Whenever you absorb new information, your mind does something fascinating. It wrinkles.

You see, when we are born, our brains are useless gray lumps inside a hardening casing. As we learn things throughout our lives, wrinkles begin to form.

Ever hear the phrase "practice makes perfect"? Practicing deepens the wrinkle, helping you perform tasks or remember facts without thinking too much about it, like tying your shoes or brushing your teeth. These wrinkles will be deeper than others that develop as your life goes on, almost like a lamp that has been left on and can't be turned off.

My brain probably looked like a shriveled raisin after reading Mom's book. Who knew a good Catholic mother of four could moonlight as the author of a supernatural encyclopedia? I'd taken a break once I reached the difference between voodoo and hoodoo and was grabbing a cup of coffee—like I was told not to—when Maggie came bounding through my back door and right into me, sending hot coffee all over me and my mug crashing to the floor.

"I am so sorry," she exclaimed, grabbing one of the towels on the counter. "Are you all right?"

I took a breath and told myself that hot coffee on vital areas of my anatomy wasn't very painful.

"It's fine, Maggie," I managed to get out, taking the towel from her before it reached the tender bits. "Zack with you?"

Maggie grabbed a few paper towels and began to clean up the mess on the floor while I dabbed uselessly at my pants.

"Yeah, I'm here," Zack called, kicking the door open and walking through with his hands full of fast-food bags and a drink tray. He paused long enough to raise an eyebrow at my pants and Maggie on the floor before continuing over to the kitchen table.

"Don't even …" I muttered, walking past to get the broom and dustpan.

"I didn't say a word."

I deposited the remains of my mug into the trash can, then joined my friends at the table.

"So," Maggie said as she unwrapped her burger, "Zack said you had a body explode on you?"

I coughed and took a few swigs of my Coke to keep myself from choking. Once the stinging in my throat disappeared and I was able to speak without squeaking, I nodded. "Yeah, and it was balloon-like, yes, but the pop came from the inside, not the outside."

"As gross as it sounds, that's so wicked."

"Um, *ew*."

Maggie smiled. "Pansy."

"In the face of what I've seen lately, I will gladly take that title."

We lapsed into silence, intent on eating. The kitchen was filled with the sounds of crinkling wrappers, the soft thumps of cups, and the occasional plop of ketchup falling from a burger to the table. Wonderful, normal things.

"All right," Maggie said, once she was done, "what do we do now?"

I chewed on my straw for a moment. "We look at everything again," I finally answered, earning a few sputters. "I missed something the first time around."

"Is that why pictures of dead things are taped to your dining room wall?"

I blinked, tilting my head a little at Zack and slowly started to shake my head.

"No, I don't—"

"Your front windows are wide open, you idiot," Zack interrupted, and Maggie started laughing. "Might want to close your curtains unless you want to give that lady next door something else to be nosy about."

I glowered at the two of them, getting up to throw away the trash. But they were right. I should have made sure the curtains were closed before I hung up the pictures. Man, I was getting sloppy.

"Well, since you already saw it ..." I said, motioning for them to follow me into the dining room. I went straight to the two windows that faced the street and yanked what remained of the curtains closed. "I put things in the same order we had on the whiteboard in the office."

I had started with Terry, putting her on the far left. I got as close as I could without taping her photos to the doorframe. It would make for an awkward situation if anyone was using the front door. Thankfully, mine was still broken and blocked off. And because I'm such a classy guy, everyone got to come through the back. Hey, closer to the food in my opinion, and the best way to leave if anything ever got questionable.

Meredith was next. Her section was full of notebook paper diagrams: notes of what happened that day, her connection to the first death, little things I remembered or observed about the area where she had died.

Dr. Wright and Madison were up there as well, their sections a bit smaller than the others. But the papers that hung there were more facts and pieces of things that I learned from the interviews I'd conducted. Some of the papers held hunches that I couldn't shake, even with the solid facts I had.

"You were quite busy while I was gone," Zack said as he studied the wall, "and not relaxing like I said."

"Yeah, well, when my keys mysteriously disappeared from the table, I couldn't go anywhere," I replied dryly. Saying a quick apology to my mother, I perched on the tabletop and planted my feet firmly in one of the chairs.

Maggie's eyes widened, but I tore my gaze from hers and let my eyes go over the photos and papers on the wall.

After a moment, Maggie asked, "This is it? Everything we know about the squishy people?"

I snickered at her choice of words.

"This," I said, spreading my arms dramatically, "is all I have so far, with a little extra."

"You think you're next?"

Zack hadn't turned when he said it, but I could hear the worry creeping into his voice.

"I don't know," I answered honestly, running a hand through my hair, "but the way things are going … seems like a high possibility."

The silence was deafening—and just a tiny bit unnerving. It's not like I was ready to skip off into the clutches of death. I still had a few things to take care of before I kicked the bucket.

"Allen—"

"The real question is," I exclaimed, jumping down from my spot, "what did we miss?"

I went to the other side of the table and moved a few papers around. I grabbed one and held it up for the others to see.

"This," I said, waving the paper for emphasis, "is what we're going to do. We are going to figure out what all of them have in common, down to the last crumb."

"And you think this will flush out whatever you missed?" Maggie asked, frowning at me.

"Yes!"

Zack turned to look at me, and I couldn't miss the unease written all over his face or all the fidgeting Maggie was doing.

"I know you guys are worried, and your mother hen instincts are working overtime," I said. "But if I stop, if I just drop it all and pretend everything is fine and dandy, it won't stop. Whoever is doing this is out for blood and is cleaning house."

My eyes flicked down at the papers. Black squiggles on white squares stared back at me, some parts were underlined or circled for emphasis.

I rapped my knuckles on the table. "So we have Madison, a doctor, a crazy nurse lady, and Terry. What do they have in common?"

"They're all dead," Zack supplied. "Wait a sec, didn't you say Terry and Meredith knew each other?"

"Yes," Maggie said, snapping her fingers. "You said they had a fight in middle school over the stone or because of the stone …."

"Two."

She blinked. "Two?"

I nodded and filled another white square with black-inked squiggles. "When I was at the iguana house, I had a conversation with a guy named Raymon. He said that the kids thought the stone would make them stronger. I believe at some point one of the groups picked up another stone without knowing it. So think—who would know about things like that instantly, even though you don't want them to?"

"Parents," came the answer in unison.

I stopped writing, a spark of thought lighting my brain. The parents …. Of course. Gah, I'm an idiot!

"Zack, call Saint Mary's and see if you can get someone to tell you if Terry Cockrill or Meredith Strong were their patients," I said, picking up my notebook from the table and flipping through it. "If they give you problems, hand me the phone."

My friend stared at me but got up and pulled out his phone. "You have the number on hand?"

Wordlessly, I pointed to the stack of files O'Hare had managed to sweet-talk from the receptionist and continued my search. I heard more than saw Zack leave the room as he started dialing. A good house makes sure people are heard. At least my house does.

"What are you looking for?" Maggie asked, watching me.

"Business card," I muttered, flinging the notebook back onto the table with a huff and rifling through the papers on the table. "Raymon, the lead iguana guy's son, gave me one so I could get in touch with him."

Maggie grinned for a moment and then she started to giggle. It didn't bother me too much. She giggled at her own private jokes all the time. But then the giggles turned into full-blown laughter.

"Uh … Maggie?"

She turned to look at me, only to start laughing again. This was the cycle for about five minutes until she could get herself under control enough to speak.

"I'm good," she said, wiping the tears off of her face. "I'm good now."

"Do I even want to know?"

Maggie shifted some papers, looking for the elusive card. "You," she said between giggles, "are actually looking for a number."

"Your point?"

"My point is that you made friends."

Oh brother. I shot her a glare as I crouched down to search underneath the table.

It was an old argument that we had occasionally—one, I loathe to point out, that she always won. After my mother passed, many of the people I knew from school drifted away, either moving to another district or just getting so involved with other things that they didn't have time for me. Maggie was the only one who stayed around. It's not that I didn't try to make friends with new people. They just didn't respond well to my wanting to hang around. As a result, Maggie said I was "unfriendable," which was kinda true at the time.

When I got to college, I met Zack, who turned out to be just as twisted as me. Once Maggie found out that I was in contact with another human being, she was overjoyed. I swear it was like I just brought home a new fiancé. She even threw me a party—an honest-to-everything party, complete with streamers.

So now, whenever I played nice with another person for more than an hour, Maggie dubbed them a "friend," whether I wanted her to or not.

"Ha ha," I muttered, finally finding the card near one of the chair legs. I picked it up and got to my feet. "Such a comedian."

I fished my phone out with my other hand. Maggie gave me a triumphant smile as she started reading Madison's file.

"If you find anything useful, write it down," I told her, nodding to the pad and several pens.

For a bit of privacy, I walked into the living room, dialing as quickly as I could. I didn't have to wait long. Raymon picked up on the third ring.

"Hello."

"Raymon, it's Allen," I said.

"I'm sorry, who?"

"Uh … Allen Miar," I said. Had he really forgotten me so quickly? "We spoke this morning."

"Ah, yes …. Yes of course," Raymon said with a sigh. "How can I help you?"

"Well, I was hoping you could answer a question for me," I said, straining to hear anything in the background.

"I'd love to hear about your prices, ma'am," Raymon said, clearing his throat, "but maybe another time would be better."

What was he talking about?

"You can't talk freely, can you?" I asked, shifting against the wall. Not a big deal, I could work on a different angle until Raymon was able to talk.

"Yes, ma'am," Raymon answered, "that is my address, but like I said, now isn't a good time."

"Call me later," I said.

"Of course, you have a good day as well."

The phone went dead in my ear. And I realized that just by meeting with them and calling just now, I may have set Robert, Raymon, and the rest of the iguanas up for slaughter. It made my stomach twist. If anyone ended up all over one of those immaculate rooms, I would have a horde of iguanas after me.

"Allen?"

Maggie's voice startled me. I put a hand to my chest. I really needed to stop spacing out when I was thinking—it was going to kill me one day.

"You all right?"

She was watching me with apprehension, not that I was surprised. I would have looked at myself the same way.

I managed a small smile and a nod. "Yeah, as good as I'll ever be."

Her eyes narrowed in concentration as she inspected my face. She crept closer until I was enveloped by the intoxicating smell of her cherry perfume. I blinked a few times when I felt my face heating up.

"Must have been a dead end if you got off the phone that quick."

I shook my head, moving a bit farther away from Maggie to pace around the living room. "He's gonna call me back. There were other people there, I think, so he probably just needed some privacy …."

Maggie grew suspicious. "Privacy … Do you think he's in trouble? What if he needs help?"

"Hold on," I said, trying to slow her down. "Just because he couldn't talk right away doesn't mean we need to rush over. We do that, I risk losing the agreement they made to let me help. Some of the family weren't exactly happy that I was allowed to help them, you know? If we show up at the house with guns blazing, the entire family could turn on us. All of us could end up as red paste. We know that the killer's style is to use the stone from a distance to kill, right? It also could mean that they need a clear view of the target. I doubt they would risk a fight with a whole house of angry reptiles. Let's just chill and wait for Raymon to call back."

"We still should go check it out," Maggie huffed.

I grinned and tried to diffuse the situation. "What? You want to go spy through their windows? You want to be a Peeping Tom?"

Maggie gave me a shove. "It's called a stakeout, Short Bus. Besides, Peeping Toms are guys."

"So what would that make you?" I asked.

"A stalker?"

That's how Zack found us. "Did I miss something?"

"Maggie wants to be a Peeping Tom," I answered, laughing so hard I ended up on the floor looking up at the ceiling.

"The term is *stalker*," Maggie said, kicking my foot. "And you're supposed to be a detective."

I rested my head on the floor as Maggie and Zack joked around. They would make a cute couple, I thought. Neither was too tall or too short, and Zack was obviously smitten. I had a feeling that Maggie was completely oblivious to his feelings though. Finally, I stretched a leg out to tap Zack's shoe with my own. "Get any info?"

Zack's face crinkled in mild annoyance as he gave my foot a kick. "Yep."

"Really?"

Zack held up a piece of paper. "Apparently, they had a tough time finding the right file because a few have gone missing."

I blinked, then shrugged. "Before you point fingers, the only files I have are on the good doctor himself and Madison. And I wasn't the one who convinced the receptionist to hand them over …. That was all O'Hare's doing. The entire stack is nothing but copies, so technically I can keep them or have a huge bonfire later."

"Allen," Maggie exclaimed, "you know that's illegal!"

"That's why I said 'bonfire.' Look," I said, getting up, "finding a judge that would sign off on a wild theory like mine would take time that we don't have. Even if we did manage to convince someone, the process would take a full day, maybe more. This way we have our information and they get the file back."

"Maggie's right," Zack said and let out a sigh as he motioned to me, "but so are you. We've already had four people die. If we can solve this case by bending a few rules, it'll be worth it."

Maggie huffed and put her hands on her hips. "Fine. But I don't have enough bail money for both of you, so don't you dare get caught."

I blinked and stared at both of them. Did all of us just agree to break the law in order to uphold it?

"So are we Robin Hood-ing this thing or not?" Maggie asked, stomping back to the dining room.

Zack and I looked at each other before following.

"It's more James Bond than Robin Hood," I pointed out, stopping in front of the scattered papers on the table, "but either works."

"No, we're pulling a Robin Hood," Maggie corrected, not looking at me. "He upheld the law. Bond blew things up and was a secret agent man. We aren't doing anything like that."

I bit my tongue to avoid pointing out that I had already blown up a building.

"So what did you manage to find out?" I asked Zack.

"Terry and Meredith were regular patients of separate doctors," he said. "Terry was seen by a Dr. Travis Willard, and a Dr. Dean Swanson was Meredith's attending physician."

"So it's a dead end?"

"Not quite," Zack said with a grin. "Both girls were treated at the same hospital the day of their fight."

I frowned and moved around the table to the wall, almost running over Maggie in the process. "Not the smartest thing to do after two kids get into a deadly fight."

"Whoa, hang on there, Sherlock!" Zack said, moving after me at a slower pace. "There's more."

I twisted around to look at him briefly before patting myself down for a pen.

"Before the girls left," Zack said as Maggie tossed a pen my way, "Dr. Swanson did refer the Strong family to a psychologist, thinking it would help Meredith work through what she was feeling at the time. So he might have picked up on something being wrong."

I paused in my scribbling, frown deepening. "Did he now?"

Zack nodded. "That's what they said was written in the file …. And I don't like that face."

Maggie tilted her head at me. "What's wrong?"

"Mrs. Strong didn't mention anything about her daughter seeking help. Then again, I didn't ask," I admitted, turning back to the wall. "And if Meredith did see a psychologist after the fight, that doctor would have to inform her mother if Meredith were a threat to herself or others. If the police ever came around with a warrant, they'd have to say something. That is, if the mother didn't strong-arm him."

"That can't be the reason for the frown though," Maggie said, picking up Zack's notes to look them over.

I grinned over at Zack. "Anything else before we get too distracted?"

Zack shook his head.

The floorboards creaked as Maggie walked over to me. "Says here, Meredith came in to have a few scrapes and bruises patched up after the fight; nothing major."

I took Zack's note from her and taped it to the wall under a section labeled Connections. Then I took a step back, letting my eyes take in what was there so far.

We had a few more pieces, but we were no closer to finding out who was calling the shots. O'Hare seemed like the right kind of person, but this whole thing was too messy and public, not your typical mob style at all. Were the actual bad guys thinking I would chase after O'Hare because of his chosen profession? Was that their plan?

Now, now, I scolded myself, *don't get ahead of yourself.*

Good luck convincing me of that, another voice interjected from a different corner of my head, and I groaned.

"Damn it, would you shut up!" I snapped aloud.

"Sorry," Zack said, clearly startled by my sudden outburst. "What—"

I waved at him. "Just thinking."

"Thinking?"

"Inner monologuing."

"And the expletive?"

"We disagreed on something."

Zack stared at me.

"Do we have anything?" Maggie asked from my other side. "Because I for one don't like being at square one."

No kidding, I thought. "Welcome to my profession. I don't think we are though."

"Translation?"

I let out a breath and scratched the back of my head. "Translation—from the moment we started looking into this case, someone has been following us. Every time we make progress, that same person is making sure we hit walls."

Maggie put a hand over her mouth. "So all those people …"

"They were the intended victims the entire time," I confirmed, grimly tapping a finger against my upper lip in thought. "Whoever is pulling the strings right now might even have one of the stones. If the stones are like a power source, what if the person using them doesn't know the full extent of the stone's power?"

"Kind of like tossing a lit match in a gas-filled room?"

I nodded my head slowly. "Um … kinda … yeah. What if the power in the stones was latching on to a person's emotions? Like one of the power rings from *Sonic the Hedgehog*, only ten times as powerful and four times as destructive."

"Good lord!" Zack exclaimed.

"What?"

"You are such a nerd!"

I glared at him and waved a hand at the wall. "Shut up. We have more important things to focus on, like who is going to die next."

"It's true," Maggie said seriously. "He is a nerd; painfully true …."

"Maggie!"

"But I have a question," she continued. "If the stones are feeding off emotions, what was the trigger for the killings to start? And how do we figure out who is using it?"

I rubbed my temples. "Who do we know that would risk everything for the stones?"

"That weird mob guy?"

"Giant lizard babies?"

"Mary Strong?"

I paused and shook my head. "I've ruled out Riley O'Hare. He's too meticulous to draw attention to himself. Unless mobsters have changed the rules in the past hundred years or so. He also got me half of the information we have. It makes me think he likes to meddle more than anything."

For right now.

"I guess the lizards are out then," Maggie said with a sigh.

"Not exactly," Zack said, moving to the wall and tapping Meredith's name. "Allen said her mother was a Komodo dragon, and they were the ones that attacked us in IHOP."

"They were the zombie slime things that I saved your ass from," Maggie pointed out excitedly, looking at me.

I smirked. "You went wild woman on them with a chain saw and then turned the hose on those freaks."

"My shoulder was a small price to pay for making sure those things didn't kill you," Maggie said. "But the next time they show up, I'll let you slay the mighty dragon."

My face flushed.

"Right," Zack said, looking a bit confused, "and the whole thing started with a fight between the Komodo dragons and the iguanas—an ongoing family feud?"

I held up a finger. "That makes sense. The girls were told all these stories about the stones, their power, their abilities, but even the elders didn't know what those rocks could do. I mean, if you really think about it, the stones can look like any old gem. It's the perfect disguise. And if two teenage girls got ahold of them—or even one, for that matter—with all their pent-up hormonal emotions boiling inside ... they plan to do something bad for once .... They pick a fight with the most popular person in school, who just happens to be part of the rival clan. They take the stone to the fight, where it felt the emotions of all the kids involv—"

"And because of that," Zack finished, his eyes alight, "it woke up."

"Exactly," I agreed. "And whoever has it now has no clue what they're hold—"

I was rudely interrupted by a zombie dragon crashing through my dining room window. Maggie let out a scream, and I ducked as glass went flying. A stream of stuttered curses came from Zack, which were soon drowned out when the dragon opened its mouth and roared. The floorboards shook, and the dishes in the cabinet rattled violently.

When the lizard began to shake itself, I forcefully yanked both Zack and Maggie to the floor as globs of acidic goo flew everywhere. Steam began to rise from the table, chairs, and wall as the acid ate through them.

I almost gagged. The fumes surrounding the creature could only be described as the aroma of something slowly rotting in the Texas noonday sun, a horrid stink that tries to crawl up your nose and permanently embed itself in your brain. I didn't get a chance to adjust to the smell before the reptile swung its head—half of which looked melted—in our direction.

"Oh … trucks," I said under my breath, getting to my feet. It was the Komodo dragon Maggie'd hit with the chain saw, and it looked more pissed than before. "Maggie, Zack, get to the kitchen."

I heard Maggie scramble in that direction, her breathing heavy, but Zack hadn't moved at all. I took a gamble and shoved behind me, hoping to nudge him into action. Maybe he'd take the hint and get moving; I hoped.

"Give it to us," the Komodo gurgled, taking a step in my direction. "Give it to us."

I scooted farther away, my eyes darting around for anything I could use for defense. Everything around me had belonged to my mother though. I didn't want to use any of it and ruin it. But I also didn't want to die. That thought led to a silent plea for forgiveness as I grabbed one of Mom's wooden dining chairs, holding tightly to the backrest with both hands, the legs sticking out in the dragon's direction, lion-tamer style.

Behind me, Zack and Maggie were moving in the kitchen. No screams or curses floated out, leading me to believe only one dragon had come this time. Hopefully, more weren't inbound.

"Allen," Zack yelled above the bangs and slams of cabinet doors, "what the hell is that thing?"

One of the Komodo's paws came up and swiped at the chair legs, almost knocking me to the floor. The thing hissed, its monstrous head swinging back and forth as more goo dissolved my floor.

"Um, remember when you jumped all over me for letting Maggie get hurt?"
I said, wishing desperately for the sledgehammer in the backyard.

"You have got to be kidding me?!"

Note to self: Work with Zack on his acceptance of what is now normal.

"Zack," I yelled, "does it look like I'm kidding?"

I didn't hear his answer as the creature let out another roar and lunged at
me, those deadly jaws snapping shut on the chair's legs. Its head thrashed from
side to side, pulling me across the floor in its direction. The air filled with the
acrid smell of rotten meat and lacquer as the goo leaked onto the only defense
I had against it. I adjusted my grip on the chair, backing up and planting my
feet as best I could. No way I was going to lose the only means of defense I
had at the moment, much less my fingers, to that thing.

"If you guys have a plan, let me know," I grunted, giving the chair another
tug. "My arms are starting to hurt."

"One second," Maggie answered, followed by a few more bangs.

The dragon snarled, a gurgle coming from deep inside its chest as if it
were trying to cough up a hair ball. But lizards don't get hair balls .... Unless
... oh crap!

"Guys, if you're standing behind me, move!" I yelled, watching the lizard's
body tense, its muscles convulsing. I was horridly fascinated and couldn't
look away or run.

I reminded myself to breathe through my mouth as more of the acidic goo
gathered at the corners of the dragon's mouth, spilling out in globs the size of
softballs. They landed with wet sticky plops, bubbling and forming several
holes in the scuffed hardwood floor.

"Allen, you need to get him outside!"

No problem, I thought, watching the growing bulge in the dragon's throat.
Let me just toss him out the back door.

"Yeah," I said aloud, "sure. Give me a sec."

Turns out, I didn't need to try and make him move because the lizard had
other plans—like dropping the chair and hocking a spitball the size of an
overinflated basketball at my head. The sudden lack of counterforce caused

me to stumble and fall backward. I landed with an "oomph" and blinked as the goo-ball sailed over me. I winced as a few stray drops plopped onto the floor and, perhaps more importantly, onto my pants. I scrambled back into the kitchen, dropping the now useless chair in the process.

I quickly got to my feet, looking around frantically for a weapon. Instead, I found Zack standing beside me with one of my mother's pots on his head like a metal hat and a broom in his hand, bristle side facing our fiendish intruder. I should have slapped him on the back and kept going, maybe make some witty remark about his choice of battle gear. But the only thing I could do was laugh.

"Shut your mouth," Zack muttered, hitting me with the business end of his broom.

Not trusting myself to speak, I just nodded. He looked so ridiculous, but then again, what did ridiculous even mean anymore?

A loud, bubbling hiss sounded on the far end of the room followed by the smell of melting plastic. I think I gave myself a small case of whiplash with how fast I turned my head. What I saw made the giggle die at once. The spitball from hell had missed me, spared parts of the floor, and landed right in the middle of my fridge. My poor appliance's door was dripping melting chunks, making mixed puddles of white, black, and gray on the floor.

"I had food in there!" I exclaimed, my blood starting to boil.

I turned to look at the creature that was slowly making its way into the kitchen. Without a word, I grabbed the pot from Zack's head, ignoring his rather creative protests, and marched over to the cause of my distress. I raised the pot as high as I could—and I do not recommend that kids try this at home—and then brought it down on the dragon's head.

What came next was unexpected. There was a sucking sound as I pulled what was left of the pot away and tossed it aside. The lizard tensed and started to stand, one of those goo-covered paws slamming into my face as it reared up on its hind legs.

There are no words in any language to describe the pain. None. In school, you are taught to stop, drop, and roll if you ever catch on fire. Stay calm and do not panic, they say. That's all well and good if you aren't the one on fire. If you happen to be the one on fire, all you want is for the pain to disappear.

The pain was so intense, I lost focus on what was around me. My senses were filled with the smell of burning skin, the tightening of my face, and the need to make it stop. Every little movement hurt.

Dimly, I heard Zack yelling for me to move and the thing roaring. That's right, I was supposed to get the lizard outside. Why though? Couldn't remember. I forced my eyes open and bit back a yell as the skin on the right side of my face pulled sharply. I counted quickly to five before trying again, this time keeping my right eye closed and allowing my left eye to adjust to the disability. I then took a look around.

Apparently, I had fallen after the paw had connected with my face, because the first thing I noticed was the crack in my ceiling. The second thing I noticed was Zack standing in front of the dragon waving his broom around wildly in a poor attempt to keep the creature from advancing. I slowly pushed myself up, stumbling as I got to my feet with a groan. Damn it, everything hurt.

"Never mind that now," I said softly, biting my lip at the throbbing pain, "have to get it outside."

I let my only eye dart around to get my bearings. I had a sudden admiration for pirates and their eye patches. I mean, have you ever tried to walk around with one eye covered? It's hard!

I had landed near the door that led to the dining room, which sucked. The creature, apparently assuming I was dead, was focused on Zack. Zack had retreated to the back door, waving his stick the whole time. The lizard hadn't dropped to all fours, which meant it was dwarfing Zack and his stupid stick. All I had to do was get Zack out of the way and make sure not to miss the lizard or the door. It was perfect—stupid even—and the only idea I had.

As quickly as I could, I plotted a goo-free path across the floor. Then I let out a breath mixed with a prayer and started running—right at the lizard and Zack.

"Head's up, Buttercup!"

My voice was hoarse, and Zack wasn't moving. I swallowed what spit was in my mouth and yelled it again. This time he heard me. Almost in slow motion, I saw a look of horror take over Zack's face. I must look pretty bad then. Oh well. He dove out of the way, landing with a grunt and a clatter somewhere outside my field of vision and leaving me a clear path to my goal.

"Get your undead ugly ass out of my house!" I bellowed, dropping my shoulder at the last minute and turning my head to protect what was left of my face. I felt my body slam into the dragon's midsection and the sweet glory of gravity take over as the creature stumbled.

The pain I'd felt earlier was mild compared to this. Then again, it had only been my face burned by the goo, not the entire right side of my body. I had a moment of panic until the fresh rush of adrenaline went through me, dulling the sensation just enough for me to keep going.

A loud crash followed by the feeling of warm air on my back told me we had made it outside. In my haste to get the lizard out of my house, I'd forgotten Newton's wonderful first law of motion. Say it together, kids! An object will stay at rest or continue at a constant velocity unless acted upon by an external unbalanced force. In non-nerd speak, it means the lizard and I would keep flying through the air until something stopped us. The back porch took the honors.

We landed with a thud, the lizard taking the brunt of the fall, for which I was very grateful. Landing with me on the bottom would have been extrabad. I tried to roll off the creature, but I didn't get very far. Pain exploded across my back as those claws dug in and began to shred my skin. I screamed, high and loud. Anyone on the block within hearing range would think someone was being murdered. To be honest, I thought I was that someone.

Blindly, I began struggling, rational thought fleeing with my screams. The porch step that suddenly dug into my back gave me a jolt so bad my vision went white. There was a brief pressure on top of me, causing those claws to sink in a tiny bit deeper.

Count the steps!

Stupid voice, leave me alone—

Would you just count the steps already!

Right, and maybe I'll get lucky and pass out before we reach the lawn. Fat chance, but what do I have to lose?

Your life, you moron!

The dragon let out a startled sound as we turned again, and I allowed myself a short sigh as my back was exposed to the late afternoon air. I could feel the skin and clothes I was wearing start to burn together. My whole body was on fire. I needed to get him off me, and quick, or I was going to look like a short version of Deadpool.

I moved back as far as I could and started throwing rabbit punches to the creature's side. Being the youngest of four and a favored target for bullies, I learned the art of fighting dirty, sometimes extremely dirty. And yes, ladies, the deadly knee to the crotch does count!

As we turned for a third time, I felt something give. Bingo! I heard the creature grunt; the claws loosening just enough for me to try and push it away. I would love to say that I kicked away from the creature, rolled to my feet, and struck a pose to match any superhero, and then came up with some witty line just before I put a final stop to the bad guy. As it turns out, if you rabbit-punch a zombie lizard hard enough, it will fling you across your backyard …. Free of charge! If you're lucky, you'll land on something soft. But if you're me, you'll cuss creatively as you slide across the yard, dirt and bits of whatever else crawling into your wounds. I finally stopped in a rather ungraceful heap in the dirt and rocks close to the alley.

Agony replaced the pain from earlier—flaming, white-hot agony. I couldn't move, the slightest twitch felt like a thousand needles being shoved under my skin. Then it rippled to other parts of me that I didn't even know could hurt.

"Allen!"

Maggie. I opened my left eye and, with my entire body protesting, turned my head toward her yell. She was manning the garden hose again, doing an excellent job of keeping the lizard at bay and making it very angry. It let out a bellow of pain as more water started to cover its body. The creature swiped its claws blindly, narrowly missing Maggie's already injured shoulder.

"Allen, get up!" Maggie yelled as Zack emerged from the house. "Allen!"

Inch by inch I pushed myself up, watching my friends fight a nightmare. With difficulty and my vision threatening to black out, I managed to get to my feet as something like a fever pulsed through me. I took a step in Maggie's direction, and the edges of my vision darkened.

Oh, not good, don't pass out now, Allen! They're in danger! They need you.

I stopped long enough for the darkness to fade.

Maggie called me a few names that were surprising even for her. I tried to smirk and hissed sharply through my teeth instead. So what if I ended up passing out? So what if I got shredded to bits? If I was going down, I was going down epically.

"All right," I said aloud, my voice coming out in a gravelly rumble, "here goes everything."

Counting to three, I started moving again. It was slow, but at least I was mobile. I turned my head as little as possible, searching for the machine Maggie had used earlier. Pain continued to crash over me as I moved. I ignored it as best I could and kept looking. I finally spotted it lying close to the toolshed and changed my direction.

"Get him on his back legs!" I yelled, my voice raspy as my hand closed around the handle.

"Are you crazy?"

It took me two tries to start the chain saw. "Stand him up!"

If they answered me, it was drowned out by a roar as Zack landed a few hard smacks to the creature's snout with his stick. It shook its head, making Zack and Maggie retreat a few feet to avoid the flying gobs of goo. A moment later, the creature started to stand.

The chain saw sputtered to life, sending tiny shocks up my arms, and I closed the gap between me and the creature.

"Go to hell!" I snarled, bringing the chain saw around for a hit, ducking my head in an attempt to keep my eye.

A violent shudder ran up my arms as the blade found its target and threatened to jolt out of my hands. I grunted, but instead of letting go, I pressed my weight against the saw, being sure to keep my head turned away. It felt like hours before the creature started to gurgle, its body seizing up as the chain saw let out a final whine of protest and died. I shook my head as black dots appeared around my vision and gave the saw one last shove.

Somehow, the creature stumbled away, the chain saw protruding from its belly, and collapsed awkwardly next to the back steps. I fell to my knees in the grass, the spent adrenaline leaving me numb. The world started tilting as I watched a spray of water peel back the zombie's soggy leatherlike armor, revealing rotted organs and brittle yellow bones. Then my vision narrowed to a small slit, blocking out everything but the lizard melting away on my lawn. The blackness closed in, and I didn't fight it. I didn't have the strength or the will to do so, so I let it take me into blissful, painless silence.

Chapter Eighteen

There are a lot of theories about dreams. In ancient times, the Greeks and Egyptians believed that dreams foretold your future, divining pending power, wealth, or ultimately death. Others believed the gods used dreams to communicate with their followers. Over the years, these beliefs were mellowed by hippies and sanitized by people in white lab coats. Now when children wake up terrified of something hiding under their beds, adults dismiss it as overactive imaginations, leaving the children afraid of their dreams.

Just to clarify, I wasn't dead—at least I didn't think I was. The afterlife is supposed to reflect what the person believes in, right? My afterlife wouldn't be an open meadow in what felt like spring. Then again, this place felt kinda nice ....

You know this isn't real, right?

... Until I heard that voice speaking up just to ruin my good time. I groaned, vehemently willing the owner of that voice to go away.

I'm not going anywhere, you know.

I opened my eyes, pointedly avoiding the direction the voice was coming from, and continued to study the clouds.

You can't ignore me either, the voice mused, *no matter how much you try.*

"What are you," I snapped, turning my head in the voice's direction, "some kind of crude inner torture device?"

My demand faded as my eyes focused on a perfect reflection of myself. Well, except his face didn't look like ground meat.

He grinned, showing perfect teeth, and shrugged. *I'm you, or at least your inner self.*

"So you're what," I asked, "my Jiminy Cricket?"

More or less.

I studied my double. He seemed real enough. Then again, this could be the beginning of a really bad dream.

"Let me get this straight," I said, carefully scooting back a bit more. "Are you messing up my perfectly good dream to have a heart-to-heart?"

My reflection shrugged. *You hardly sleep. How else was I supposed to talk to you?*

He had a point, but I wasn't in a talking mood. "What do you want?"

He sighed, and I saw him run a hand through his hair from my peripheral vision. It was shorter than mine; not by much, just enough to clear his shoulders.

Nothing really, he answered, *just making sure you're all right.*

That caught me a bit off guard. I turned my head to look at him again. The more I studied him, the faster I was able to pick out the differences between us. Where I had gained a bit of muscle, filling out as much as I ever would, he was lanky. He was in the stage of growth where kids are all leg and have to figure out how to walk again. The look on his face was one of genuine concern, but what I saw in his eyes made me believe he was real, no matter how much I didn't want to. This was me before the abuse started, before I started having problems with touch, with my anger, with … everything. The age of innocence. My eyes flicked to his clothes, slightly baggy as if they were just a tad too big for him. He even had my Converse on.

It's hard to fathom, isn't it? he asked, a small smile pulling his mouth up.

"Do you blame me?"

He let out a short laugh. It was clear and still full of innocence. *Not really.*

We sat there for a moment staring at each other, neither of us moving. It was a bit disturbing looking at my double—neat, but disturbing.

I finally broke the silence. "I'm doing fine, you know."

Really?

"Yes."

He raised an eyebrow. *You're sure?*

"Absolutely."

My voice lacked conviction. My double seemed to hear it, and he let out a sigh.

Have you solved the case yet? he asked, settling on the ground beside me.

I picked at the grass. "No …. Everything is still too jumbled. I have four victims that died by way of explosion, and I have not a clue which direction to go."

Are you sure?

"You think I missed something?"

My double shrugged, his mouth threatening to turn up again. The brat was enjoying this.

Go over it again, slowly this time, he said, tilting his head back to look at the sky.

We lapsed into silence, the air around us filling with the sounds of birds and rustling grass. The sky began to darken, and the temperature dropped. A storm was coming. The fluffy white clouds twisted into gnarled black hands in the distant horizon, as if someone had taken a paintbrush and attempted to ruin their purity.

Purity …. I blinked and got to my feet. Why hadn't it dawned on me before?

Figure it out? my reflection asked, watching me with amusement.

"Yeah," I said, glancing from the other me to the sky above, "something I should have figured out a long while ago. What's up with the sky? It was nice and relaxing a moment ago."

As if in response, the wind kicked up and yanked on my hair, like fingers pulling me toward the horizon. My footing faltered, and I felt myself sliding. When a hand landed on my arm, the pulling sensation lessened, but it was still there, lingering in the empty space around me, waiting for another chance to grab me.

"What the hell?"

My reflection had his hand on my arm. He was keeping me grounded. The nervous expression on his face had morphed into something closer to fear. I realized then all the differences between us.

We weren't quite the same height; he only came up to my shoulder. His hair was tangled, and bruises were blossoming on his face, slowly becoming darker and more sinister. The worst part were his eyes. There was terror in those blue orbs. Only a child who had seen true evil—an evil that wouldn't vanish no matter how hard you prayed or begged—would look that way.

You need to wake up.

"What, why?"

Wake up, the reflection said, a bit exasperated. *You need to get back to your friends.*

I expected his hand to be cold, but it was surprisingly warm. I felt his warmth spread through me as if he'd gently shoved a sunny spring day into my chest, and it was trying to defrost something deep inside me.

Now go! he yelled, giving me a push backward.

Panic welled up when I felt the ground fall away, sending me into a free fall. The wind howled and reached after me, its claws screeching as if scraping against metal. I'd felt them earlier, but now I could see them—bony, gnarled, and twisted—reaching out to me, the tips curling into wicked-looking claws. I yelped when they came dangerously close to my eyes, a wave of cold following in their wake. Another howl echoed above my head, and I raised an arm to fend off the rising wind.

***

An elephant was tap-dancing on my chest.

"Ease up, Maggie. He's breathing again," Zack said.

Breathing was a totally different thing from what I felt I was doing at the moment. To me, it felt more like swallowing fire.

"I'll ease up as soon as I kick his ass."

Oh, how I love my friends. I started coughing and felt someone gently lift my head enough to pour something into my mouth. It was cool, crisp, and felt like heaven. I gulped it down as fast as I could, a bit escaping from my mouth as the source was pulled away. Never again would I make fun of those water-pushing health freaks.

"Ow," I croaked, my voice coming out like sandpaper. "What landed on me?"

"Maggie performed a rather interesting version of CPR that looked like she was struggling to pack an overstuffed box," Zack said as he lifted me to a sitting position, pausing when I groaned.

I grumbled and tried to open my eyes, only to find out I had a small problem. "Uh, guys?" I said, my voice tinged with panic. "Why can't I see?"

"Well, you kinda face-planted," Zack said carefully.

Anxiety crept in. "Please tell me it wasn't into the acid goo."

Silence was answer enough. Shit. Sounds of protest erupted when my hands came up, fingers brushing a web of gauze bandages encircling my head.

"No, no, no," I growled and began tearing at the offending fabric. I couldn't be blind! I didn't go toe to toe with a gooey zombie lizard just to end up blind!

"Allen don't," Zack said as he tried to grab my wrists, "you'll hurt yourself more."

"Get them off," I demanded, continuing to paw at the bandages.

"Allen, I don't think—"

"Get them off my face!" My voice came out in a panicked cry. "Now!"

A stretch of silence was filled with my heavy breathing until I felt the bandages being removed. Once the last of the gauze had been taken off, I very slowly opened my eyes. I never thought light could physically hurt. I mean, I've walked out of a dark movie theater into the sun, but I never stopped to figure out if that pain was physical or just mental. This pain was not mental, and it hurt like hell—like a hundred tiny needles were stabbing places that were best left alone.

"You all right?"

I lifted a hand, shielding my somewhat useless eyes from the sun, and nodded. I was really beginning to hate getting thrown around. My whole body hurt—skin, bones, even the roots of my hair.

"Give me a sec," I muttered. "You two good?"

One of them kept a hand on my shoulder, making sure I didn't fall back to the ground. From the cool touch, I was guessing Zack. I couldn't smell anything beyond the rancid zombie goo, and my eyes were still adjusting to the ball of burning pain that lived in the sky. I didn't mind my eyes not being useful. I could have one of my friends help me around for a bit. But my brain did point out a rather suspicious draft everywhere on the front half of my body.

"We're more concerned about you," Zack said, his voice close to my ear. "You sawed that thing in half, then keeled over. We thought you were dead."

I took another chance at opening my eyes again. Not as much pain now, but they still burned. Less like acid and more like a bad sunburn. I shaded my eyes once more and looked around at the damage—or tried to—everything was blurry, and all I could make out were lumps of color.

From what I could tell, what used to be my only working door now matched the front. Pieces of the frame and the door itself were strewn around the backyard. From where I was, I couldn't see the steps, but I assumed that they were in worse shape than the door.

"Where's the body?" I asked, looking to my left at Zack's fuzzy form.

"Well," Zack started, "there was one, until someone went on a rampage."

Maggie let out a sound of protest. "I wanted to make sure the thing was dead!"

"You hosed the body down to watch the thing melt," Zack said matter-of-factly.

"I was doing a thorough job—"

"Guys, as much as I would love to sit here and listen to you bicker," I interrupted, rubbing my temple and grimacing at the rough texture of my hand, "I'd like to go inside now."

I started to stand and felt a hand on either shoulder, forcing me to stay seated.

"You stay put for just one sec," Maggie ordered. "Don't move!"

I felt a frown pull my mouth down. *Stay put?! I almost died! She can't boss me around right now*, I thought as I shifted my weight to stand up. My eyes widened when I realized I was naked except for a shirt draped across my lap. My face heated up.

"Um, where are my pants?"

"Hmm?" Zack asked. "Oh, the goo ate away your clothes. We had to cover you with a spare shirt from the car."

I put my hand over my face and groaned. My clothes had been destroyed by a lizard goo monster, which meant Maggie had seen all my bits. I needed to crawl into a hole and stay there, possibly forever.

"Please tell me that you covered me up," I pleaded, peeking through my fingers at my friend.

Zack chuckled and shook his head. "I tried, but Maggie was very insistent on making sure that all of your parts were intact."

I almost flopped back down in embarrassment, only to have Zack stop me. He helped me lie down carefully as the shock wore off and pain slowly took its place. The rocks I felt pressing against my back were uncomfortable but nothing near the level of the pain cycling beneath my skin. I looked like ground meat, felt like I'd been put through a wood chipper, and the girl I liked had seen me in all my nudie glory. All I needed was a cherry to finish off this embarrassing adventure.

"You are the worst best friend ever," I groaned, closing my eyes.

"If it makes you feel any better, she looked rather impressed."

I risked the burning rays of the sun to look at him and see if he was yanking my chain. He was grinning. "Really? She say anything else?"

"She," Maggie put in from the porch, "is right here, and once I knew you were in one piece, I let Zack take over." She tossed a blanket out to us.

I couldn't move around too much for fear of showing the world my most private attributes. That, and every movement pulled the wounds on my back. It's funny how you don't realize how often you use your back muscles until something happens where you can't, like a giant lizard playing tic-tac-toe on your spinal column.

I did manage to move my head enough to see that she had grabbed one of my favorite blankets. It was big, fluffy, and a shade of green that would make any sane person's eyes hurt.

Very carefully, and with Zack's help, I managed to get back on my feet. He wrapped me in the blanket, making sure I could still see before we slowly made our way up the stairs. The fun part was making sure that neither of us stepped through the stairs instead of up them. The blanket also caught occasionally, and Zack would stop long enough to unhook it before we continued our trek.

Finding where the lizard and I had landed once we'd crashed through the door wasn't hard. In fact, it was impossible to miss the lizard-sized hole in my porch. I paused to look at the landing and took a calming breath. If the porch looked like this, I dreaded what was waiting inside for me.

"Is the inside bad?" I asked.

He bit his lip. "You know how you've been wanting to remodel?"

I let him lead me inside and stopped when I saw the state of my kitchen. It was in shambles, all because of that dragon. Technically, the person who sent the zombie lizard was at fault, but I didn't know who that was yet, so I blamed the undead animal.

"Well," I said, starting forward, "hopefully, this falls under the iguana family's offer to fix my house."

"I don't think they meant your *entire* house," Zack answered as he followed close behind me.

"Their fault for not being specific then." My poor kitchen was a disaster, making my heart twist just a little. This space was supposed to smell of cookies and dish soap with maybe the faintest hint of coffee, not slowly cooling plastic or scorched metal.

I made my way around the warped pools of plastic and singed wood. There were also a few perfect dragon footprints embedded in the linoleum, and I made a mental note to remove them before anyone else saw the house again.

The physical damage wasn't as bad as I thought. I had lost a fridge, not to mention the linoleum and a good chunk of the cabinets. With a little paint and elbow grease, it'd look good as new. That is, unless something else decided to add to the damage.

Maggie was by the fridge trying to salvage what she could. A small stack of food sat on the counter and the ground around her, safely out of the reach of the linoleum sinkholes. I sank gratefully into a dinette chair and watched her work.

"How much is left?"

She turned enough to look at me and sighed. "Everything on the door and the main shelf are lost. So far, the only thing that isn't melted or spoiled are these here."

My eyes widened a bit at the carefully wrapped tinfoil package in her hand. Great glory above I still had food.

"What is this anyway?" Maggie asked as Zack moved into the kitchen, medical bag in hand.

"Layers of tinfoil protecting yummy homemade goodness," I responded and tried to ignore the throbbing sensations emitting from wherever Zack poked me.

"He can't cook, so he mooches food from other people," Zack translated, pressing on a patch of skin when I started to protest. "Does this hurt?"

"Ow, damn it, yes!" I snapped. "What was that for?"

Zack stepped back and started unwrapping the bandages that encased my chest. "I was seeing how they were healing."

When I didn't answer, Zack sighed and moved back far enough for me to focus on both him and Maggie.

"What?" I snapped again.

"Allen, how's your leg?"

I blinked owlishly at him. I just went head-to-head with a zombie, then face-planted in a puddle of toxic goo, and he's asking about my leg?

"My legs are fine," I said, bending both of them for emphasis. "See? Nothing wrong with them."

"Leg, Allen," Zack said with practiced patience, "the one the iguana sliced up?"

"What? … Oh."

I shifted and looked down at my leg or tried to through the layers of fluffy blanket. The bandage was gone, presumably eaten away by the goo, and all that remained of the wound was a slightly puckered white scar.

I leaned down to touch the scar with a finger. It was still a bit tender, but the tightness of the surrounding skin told me it was healing. How in Casper's name could I just forget about it?

"I remember the pain," I said, sitting back. "It lasted for a few days, but then it faded. I thought it was the aspirin."

Why hadn't I noticed when my leg stopped hurting? I was telling the truth when I said I thought it was the aspirin I'd been taking. I'm not the type to keep up with something once it stops hurting. But even then, I should have noticed, right?

"Wait a sec," I said aloud, causing both of my friends to look at me, "if my leg healed in a couple of days, what about this?"

The two stared at me, unmoving. Probably thought the goo had melted my brain too.

Amid protests, both from my body and my friends, I made it to my feet and began a shuffling march to my dining room—or what was left of it, that is.

The front window was smashed, letting in a slightly warm breeze that fluttered the curtains. My mother's prized oak table was in pieces from the lizard's goo. Whole chunks were missing from one end, and it teetered dangerously to one side on a half-eaten leg. Most of the chairs had fallen in battle or had been so eaten away by the acid that they couldn't be salvaged. How would I find a table to replace my mother's?

Papers that had been on the table were now scattered all over the floor, a few eaten away by the creature's sudden appearance. The murder wall was still intact. Only a few pieces held slightly crispy edges from narrow mishaps. But other than that, they were fine.

Tallying up the damage in the dining room, I had no front window, no dining room table, no chairs, and a reptile-shaped hole in my floor where the thing landed after coming through the window. I took a deep breath and told myself it was just a table, that I could buy another one, before I directed my feet to the downstairs bathroom in my mother's old room.

I groped for the light switch and momentarily blinded myself when the small space flooded with light. When the dots had disappeared from my eyes, I turned my attention to the man in the mirror and held in a cringe the best I could.

I looked like a walking tanning-bed accident. The skin on my chest was bright red with darker patches where I assumed more of the goo had fallen. My entire right shoulder looked like an overcooked marshmallow. A creamy white mixture had been smeared over it; Zack's work. He was possibly the reason why I wasn't swearing in pain as well. He must have administered some kind of numbing agent not long before I woke up. I pressed a finger into the blackened skin and grinned when I felt nothing. Novocain was a wonderful thing. Good ol' Zack. I was definitely getting him a fruit basket.

My face wasn't Deadpool, or even Jason, but it did look pretty bad. The side of my face that had gotten slapped was a dark, angry red with a bit of black near my hair and jawline. Not bad. I could deal with that. Plus, I still had my ear. Losing it would have been rather interesting. The other half of my face was a few shades lighter but still red. My eyes were intact, a bit bloodshot and tender to the touch from my face-plant, but I still had eyebrows, a nose, and a mouth. I was good.

I stood there studying the red skin, a bit disappointed that nothing magically healed while I was watching. But if I could pull a Wolverine, I think I might have noticed before now.

Just what the fuck was I? Normal people take days, sometimes years to heal from burns like this but I healed in a matter of minutes? I should look like a walking corpse right now. I should be seeing bone and muscle. Hell, I shouldn't be able to walk, much less talk. So what did that make me? Was I a monster now too? I vaguely remembered my mom getting cuts on her hands that would seem to disappear. Did I get this from her?

"This is so screwed up," I muttered, staring at my blurred reflection.

Calm down, or you'll give yourself an anxiety attack, my double's voice sounded, soothing my nerves.

Maybe I could get Zack to run some tests later. Yeah .... Yeah that could work.

Finally, with a bit of reluctance, I turned around to look at my back. It looked like a train wreck. Chunks of flesh were missing where the lizard had really dug in. Black surgical thread showed against the irritated skin in a jagged crisscross pattern, reminding me of Frankenstein's monster. Luckily, everything close to my spine was intact, or I would have been more freaked out. I was a bit surprised I was so calm, probably because I couldn't feel anything at the moment.

"I tried to tell you it was bad."

My eyes drifted in the mirror to find Zack standing in the doorway. He seemed a bit more at ease than when I first woke up. Zack walked over, gently turning me sideways so he could inspect my back. His touches were light, and with the Novocain, I barely felt them. What I could feel was the tension that floated around Zack as he worked. It was the same kind of tension I had while working, and it worried me a bit. Zack was never tense. He was Mr. Mellow at work.

"You all right?"

Zack paused briefly, and I watched in the mirror as he started cleaning the superficial wounds. He must have done the worst of the sewing while I was still out. Smart man. His face became a mixture of panic and anger before he started speaking again.

"After you got that ... thing," he said, spitting the word out, "out of the house, I just sat there, shock probably, and tried to figure out what the hell I just saw."

"When did you get outside?" I asked, a bit of guilt rising up.

"When I heard Maggie yelling at you," Zack said with a small grin. "Loved the bit with the chain saw though. I have to say, you looked pretty awesome, very Ash Williams."

I shrugged. "That's what I was going for."

Zack shook his head a little, his grin disappearing as he started cleaning the claw marks again. "But when you collapsed afterward … Allen, you were covered in blood. I'm surprised you were even able to get up and charge that thing. I got to you first and pulled you out of the goo while Maggie hosed you off. I started to patch you up and went back in for more supplies. I was only gone a few minutes before I heard Maggie yell that you weren't breathing."

My heart twisted. Poor Maggie. No wonder she was so pissed when I finally woke up.

"Anyway, you know the rest," Zack finished, tossing the rag he'd been using onto the counter. "Let's see if I can finish this up on one of the beds," he said, pointing to my back

"No," I said, adjusting my grip on the blanket, "not yet."

Zack looked at me, his face starting to harden at my words. "You do realize I need to do this regardless, right?"

"And you will," I assured him as I heard faint sounds of Maggie moving around in the kitchen, "but I'd like to debrief with you both before anyone else decides to destroy my house."

"On one condition," he countered, still not looking pleased with the decision. "If you start feeling pain, you're going to bed."

"Fine," I answered, looking at the bedroom door. "You can poke and prod then." I limped out of the bathroom and across the bedroom, pausing briefly to catch my breath.

"Go ahead and set up in Mom's room," I told Zack over my shoulder, and started back to the kitchen.

I navigated my way through the dining room, stopping at the kitchen door to peek in at Maggie sitting at the dinette table. Carefully, I walked over and slid an arm around her shoulders from behind. She stiffened in surprise before leaning back against my hold.

"I'm sorry," I said quietly. "I didn't mean to worry you like that."

Maggie moved a hand up to gently squeeze my arm.

"I know you didn't," she said, her voice shaking. "I … I thought …"

"Hey, I'm in one piece," I said softly. "A bit crispy, but one piece. And I promise to be more careful next time."

Maggie coughed and glanced back at me. "Promise?"

"Scout's honor."

"You were never a scout."

"We can pretend."

Maggie's mouth turned up, and she patted my arm, signaling me to move.

"You're hopeless," she muttered, getting to her feet. "Come on, let's see if Zack can make you less creepy. And maybe find you some pants."

***

I let Maggie pick out my clothes after a bit of debate and a lot of vetoes on my part. I was finally dressed. It had taken ten or fifteen minutes to get it done, but I'd like to see you try getting dressed without messing up your bandages or raising your arms over your head.

While I had been fighting with fabric, Maggie and Zack managed to cover the damaged window with what remained of my dining room table. That way, there wasn't one more way for people to get into my house.

The two of them had also gathered what they could from the murder wall and moved it to the living room. I had claimed the remaining living room chair.

"I think I have an idea of who's behind all of this. Well, the monster part at least. Right before the lizard came through the window," I said, leaning forward a bit, "what were we discussing?"

"Who the hell was killing people these past few days," Zack said, frustrated. "We already went over this, Allen."

"Patience," I said. "We were discussing the stones and the families. Then a zombie lizard came through my front window. Correct?"

"What's your point?"

"Point is, every time we get some kind of new information or theory, I get attacked."

Maggie's brow furrowed in confusion. "What do you mean? It attacked us, too, you know."

"It only attacked you and I, Maggie, after we hit it," Zack pointed out, "not before."

"Because I was the intended target," I added quietly. "I was getting too close to figuring out the answer to our problem."

That was the simple version and the best one I could give at the moment. However, figuring out how those lizards knew what I was doing and thinking was a different story. And just my luck, it would be several times harder to figure out who was behind this now that I had someone who wasn't O'Hare following me.

"So we have a why," Zack said, "now we need a how."

"I might be able to help with that," I said. "It's a bit out-there, so bear with me." I started mapping out what I'd thought of before we'd been interrupted.

"We know it's the dragon family that's been attacking us; the iguanas don't have their stone, right? So I doubt that they are going to do anything. We know that Meredith was referred to another doctor, and nothing of the sort was mentioned during the interview I conducted with her mother."

"So what are you saying?" Zack asked.

"I think that sometime during the school fight, the stone's power attached itself to Meredith, almost piggybacking her. She was an easy target, being full of emotion. When she finally calmed down, Dr. Swanson had already suggested a psychologist, which is the only thing a human doctor could do. Then we know she transferred schools—my interview with the iguanas backs that up. She doesn't make any more trouble until her death lands on my desk. There also isn't any indication that the stone was used again until Terry's death."

"Cut to the chase, Allen," Maggie said.

"I think we've been duped into believing that O'Hare had the stone. He wants one, which is where I came in. My mom has the stone that belongs to the iguanas, but that's only one stone. The stone that is unaccounted for after the fight is the one from the dragons. Mary Strong has to have the other stone," I explained, moving to the edge of my seat as I awaited a response.

After a moment, Maggie finally spoke up. "If Mary Strong does have the stone … what if the power could, I don't know, possess someone?"

Zack groaned. "Why are you encouraging even more craziness?"

"Because," Maggie said, not looking up as she rifled through the evidence, "unlike close-minded people like you, I have a faith and fascination in what cannot be explained or seen."

I watched them with amusement. How Maggie handled people had always floored me. She worked in a bar for a bit during college, so I guess that helped. But I got the most laughs watching her go head-to-head with someone in a religious debate. She was a whirlwind of rainbow-haired fury.

Zack's shoulders tensed and relaxed in a silent defeat. "Listen, before this case, I didn't think zombie lizards could exist outside of a B-rated movie. But now we know that things we previously thought were impossible are in fact possible."

Maggie patted him on the shoulder, then held up what was left of one of the files. "We have a problem," she said. The folder was pocked with goo burns. It was useless. Good thing I'd gone through it earlier.

"I already read it," I answered. "No worries, Mags."

"I keep forgetting you have that whole photographic memory thing," Zack said, moving over to inspect my face as Maggie tossed the file into a slowly growing pile.

I squirmed a little in my seat as he pressed his fingers against my face. "It's more like a supermarket of useless facts and figures. It's also a pain in my ass, but it does come in handy at times."

Zack made a sound of agreement and started feeling along my shoulders, his eyes never leaving my face as he watched for any sign of pain.

"So say the stone's power could possess someone?" Maggie pressed on. "When did it jump to Mary Strong?"

I forced myself to stay still when Zack's fingers found a benumbed spot. "It had to have jumped over after the school fight—probably at the hospital, if I had to guess. By the time Meredith transferred to our school, she was reserved and shy."

"So she went back to normal?" Maggie asked, reclining against the skeleton couch.

"Normal isn't the right word for it," I said, shifting away from Zack's prying fingers. "My bet is that— Ow, damn it, stop!"

Zack stepped back from the chair and pointed at the bedroom. "Time to go."

"But—"

"We had a deal."

"I'm—"

"Don't care," Zack said flatly, still pointing. "Now."

"We can talk while he works," Maggie said, getting to her feet and looking at Zack for confirmation. "Right?"

Zack nodded and pulled me to my feet. "Come on, let's go."

A small sound of pain escaped as I was hauled to a standing position. Okay, so it might have been closer to a very loud gasp than a whimper, but you try sounding manly after being used as a scratching post.

I let Zack guide me to my mother's room. I walked in and flopped face first onto the bed. Maggie settled on Mom's old wooden rocker as Zack started looking through his bag for what he needed. I got comfortable and buried my face in one of the pillows. It smelled like her. Warm, inviting, and safe. I sighed and turned my head to look at Maggie, then past her to the window.

Prior to this case, it had been a while since I'd let myself actually think about Mom. Sometimes it was too painful to even look at the room we were in now. It left me drained for days and put me in a foul mood. One episode was so bad that Maggie and Zack locked me in a room by myself for a few hours until I cooled off a bit.

Other than the day Mom died, that was the least favorite day of my life. But now they both kept an eye on me, maneuvering me away from the general public when I got really bad. The only time they hadn't been around was when I'd been asked to help with a child abuse case .... Yeah, what a disaster.

"So," Maggie prompted once Zack settled on the bed beside me, "the stone's power jumped?"

I smiled a little at her attempt to distract me. It wasn't the best attempt on her part, but I did appreciate it all the same.

"Yes," I said, turning my eyes back to her. "I think that when the power sensed a more suitable candidate, it jumped into Mary Strong, which let Meredith return to her original self. Then she moved out of town to attend college in hopes of getting away from everyone here."

Maggie gave me a curious look. "What do you mean? She wasn't bullied in our school. She got along with everyone."

I nodded, hissing as Zack cleaned the rest of my wounds.

"True," I agreed with a small sigh. "But what if it wasn't the students she was trying to get away from? Other than school bullies, who else do we leave home to avoid?"

Maggie stared at me, and for a moment, the only sound in the room was Zack's scissors snipping a thread. I didn't attempt to look over my shoulder at him. He'd just shove my head back down onto the bed.

"Your parents," Zack supplied. "If it's not your peers you run from, it's your own family."

"Yep, exactly."

"You think Meredith's mother would be able to kill her own daughter?" Maggie asked slowly. "Why would Mrs. Strong do that? That doesn't make sense."

I felt my back spasm as Zack found a live patch of skin. She had a point. Why would Mary Strong kill her own daughter?

"Misdirected rage?"

"If that's misdirected rage, keep it away from me," Maggie said firmly, holding up a hand. "I have plenty of my own."

I snorted and Zack chuckled above me. Neither of us would deny that.

"You almost done?" I asked, subconsciously moving away from the pull of the needle's thread.

"Everything benumbed?"

"Am I imagining all this pain?" I asked through gritted teeth. I sighed, letting my eyes shut and pretending my back wasn't slowly turning into fire.

After a pause, I heard a small clink as Zack picked something up. He moved back, and I felt the tip of something against my skin. I froze.

"You're going to feel a slight pinch."

"That had better not be what I think it is."

Zack ignored me and pushed that horrid thing into the soft flesh of my hip, making me flinch.

"I hate you," I grumbled. I hated needles.

"Hmm?"

"Seriously, who stabs their friend with a needle like it's the most normal thing in the world?"

Zack didn't have to answer. The feeling that hit me soon after was answer enough.

For those of you who have been in the hospital for surgery, do you remember when the nurse gives you a shot of the good stuff for pain? The medicine that gives you the feeling of floating, like nothing will be unpleasant ever again? The medicine that wraps you in a warm fuzzy feeling when it hits your system. Bless the sweet doctor that created it.

"Oh," I sighed, grinning, "I take back what I said .... I love you."

Zack chuckled, and I heard him moving around. "I love you too."

"What did you give him?"

"Morphine."

I tried to listen to them. I really did. But it was like listening to an echo in a long tunnel. While focusing on the echoing voices of my companions, more than one golden ball of light floated into my line of sight. The lights shifted and molded into various things: butterflies, birds, dragonflies, and even a few that looked like ladybugs. All of them golden and beautiful, dancing in my field of vision. I giggled as I moved a hand to grab at a golden butterfly that fluttered past my face and frowned when my fingers passed right through it. My frown deepened when I failed again to grab a passing illusion. Stupid butterfly, hold still, damn it. It was getting hard to move my arms, but I wanted that butterfly.

"Don't worry, Maggie, I only gave him a small amount. He'll either wake up in pain or wake up healed."

Their voices faded away, and I felt my eyelids get heavy. I didn't want to sleep. There was something I had to do. Couldn't remember what ... or why

I had to do it that very instant. I tried to shrug, smirking at the sensation the sheets gave me when they rubbed against my bare skin.

Bare skin. It sounded so dirty but felt so wonderful, like a thousand velvety kitten paws kneading my skin all at once. I loved it, and I never wanted it to stop. I giggled as the weightlessness gently pulled me into an embrace of those dancing orbs and kitten massages.

Chapter Nineteen

I woke up to pain. My back felt as if someone had skinned it and then tried to fit me back inside it; like forcing yourself into a pair of jeans you love but are obviously too small. Yeah, that times ten thousand.

I took some deep breaths and then very carefully opened my eyes. I remembered going to my mother's room with Zack to get sewn up, talking about the stones, and being injected with something, but that was about it.

My eyes found Maggie asleep in my mother's chair, curled up under a well-loved quilt of many colors. I smiled a little and began the painful process of sitting up without crying or throwing up. It soon became apparent that while pushing myself up was laborious, convincing my legs to move was a bit harder. I glanced over at Maggie, making sure she was still asleep, and uttered a few colorful words under my breath.

"Stupid legs," I muttered, hissing softly as the muscles in my lower back spasmed slightly, but then one of my legs moved the tiniest bit.

Oh yes, my inner voice spoke up, sounding as disgruntled as I felt, *let's blame the only part of your body that hasn't been used as a chew toy.*

"Shut up," I growled, keeping my voice low. "What do you want now?"

I can't do both, you know, the voice mused.

"Just answer the question."

My, my, that dip into monster goo made you snippy.

I took a breath as my legs folded themselves under me. This was not the time to get into an argument with myself. I had a possible homicidal mother out there being influenced by a rock, plus a mob boss who was less than happy with me. I couldn't afford to let my guard down.

"Allen?"

"Mother of China!" I exclaimed as I tumbled onto the floor in a tangle of sheets, pillows, and comforter. The impact wasn't too bad as it was cushioned by the bedding.

"Oh my—are you all right?"

Maggie was standing over me with a worried look on her face.

"I, uh, um," I stuttered, gazing up at her, "I think so …."

Real smooth.

I ignored him and cleared my throat in a failed attempt to recover my dignity. I was also trying extremely hard not to stare at the particular curves I could see from my vantage point.

You're staring.

Mind your own business! I snapped at myself, but even as I thought the words, I could feel my face heating up.

"Not that I don't appreciate you checking up on me—"

You know, if you raise your left hand just a little …

"But could you please move?" I finished, my face now blazing red.

Maggie grinned a little but did move back, her shirt settling enough for me to know that there was nothing underneath. I averted my eyes, but not before Maggie started laughing.

Someone's really brave.

I stared hard at the ceiling and made myself think about other things: puppies, dictionaries, potato chips, anything but Maggie at the moment.

"Where's Zack?" I asked, starting to sit up.

"He went back to his lab," Maggie said, helping the best she could without touching my back. "He used a lot of bandages on you. He should be back any moment."

Once upright, I glanced at the window. Even with the curtains drawn, I could tell it was dark outside. I sighed and ran a hand through my hair, wincing as I snagged a tangle.

"How long have I been sleeping?" I asked, using my fingers to work out the snarl.

"Um," Maggie said, looking at her watch, "about six hours."

"What?!" I yelled. "Six hours? Why didn't you wake me up?"

I kicked viciously at the covers but only succeeded in getting my feet even more twisted in the fabric.

"Allen—"

"Don't," I said, not looking at her. "Have to catch a bad guy."

Maggie, the ingenious woman that she is, took the blankets that I had been fighting and proceeded to retangle my legs. That is, until I almost kicked her in the face, then she quickly grabbed my free ankle and held it down with both hands.

"Do I have your attention now?"

I nodded in defeat.

"Good," Maggie said, firmly pressing on my sheet-covered leg. "Now listen to me: Zack stuck you with a low dose of morphine and sent you off to dreamland with the intention of making you heal up before you tried to commit suicide. He came back a few hours later, and pieces of your back had started to close. Not the big ones that he had to sew up, but the scrapes and minor burns. We thought the sleep was helping, so we let you keep dreaming. Zack left to restock his bag and to provide your chief with an excuse as to why you didn't go back to fill out your report."

I groaned and rubbed my eyes. The chief .... I was in for an earful. Hopefully by then I would be fully healed, in body anyway.

"Just remembered that, didn't you?"

"Yes," I answered, not moving my hand away. "And I have a feeling that I won't have such an easy time explaining this one."

Maggie smirked and released my legs. "You'll figure something out. You always do."

I fell silent and sat there watching her. It wasn't that the statement surprised me—it was the carefree attitude wrapped around it. I knew Maggie had faith in me. She'd shown it a few times, mostly right after I did something that landed me in hot water with someone fairly important. But it never failed to amaze me how she was able to roll with life's punches. I was kinda jealous.

"Thanks?"

"Want help up?"

"I think I'm good," I answered, firmly ignoring the laughter in my head. "I need to catch my breath anyway."

Maggie gave me another one of her smirks before moving away. "I'm leaving to get food. You and Zack play nice."

She disappeared from my line of sight, so I turned my attention to getting up. Figuring out how to untangle myself and get up—without falling back into the white entrapment on the floor—took me a moment. After a few failures and more than one windmill maneuver, which did nothing but create waves of agony through my shoulders and upper back, I succeeded in moving to one of the walls near the bathroom in my mother's room. I glanced around briefly for any creepy crawlies before I carefully put one foot in front of the other and, keeping a hand on the wall, made the slow shuffle to the living room. I could hear Zack in the kitchen.

"Are we sure that there's nothing left from those undead dragons?" I panted once I reached the hallway. " 'Cause I'd like a souvenir for all this trouble. Hell, even a toenail."

Zack yelled instructions that included going back to bed. I didn't pay much attention as the pain in my back was slowly creeping to a level that I was pretty sure was reserved for torture. I leaned my shoulder carefully against the frame and took a breather, closing my eyes to block some of the light coming in from the dining room. It wasn't horribly bright, but it was enough to make my still-sensitive eyes hurt. I was also being a tiny bit lazy and didn't want to move any farther. But I knew that if I stayed in bed, I'd run both my friends up the wall.

"What are you doing out of bed?"

I cracked an eye to watch Zack stalk toward me in a strangely graceful manner. He'd changed clothes and shaved since the last time I'd seen him. I probably needed to do the same. I couldn't get any work done smelling like blood and zombie goo.

"Standing," I said as he stopped in front of me. "What does it look like?"

Zack glared and pointed stiff-armed to the room behind me. "Get back in bed."

"The sheets are covered in blood and lizard smell," I protested. "I'm not going back in there."

"Oh? Then where else are you going to sleep?" Zack snapped, crossing his arms over his chest. "Because it's not going to be upstairs or the floor."

I scowled at him, trying to gauge if he was bluffing or not. I really didn't want to go back in that room. Besides … bad guy.

"Your bedside manner sucks," I finally answered. "And I'm sticking to what I said: I'm not going in there …. You've forgotten that we have to put a murderer behind bars."

Zack studied my face as silence stretched between us. Finally, he nodded and stepped aside.

"Promise me something though," he said when I took a few shuffling steps away from the doorframe. "When this is all done, take some time off to recover? You don't know how much your body can take; a normal human would be dead by now."

He was right about the human body only being able to take so much. I nodded. "I know, and don't worry, I will."

"I mean it, Allen," Zack said. "Promise me."

"I promise."

Some of the tension drained from Zack's shoulders, and he stepped over, carefully putting one of my arms across his shoulders. Together we made it to the kitchen, with me stumbling only once or twice. Once Zack deposited me in one of the chairs, he checked on the stitches and a few more questionable scrapes. He was inspecting the damage to my face when Maggie walked through the door, plastic bags in both hands.

"You should really get that fixed," she said, picking her way through the mess. "Weirdos could just walk in."

Zack snickered.

"Yeah, I'll get right on that," I answered as Zack moved away. "Top of the list. Right along with a new fridge, floors, table, and a bunch of other stuff."

Maggie ignored me and set the bags on the table. My mouth watered when the heavenly scent of fried chicken filled my nose.

"Please tell me that's Bubba's," I said pulling a foam container out and placing it on the table before reaching for another one.

"Duh," Maggie answered as she set three cups on the table. "Where else in this dinky town would I go?"

Bubba's was run by a family on the south side of town, and they were as redneck as they came. Sweet folks though. They would be more than happy to help you out and would put extra food in your order if they declared you "underfed." However, if you started any trouble in the restaurant, or just with the family in general, you would feel the deadly wrath of Miss Bessy. And no one wanted to mess with Bess.

"So what was my excuse for missing work?" I asked and then sank my teeth into a piece of deep-fried golden bird, reveling in the grease that trickled onto my hands.

Zack shrugged. "Told him that you caught a nasty case of food poisoning and had to stay home."

"He bought that?"

"Seemed to."

I nodded and continued to munch on my chicken. Oh, how I loved the person who invented the deep fryer. Glorious grease and crispy skin with warm succulent meat underneath. Bubba's got it right every time.

Our meal was pretty quiet, except for the contented sounds of crunching and the occasional slurp of sweet tea. By the time our eating slowed to a crawl, there wasn't much left.

"Oh, wow that was good," I said, leaning away from the table. "I didn't realize how hungry I actually was."

Zack dumped his chicken scraps into the box. "You almost bit me when you figured out there was only one piece of chicken left."

"Cry me a river," I responded with a grin. "I didn't eat breakfast or lunch. I needed food."

"And I'm considered food?"

"Only if you get in my way."

Zack let out a sputtering sound, and I grinned, dumping the remains of my meal into the box as well. Now that I had food in me, I felt a bit better. Sure, my back was still killing me, but it wasn't anything some aspirin couldn't fix. That would at least take the edge off enough for me to finish working.

"What's our next move?" Maggie asked.

I shifted in my chair.

"You have no clue, do you?"

A groan escaped me. "I'm in a fried chicken coma …. I need a minute." My eyes flickered between the two people staring at me expectantly, and I stretched a little but stopped when my back started protesting.

"Okay," I said finally, "we already established the possibility that the stone's power can jump into whoever it wants. And we think that Meredith was the only logical candidate for it to jump into the first time."

Zack nodded. "You also accused Meredith's mother of being the killer."

"I don't accuse unless I know I'm right. You know that."

"So we investigate her," Maggie said, frowning a bit. "That still bugs me though."

"Her daughter being a victim?"

Maggie nodded. "It doesn't make any sense for her to kill her own daughter."

To tell the truth, it was stumping me too.

"Tell you what," I said, looking at Maggie and then the empty hole where my back door had been, "it's dark, and we won't be seen. How about a little stakeout?"

To be continued in Part Two ….